The Ashes Know Her Name

By Denise Nussbaum

The Ashes Know Her Name

Copyright ©2025 by Denise Nussbaum

ISBN Paperback: 979-8-9987985-0-4

ISBN eBook: 979-8-9987985-1-1

Publisher: Neesey Designs
PO Box 10549, Lahaina, Hi 96761

Printed in the United States of America.

ACKNOWLEDGMENTS

The author would like to thank Betsy Chasse for her brilliant mentorship and guidance; Claudia Micco and Christine Judal for their skilled input and editing; Nisim Asayag and Aliya Nussbaum for their perspectives on the diverse relations between Jews and Arabs in Israel; my medical consultant, Dr. Mike Keller; my spiritual advisors, Nicole Angove and Dr. Joel Friedman, and my husband Barry Nussbaum for his unwavering love, support and encouragement.

About The Author

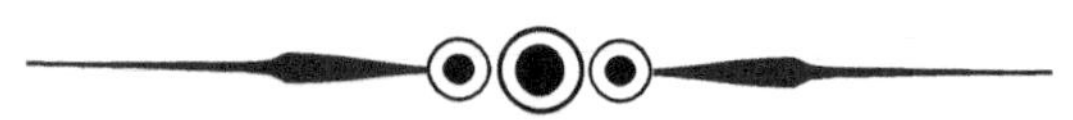

After backpacking around the world on a ten-dollar-a-day budget for nearly three years, **Dr. Nussbaum** returned home with a deep appreciation for the complexities of human connection and cultural identity. She earned her Ph.D. in sociology in 1999 and went on to serve as a Professor and Department Chair at Mt. San Jacinto College for 22 years. During her tenure, she taught and mentored hundreds of students in critical thinking, focusing on topics like social inequalities, prejudice, and the lasting impact of trauma.

Her academic work includes published articles and book chapters on discrimination and systemic injustice, and in 2003, she was honored with the prestigious **Stanback-Stroud Diversity Award** by the Academic Senate for California Community Colleges.

Now retired from academia, Dr. Nussbaum continues to explore how social institutions shape our identities and lives—this time through fiction. *The Ashes Know Her Name* is her debut novel, a powerful blend of global thriller and emotional reckoning that reflects her lifelong commitment to understanding the forces that bind and break us.

DEDICATION

Dedicated to the victims and survivors of the Lahaina fires and the October 7th terrorist attacks. May our strength and faith pave the road toward a safe and peaceful future.

Woe to those who call evil good and good evil,

who turn darkness to light and light to darkness.

-- Isaiah 5:20.

CONTENTS

PROLOGUE

October 31, 2006
Northern Israel

The setting sun casts a warm glow over the kibbutz in Northern Israel as children dart between tables adorned with colorful streamers and balloons, their laughter filling the air. Parents and neighbors gather around, chatting and smiling, while the aromas of challah bread baking and shish kabob grilling waft through the still evening air.

Eleanor, Ellie to her friends, catches Pua's eye from across the dining hall, and they both laugh. Pua yells, "Oy vavoy! People, people … this is like herding mongoose!"

Ellie and Pua, despite their relative youth, are the matriarchs of this large extended family. Their two families may as well be blood-related. Their story began when Lou Cohen and Kalama Akamai met as young men in the Marine Corps. They had both enlisted right out of high school in 1981: Lou in California after the tragic death of both his parents in a car accident; Kalama in Hawaii, looking to make a better life for himself and his high-school sweetheart and wife-to-be, Pua.

Kal and Lou went through Basic Training together and bonded over their similar cultural upbringing. Lou was raised by a Jewish-American family on a kibbutz in Israel, farming and growing crops, Kalama on a large communal, multi-generational property on Maui, living off the land in a similar way. Both were very spiritual, hardworking, family-oriented men. They'd often talked about living on a kibbutz, growing crops, raising cows, and raising their families together.

On August 20, 1982, Lou and Kal were two of 800 U.S. Marines from the 32nd Marine Amphibious Unit that arrived in Beirut, Lebanon. They were 19 years old. Two months later, they were both at the Marine base in Beirut when Hezbollah murdered 241 US military personnel in a horrific terrorist bombing. Kalama was gravely injured. Despite Kal's plea that Lou leave him there and save himself, Lou refused. Somehow, although wounded himself, he managed to get Kalama to safety, single-handedly saving his life. Lou had received the Medal of Honor, the Navy Cross, and a Purple Heart. Kalama had been awarded the Bronze Star for Combat, the Silver Star, and a Purple Heart.

Both men are badass war heroes. They had forged a lifelong bond and truly considered themselves brothers. After the Marine Corps, they both entered Special Operations together, followed by a stint with the CIA.

Lou and Kal moved to the kibbutz when the two officially left the CIA in 1995, and Ziva was born a year later. Both families had had enough war in their lives and wanted to pursue their common dream of raising their families in peace on a working farm in Israel. Kalama had married his high school sweetheart, Pua, years before, and Lou had just married Eleanor, an ex-Mossad agent he had met during a mission a few years prior. Today, Lou and Kal are both "paycheck warriors" – private soldiers for hire, which is why they were late to the birthday party.

Ellie joyfully but sternly shouts orders to the growing crowd of friends and family. It is a happy day—her baby girl is turning ten, and her beloved husband is returning from a long stint overseas.

"Let's go, let's go!!! Ugh, who can get a word in here?"

She shakes her head and turns to Pua, who is wrestling with the enormous birthday cake. Ellie had insisted on a ten-layer cake, one for each year of Ziva's life. Pua fears it may topple over under the weight of the Wizard of Oz characters on top. Ellie laughs as Pua barely gets the cake to the table in one piece.

"Okay, I may have gone a little overboard for Ziva's birthday."

"Can you believe these mishugat?" Pua laughs and turns to the group of children as they wrestle, laugh, and play.

"Noa, get your brothers! Tali, stop that and come over here! Kimo, get these shovavim to stop fighting and come to the table! Lilikoi, baby, go stand next to Ziva."

Like her mother, Ziva enjoys the happy chaos of the kibbutz and giggles affectionately at the crowd before her. Her large extended family gathers around her in the dining hall, her beloved mother standing front and center, barking orders at children and officers alike. Pua gathers the last stragglers to the table.

Ziva laughs at the way her mother whistles, yells, and pushes the people toward the table. As tiny as she is, when Ellie Cohen barks, people listen. That's why Daddy calls her 'General'. Ziva feels happy, loved, and safe.

"Come on, come on! Everyone gather around, gather, gather! It is time we sing for Ziva … gather around!" Ellie begins to sing, and the crowd joins in, still talking and laughing. Kimo and his 3-year-old sister, Lilikoi, join Ziva at the front of the table, and the three hold hands.

"Haappy birthdaay to youuuu. Haappy birthdaay to youuuu …"

Ziva scans the crowd for her father. He promised he'd be back for her birthday.

"Happy birthday, dear Zivaaaaa …."

Daddy promised to bring her the new Nintendo Wii from America.

"Happy birthday to youuuuuuuu!!!"

The crowd cheers and laughs as someone yells, "Now in Hebrew!"

Ziva closes her eyes and makes a wish. She bends down to blow out the ten candles that hiss and sputter atop her giant pink birthday cake. She can smell the sweetness of the icing as she lowers her head to extinguish the candles with one last joyful exhalation.

The sound is deafening. Explosions rock the building. There is shouting, gunfire, confusion, more explosions, and endless rounds of gunfire—screaming!

Ziva is thrown to the ground amidst the toppled cake and table. All she can hear is screaming and explosions … one after another. Blinded by smoke, Ziva reaches for Lilikoi's hand and finds emptiness.

"Lilikoi!" Ziva calls out for the child. "Lilikoi!" No response. Ziva panics and screams for help.

"Ima! Ima!" Ziva calls for her mother, but can see nothing through the smoke and flames.

"Ima!!!"

CHAPTER 1

Lahaina, Maui
August 8, 2023

Ana's early morning lesson at the Krav Maga halau is interrupted by a power outage as the winds from Hurricane Dora batter Maui's tropical landscape. She looks out the window to see the palm trees bent over, large fan leaves dancing frenetically in the wind. Dora had been lurking outside the Hawaiian Islands for a few days, but it hadn't appeared she would hit Maui in full force. Now, the gusts are kicking up, and Ana is becoming concerned, as is her large dog, Koa, who watches nervously out the window as the weather turns ominous.

Ana apologizes to her students. "Sorry about the power, girls. It looks like we have to cut this short today. We'll reschedule your lesson for this Monday, yeah?"

Six-year-old Iki bows with respect, then playfully throws Ana a shaka. "Yes, sensei."

Ana returns the shaka and waves goodbye to Iki and her mother. She turns to Koa. "C'mon, boy. We don't need electricity to walk on the beach, do we?"

Later, as Ana and Koa wrap up their 5-mile beach walk, the willful winds rage with up to 60 mph gusts, and Ana begins to feel uneasy.

"Koa, let's go, boy!" The dog ignores her as he digs at the shoreline for the quickly vanishing critters. Frustrated with his lack of compliance, Ana uses her sterner command voice.

"Koa, come now!" Koa jumps up and hastens to sit by Ana's feet. "Good boy. You've been trained to military standards; why don't you act like it?" Koa shnortles as if offended; this was supposed to be a fun walk.

As the pair walk quickly toward her truck, Ana sees a male figure off in the distance, waving his arms. As they get closer, she sees it is her best friend Kimo Akamai, and Koa runs off to greet him. As Ana gets closer, Kimo yells over the moaning wind.

"The power is out over at the retirement home. Mama sent me to get Auntie Pakalana and bring her to the homestead. I saw your truck and thought you may want to come with."

Ana nods but is distracted by a plume of smoke growing larger a few miles to the north of them. Kimo's eyes follow her gaze, and he feels a rush of concern. This doesn't look like a normal brush fire.

"Do you see that, Kimo?"

"Yeah. Crap. We've had a drought for over a year now. With all this dried vegetation, that fire will spread lightning fast. We gotta go, Ana."

The three run toward their cars. Kimo has a bad feeling and insists on keeping Ana close. "Come with me, Ana. I'll bring you two back to your truck later." She recognizes his firm tone, acquiesces, and jumps in his truck with Koa between them.

As they rush toward Lahaina Town, they immediately realize the gravity of the situation. The relentless winds demolish everything in their path. Hundreds of downed power poles litter the only road in and out of town, and live wires dance perilously, lashing out in every direction. Cars speed frantically over the live power lines as panicked drivers rush toward the only way out. The wires spark new fires in all directions as people and animals run frantically for their lives.

Ana can't believe her eyes. "Kimo, what the hell? It looks like the end of the world! Why hasn't HECO turned off the electricity to the power poles? This whole place is going to burn!"

Kimo drives on single-mindedly through the chaos. Dozens of cars speed toward them, swerving around downed poles, trees, and massive pieces of flying debris, desperately trying to flee as Kimo drives into the fray toward the mayhem. People are screaming at them out of their windows.

"Turn around!!! FIRE!!!"

"The road is blocked! Turn around!"

"There's no way out!"

Flames are erupting in every direction. Enormous blocks of fire are lifted by the winds, shooting hundreds of feet in the air, just to put down in a new area with more fuel to consume. The fire blazes north, carried by Dora's rageful winds, as Lahaina Town and the homes above it are recklessly, horrifically devoured without prejudice.

Kimo floors the engine and drives off-road over sidewalks, through fences, and parking lots to get to the retirement home, which has already succumbed to the blaze. The smoky scene is right out of Dante's Inferno. Although it's only 3:30 pm, the skies are as dark as night. There are hysterical, shrieking, and suffering people everywhere. The cacophony of screams is excruciating to witness. Many are injured or have collapsed from smoke inhalation. A few people try to get into adjacent homes to save loved ones; others are clawing to get out of what would catastrophically become their final resting place. There are lines of cars pulled over haphazardly on the sides of the road as the flames or the ill-placed police roadblocks obstruct their escape.

"Oh my God, Kimo! These people are all trapped!" Ana jumps out of the still-moving vehicle and runs toward the burning building, Koa on her heels. She looks around for help but sees no one. Where are the first responders? Where is security? Finding themselves alone in a large foyer hastily filling with smoke, Ana and Koa run to the north wing toward Auntie Pakalana's room.

"Ana, wait!" Kimo arbitrarily pulls over and runs after the pair into the building and down the hallway as the dense smoke billows. People cough and scream for help. Kimo catches up to Ana and Koa in Auntie's room, where Ana struggles to get an unconscious woman into her wheelchair, Koa barking excitedly.

"I found her on the floor next to her bed. I don't know, Kimo …" Ana begins to cough and realizes they don't have much time. Kimo quickly loads Auntie into the wheelchair.

"Get her to the truck, Ana! I'll try to help here!" Kimo turns to enter another smoke-filled room as the fire reaches the building's propane tank, and an explosion rocks the back of the burning building. They are both thrown to the ground.

Ana quickly rises and starts shouting orders. "Koa, go to the truck and stay. Now!" The dog obediently takes off running as Ana turns to Kimo, who is already up and heading toward the worst of the blaze.

"Kimo, no! You're not going back there; you'll die." Flashbacks of the kibbutz attack all those years ago threaten to crack Ana's armor. How can this be happening again? It's too much. Ana begins to panic.

"Kimo, please don't go! Don't leave! I can't do this without you. We need you, Kimo. I need you. I can't lose you, too."

Somehow, through the smoke, Kimo and Ana lock eyes, their shared trauma flooding back to them. It was 1996 all over again. The smoke, the screaming, the explosions, the terror. Kimo looks at Auntie in the wheelchair, takes her pulse, and realizes she's already passed from smoke inhalation. He takes off, pushing the wheelchair toward the parking lot at a dead run, Ana right behind him. Tragically, the sound of coughing and screaming behind them begin to slowly subside as the fire engulfs the entire complex. Ana and Kimo rapidly approach the parking lot and hear Koa barking persistently at the truck. They look to find the flames have already engulfed the truck bed, the fire rapidly consuming everything in its path. They have only one chance now, only one way they will survive. They have to run.

Kimo grabs three towels and a water bottle from the cab of his truck just before it bursts into flames. He soaks the towels with water, wraps one around Koa's head and snout, leaving his eyes free, and hands another to Ana. "Here, wrap this around your head, cover your nose and mouth, and stay low. We have to run for it, Ana. Take Koa and head straight for the ocean. I'll be right behind you." Kimo covers his own head with a wet towel.

"Kimo, that's six blocks! The fire is coming so fast; we'll never make it!"

"It's our only chance. The whole town is burning to the ground, Ana. Run! Run like hell toward the ocean, and don't stop, no matter what you see. RUN!"

CHAPTER 2

Maui, Hawaii
July 28, 2024

Ana bolts upright in bed, screaming for her mother, "Ima! IMAAAA!". Her flailing arms knock over a half-empty glass of water.

"FUCK!"

Ana's dog, Koa, lifts his supersized head off the pillow beside her. He groans from under the down blanket and snuggles deeper into his satin pillow.

"This fucking dream again!" Koa commiserates with an empathetic whine, stretches lazily, spins around, and lies back down with a huge sigh and a considerable thud. Nobody can accuse Koa of being too lively in the morning. Usually, he can count on Mom to sleep in a little later, but apparently, not today.

Ana jumps out of bed and catches her pinky toe on the nightstand.

"SHIT!" Remembering her promise to her little "sister" Kalia to clean up her potty mouth, Ana hobbles over to the dresser and removes three one-dollar bills from her wallet. She counts them one by one while repeating the offending words as each bill pays its debt.

"Fuck. Fucking. Shit." Ana stuffs the bills into the overflowing swear jar and looks at Koa.

"At least I got my money's worth."

Koa whimpers in agreement. Kalia's college fund is looking healthier every day. Even though Kimo's little sister is only 15, she's an old soul. Kalia wants to attend university at the University of Hawaii on Oahu, earn a law degree, and then return to Maui to serve the local people of Lahaina. She's a good kid. Kalia has become a passionate and outspoken advocate for the Lahaina Strong movement in the wake of last summer's devastating fires, volunteering and pitching in wherever she can. She camped out with her cousins in a tent on Ka'anapali Beach for five months, protesting for housing and support for the fire survivors. Ana sees a lot of herself in this clever and spirited girl. Without all the bad shit. Ummm, stuff.

The Lahaina fires. Uggh. Ana is overwhelmed with grief as she realizes it will be a year next week. One whole year since historic Lahaina Front Street -- a 200-year-old whaling town -- burned to the ground. One year since 2,200 homes were lost in the terrifying blaze. One year since over 1,000 businesses went up in flames like so much keawe wood at a luau. One year since over 1,000 people died in terrifying and tragic deaths, ten times the official death toll. The aftermath has been horrifying. Untold 1,000s of local people were forced to move off-island due to a lack of housing, jobs, and resources.

Every local knows a friend or loved one who died that horrible day. The losses are immeasurable—loss of property, loss of history, loss of cultural heritage, loss of life. Not to mention a community-wide mental health crisis. Almost everyone on Maui was traumatized in some way by the devastation on August 8th.

Ana was glad the community had organized a memorial Paddle Out for the one-year anniversary. She doesn't usually attend large social events, but this one is different. This one is sacred. The paddle-out is a traditional Hawaiian tribute to the lives and legacies of those who have passed away. It is a floating memorial a few yards offshore, where mourners sit atop their paddleboards and join hands, forming a human circle symbolizing eternity. Each mourner carries flowers or Hawaiian leis on their boards and in their teeth. Some people sing songs, some "talk story" or say a few words about those who have passed. Often, the ashes of loved ones are sprinkled in the water, symbolizing the reunion of those passed with the ocean. Sometimes, the board of the deceased may be brought out by family or friends and adorned with flowers. There is chanting, and at the end, everyone splashes the water vigorously to help release grief and emotions. It is a deeply spiritual experience.

Ana wouldn't miss the opportunity to mourn and honor those who were lost. She personally knows scores of folks who'd lost their homes and more than a dozen who'd lost their lives. She thinks of good old Thumper, perpetually parked at the end of the bar at Lahaina Yacht Club. He was the sweetest old man. Thumper used to call her Wonder Woman because he thought she was the spitting image of Gal Gadot, the Israeli model and Hollywood actress. A lot of people told her that. The rumor was that Thumper was the voice of the character "Thumper" the bunny in the movie Bambi, and Ana didn't discover it wasn't true until years after she'd met him. He got a real kick out of the fact that she'd believed the rumor for so long, and he teased Ana every chance he got. Lovable, adorable Thumper always had a big smile and a bigger hug for Ana. They'd had a special bond. Ana is reminded of a quote from her favorite childhood movie, *The Wizard of Oz.*

"Scarecrow, I think I'll miss you most of all."

The Lahaina Yacht Club was Ana's go-to place for great food and cool, laid-back locals. She wasn't a big fan of crowded places or fancy restaurants, but this wasn't your typical yacht club, and these weren't your typical yacht club members. While there were plenty of folks there who sailed and fished and some who owned boats, the main focus of this yacht club was the social interaction. The members like to say, "We're not a yacht club with drinks, as much as a drinking club with yachts." Well, maybe a few large boats.

Locals loved the yacht club because, as a private club, it was the only place on Front Street where you could always get a table when the rest of the town was overflowing with visitors from around the world. The only tourists there were either guests of a member or the occasional visitor from a "real" yacht club off-island, who were generally surprised at the casual atmosphere and the regulars whooping it up at the bar.

The Akamai family was awarded a lifetime membership for Uncle and Auntie's charitable contributions to the community. It probably doesn't hurt that Uncle Kalama is "ali'i" - Hawaiian royalty. It turns out Uncle's family are direct descendants of King Kamehameha I. The whole family had their names on the back of chairs in the restaurant there, purchased during a fundraiser that Auntie Pua had organized. She sits on the Board of the women's auxiliary group, the Boomvangers, and also runs the Chili Cook-Off every year. Auntie Pua is deadly serious about her Chili.

Before it burned to the ground, the Yacht Club had a Keiki Sailing Program, where Ana volunteered to teach the local kiddos how to sail in tiny, pint-sized sailboats. She loves working with kids. They're brutally honest. What you see is what you get. No expectations. No broken promises. Membership at the Yacht Club is especially handy on big nights like Halloween, New Year's Eve, and July 4th, when you could sit out on the lanai and watch the myriad of people drinking, dancing, laughing, and enjoying a party in paradise, but still have access to bathrooms, dinner, and cocktails.

Three nights a year, people from all over the world traveled to Lahaina Town to celebrate. The local cops closed down Front Street to vehicles, and the whole downtown area became one big party from one end to the other. On Halloween, folks paraded up and down the street to loud music, dancing, partying, and displaying their costumes. The evening culminated in a costume competition at the Banyan Tree for the best and most creative costumes. It was quite a scene, but even Ana had to admit it was a good time. When they were younger, Ana, Kimo, and the cousins used to walk Front Street in the Keiki Parade every year. They had even won "Best Group Costume" one year for their Wizard of Oz regalia … Ana's idea, of course.

Ana makes coffee and feeds Koa his breakfast of raw meat, vegetables, and pumpkin, which he wolfs down ravenously as she watches in amazement. Ana has tried every trick in the book to make Koa slow down his eating, including the old tennis ball in the bowl trick and wasting money on every special vessel invented to slow him down, to no avail.

"Geez, Ow, Coco Puff! It's no wonder you're 140 pounds! You ate that faster than a prairie fire with a tailwind!" She smiles warmly at the memory of her mom's father, Grandpa Sid. He is an ex-Texas Ranger who is "tougher than a two-dollar steak" and has a veritable plethora of old Southern sayings that Ana likes to use from time to time. Between her mix of Hebrew, Hawaiian, and Southern aphorisms, it's a wonder anyone understands a thing she says. Just another reason not to socialize. Ana makes a mental note to call Grandpa Sid before it gets too late. Texas is a 5-hour time difference from Maui.

"Koa, remind me to call Grandpa Sid." Koa looks up and tilts his head. Grandpa Sid? Grandpa Sid brings chew toys and liver treats from the mainland. Koa pants appreciatively at the sound of his name. "You love you some Grandpa Sid, don't you, Koey?"

Although Ana had gone to live with Uncle and Auntie immediately after the massacre at the kibbutz, she stays in close contact with her mother's dad. They bonded over their silent grief, never discussing her missing parents. It was too painful for both of them to think about, so they remained tough and soldiered on. It was Grandpa Sid who encouraged her to continue her martial arts training – she'd studied Krav Maga in Israel for four years and had shown real promise. After what happened to his daughter, Sid insisted that his only grandchild be prepared as much as humanly possible for any type of danger. Grandpa Sid comes to Maui every few months to spend time with Ana. They go off-grid for weeks at a time, and Sid has taught Ana everything she needs to know to survive off the land. He taught her how to hunt with both a rifle and a crossbow. Ana easily mastered everything she was taught and became so proficient with her crossbow that she won a statewide competition when she was in high school. Ana was also one of the best spear fishers on the island. Today, at 28 years old, she is a Krav Maga instructor and uses her survival skills to live off the land on her little plot on the Akamai ancestral property.

Ana settles into her favorite chair on the lanai and melts into an array of mismatched throw pillows. Sipping her coffee, strong and black, she enjoys her solitude and peruses her tiny little slice of paradise. Ana hugs her knees and sighs deeply, looking off through the ohia trees that border her yard. The red and yellow blooms remind her of the legend of Ohia and Lehua.

Soon after they'd all moved to Maui, almost 20 years ago, Auntie Pua had told Ana the story of two beautiful young lovers, Ohia and Lehua. The legend says that one day, the volcano goddess Pele met a handsome warrior named Ohia, and she asked him to marry her. When Ohia explained he was already engaged to his beloved Lehua, Pele was so enraged that she turned him into a gnarled and twisted tree. Lehua was devastated when she saw what Pele had done to her one true love. She was inconsolable, sobbed uncontrollably, and declared she could not bear to be apart from Ohia. The gods, chagrined by Pele's vengeful act, took pity on Lehua and transformed her into a flower born from the Ohia tree, so that the two lovers would be joined forever. This is why the ancestors say if you pluck the Lehua flower, you are separating the two lovers, and that day it will rain the tears of the brokenhearted couple.

Ana remembered after the story, Kimo chimed in, "You know, Ana, the Ohia tree was used to create weapons and kapa cloth for the ancestors. Today, its leaves are used for medicinal tea, and its flowers and seeds feed the native birds." Kimo is such a know-it-all.

Auntie Pua said the story's message was about true love, about finding your soulmate. Ana figured the lesson was one she'd already learned on her 10th birthday: Love equals loss and abandonment. People leave. Hearts break. It's better to avoid the entire unfortunate ordeal.

Regardless, Ana loves learning about the "aina," the land of Maui. Sometimes, she can't believe she lives here. The sweet smell of pua kenikeni permeates the air. She snickers to herself at the memory of Kimo planting them around her lanai while, of course, enriching her with yet another Hawaiian cultural lesson. Kimo is like the Hawaiian Cliff Claven.

"You know, Ana, pua kenikeni means 'flower nickel nickel.' It is associated with love and beauty. Back in the day, the Aunties used to sell them for ten cents each to the cousins to make leis for the haoles, your ancestors, yeah?"

"You callin' me a haole, Bruh?" Kimo had laughed and thrown dirt at her. He's so flippin' adorable.

It is touching how Kimo regularly comes by to check on Ana and help around her home, despite him no longer living on the family property. Even after he joined the Marine Corps, he would fix things around her place when he was home on leave. Kimo is endlessly handy. He can single-handedly build a home from the ground up. And he has. Ana's piece of the Akamai family property retreats into the West Maui Mountains on the slopes of a 1.7-million-year-old volcano they call 'Mauna Kaha'la'wi.' It means the house that holds water. Ironic since the fight over water rights between the Hawaiians and the government types has endured since Hawaii became a state in 1959.

For generations, Ana's adopted family, the Akamai ohana, have cared for, hunted on, and farmed this land, which is in the shape of a wedge, reaching from the mountains to the ocean. The property yields more bananas, dragon fruit, papaya, mangoes, lilikoi, and breadfruit than the large, multigenerational family can eat, so they share it with the local community. Fruit orchards and mixed gardens – the native Hawaiian "kanaka" way -- thrive without the need for irrigation. Her family hunts boar and deer in the mountains, grows crops in the hills, and casts lines in the ocean for Ahi, Ono, Ulu, Mahi, and more. Paradise.

Ana's serene moment is abruptly interrupted as Koa barks, leaps from the lanai, and takes off, sprinting across the yard toward the gardens and the chicken coops. Suddenly, chickens are squawking, pigs are squealing, and Koa is barking playfully. Ana jumps up, spilling her coffee. "Shit!" She runs barefoot down the gently sloped yard toward the mayhem, pulling up her too-big boxer shorts as she yells, "Koa! Koa, leave it! Leave it! Oh shit! Koa, leave it!"

Ana runs around like she's pitching a hissy fit with a tail on it (another Sid-ism), chasing the pigs and waving her arms frantically.

"Get out of here! Get out of here, you fucking troublemakers! Get out of my lettuce patch!"

The squeals of the wild boar are deafening, nearly drowning out the frenetic screeches coming from the chicken coop and, of course, Koa's persistent barking. After wreaking havoc in the garden, the boar run off into the woods with Koa happily barking and nipping at their heels. Koa loves this nearly daily ritual. Ana hates it. She trips and falls in the middle of the muddy eggplant patch.

"Fuck!"

"That'll be one dollar." Kimo stands there with his soul-crushing smile, holding a fresh cup of coffee. Ana wonders how much of that shit show he caught. Ugh. She hadn't even brushed her teeth yet. Why is he so fucking gorgeous? Why is she so awkward and clumsy?

Ana brushes her long, dark hair from her face, rises from her humiliation, and takes the coffee. "Looks like it's going to be an expensive day."

Kimo follows Ana up toward the house. "I don't know why you made this promise to Kalia. I think you're cute when you cuss."

"Shut up."

Kimo laughs. Ana thinks she's a hard ass, but he knows better. Kimo knows her better than anyone in the world. Even Ana herself. Somewhere underneath that rough, tough, *vulgar* exterior is a gentle, sweet, compassionate woman. Somewhere. Deep down. Deep.

Ana stomps up the lanai steps, enduring Kimo's teasing.

"I love this look for you. It says, 'I don't care what anybody thinks'. It screams confidence."

"Shut up. Why are you here, anyway? I haven't seen hide nor hair of you since you've been shacking up in town with the young and beautiful Leimomi. Did I say young?" Ana smiles at her own dig and takes a sip of her coffee as they settle in on the lanai.

Kimo smiles back. "Leimomi is a great girl, she really is, and she's going to make someone a wonderful wife someday. It's just not me. She deserves more than I can offer her. She deserves better."

Ana knows no one would be a better husband and father than Kimo. He is sweet, considerate, compassionate, hardworking … not to mention HOT: 6'2, wavy dark hair, muscles on his muscles. Every single woman on the west side stands a little taller and smiles a little brighter when Kimo is around. Smile, giggle, hair-flip—the trifecta of the female mating ritual. Kimo is like a big, sweet, gorgeous, charismatic teddy bear. What's not to love?

They both know he's not being completely honest about the situation. Though they've become experts at dancing around it, they both know why Kimo can't commit to

Leimomi or any other woman, for that matter. He's waiting for Ana, waiting for Ana to heal. Waiting for Ana to forgive. Waiting for Ana to open her heart. Then maybe she'll realize what everyone who knows them understands: Kimo and Ana belong together.

Ana can't see the forest for the trees. Although she recognizes the connection between them, she won't let him in. She can't bring herself to believe she could be happy with Kimo, or with anyone else. She's broken. Ana encourages Kimo not to give up on Leimomi.

"Kimo, Leimomi adores you and wants to raise beautiful Hawaiian babies with you. Are you going to throw away yet another good relationship? You deserve a woman whose heart is whole and whose mind is open, not an angry, fucked up, foul-mouthed agoraphobic loner with a bad attitude and daddy issues."

Kimo laughs and rises from the comfort of the overstuffed chair. He kisses the top of Ana's head and hops off the lanai into the flower bed. He turns and teases, "You know, Ziva, that was a very self-reflective rant. You'll have to send my compliments to your therapist."

Ana throws a pillow at Kimo as he sidesteps the incoming missile. "Get out of my pua kenikeni and don't call me Ziva!"

Ziva. They were both laughing, but inside, Ana ached

with the memory of that day. Her 10th birthday. The day her whole world changed forever. On that day, Ziva prayed to Hashem, to God, to give her another life: a life without pain, without loss. To let her be someone else, anyone else. She couldn't bear to live her life any longer. She couldn't bear the loss, the fear, the abandonment, the betrayal. That day, the world as she knew it vanished, replaced by a new reality in a new place, halfway around the world.

The trip to Hawaii had been the longest 28 hours of her life. Young Ziva experienced every ingredient in the emotional cookbook during that trip. Eventually, she settled on a recipe to move forward: two parts anger, one part acceptance, with a pinch of hopelessness.

By the time the plane landed at the Kahului airport on that early November day in 2006, Ziva had changed. She felt like an entirely different person. Ziva decided then and there she would change her name and leave her life in Israel behind. She would combine her middle name with her mother's maiden name and create a new identity for herself. She was no longer Ziva Anastasia Cohen, war orphan. She would become Ana Summer, survivor, and lone wolf. She'd show this fucked up world she would never be hurt again. No one would ever leave her again. She'd show them.

The day after the attack, they left the only home Ziva

had ever known. After three planes and a long jeep ride into the mountains, they arrived at the Akamai family property. Ziva, now Ana, stepped out of the jeep and looked around at the lush rainforest around them, and she felt desperately lonely and sad. Her parents were gone, and now she had nothing. Ana knew she had to be strong for her mother; she'd promised. She knew what she had to do to protect herself.

"Gotta run!" Ana was startled out of her reverie.

"Mama is making poi today; I'll bring you a big bowl!" Always the prankster. Kimo knows Ana HATES poi.

Ana rolls her eyes. "Send Auntie Pua warmest aloha!"

Ana walks down the steps of her lanai and watches as Kimo trots off across the lawn and through the monkey pod forest toward Auntie's hale. It starts to softly rain. Ana loves the rain. It's cleansing. It's life-giving. It's nourishing. Again, as she does every day, Ana marvels at the beauty of the West Maui mountains. She looks up at the cloud-covered sky, raises her arms, and smiles as she mimics Kimo, lowering her voice and puffing up her chest like a bodybuilder.

"You know, Ana, the West Maui mountains are the second wettest place on Earth."

Ana's smile slowly retreats. The fleeting weightlessness of the moment quickly succumbs to the hefty burden of the past as Ana becomes absorbed again in memories of that time.

Ana's father, Lou, had arrived at the kibbutz the day after the attack. He had been away on a joint CIA-Mossad mission – what was to be his last mission -- with Uncle Kalama and Uncle Lior, Eleanor's brother. They were supposed to have returned days before Ana's (Ziva's) birthday, but had been detained in Turkey. The three men arrived the day after the terrorist attack to find the ruins of what was once their safe haven, their farm, their home. The survivors had gathered down at the stables, which miraculously still stood after the bombings. There were scores of ambulances, police cars, military vehicles, and civilians helping. When the men found their families, they learned the unthinkable. Ana's mother, Eleanor, was missing; there was no sign of her, and Kalama's three-year-old daughter, Lilikoi, was one of the innocent victims of the soulless terrorists. She had perished in the attack.

Pua and Ana were traumatized and inconsolable. Thirteen-year-old Kimo was doing his best to remain stoic and strong, but he was clearly shaken and terrified. There were people everywhere, everyone trying to help, but nothing was helping. Ana's memories of this time are patchy, but she remembers the fear, the aching. The pain was unbearable. Watching Auntie Pua suffer the loss of her baby girl was unendurable. The agony of not knowing where her mother was and fearing the worst was excruciating.

Ana remembers the men speaking in hushed voices, strategizing their next move. She'd never seen her father this way, and the look in his eyes was haunting. Ana was terrified by what this all meant and by what would happen next. What would they do now?

That night, Lou and Kalama sat down with Pua, Kimo, and Ana and laid out their plan. Uncle Lior would take his family and the others to a kibbutz in the Jezreel Valley, Mishmar Ha'emek, where they had relatives. They would join a special ops team that was already tracking the terror group into Lebanon. Lou would entrust Ziva with Kalama and Pua. Kalama would entrust Lou to avenge Lilikoi's death. The two families were bound together for life by the sorrow and loss of that dreadful day.

Since their kibbutz had been all but destroyed and the threat to their families had not yet been eliminated, Kalama would take Pua, Kimo, and Ana to his family's property on the island of Maui in Hawaii, where they would be safe. Lou would go with Lior to find Ellie and unearth Lilikoi's killers. Ana was hysterical. She had just lost her mother, her father was leaving her, and now she had to move to some island in the middle of nowhere?!

"Please don't leave me, Abba, please don't go!" Ana clung to her father, desperately begging and sobbing. "Please,

Abba, please!" But there was no dissuading Lou Cohen. He would find Eleanor. He would exact vengeance for Lilikoi. Lou cried as he hugged his little girl goodbye and promised her he'd come for her soon. There was a look in his tear-filled eyes that Ana had never seen before. Rage. Blind rage. It terrified Ana. She clung to Auntie Pua as she watched her father drive away in a dirty old jeep. It would be almost 20 years before she would see him again.

Koa's barking snapped Ana out of her stroll down bad memory lane. "Shit. Now what?"

CHAPTER 3

Beersheba, Israel
October 3, 2023

The sun rises over Beersheba, Israel, as Zara awakens to the discordant noises of honking cars and screaming motorists. Though she is all too familiar with the sounds and smells of the urban center -- she was raised in Gaza -- Zara longs for rural living. It is her dream to move to America, to the great state of Texas, marry an American, and live on a ranch with horses and cows. Zara has been obsessed with American television since she can remember. She grew up watching reruns of *Dallas* and *Dynasty* and even got her hands on some old *Bonanza* DVDs. Zara longs for the vast open spaces of the American West. Most recently, she became obsessed with *Yellowstone,* starring Kevin Costner, and admitted that Montana seemed like a pretty good option as well. Zara gets a kick out of the "Beth Dutton" character. Boy, is she full of spit and vinegar – an American saying Zara had learned from watching reruns of *The Golden Girls*- but she could never imagine being that outspoken and brazen.

"Zara, come please and help Iman with breakfast."

Zara's host mother, Farrah, treats her like one of her own children, and Zara feels no less loved. She came to live in Israel four years ago when she was 15. Her parents sent her to live with an Arab Israeli family so she could have a better life and chase her dreams. Zara's parents, the al Tajirs, were not wealthy, nor did they support the Hamas terror group that ruled Gaza, but they did not have the means to escape. Regardless, they wanted freedom, opportunities, and happiness for their daughter, so when the opportunity arose, they jumped on it.

Zara's family had suffered an unfathomable loss. Hamas had murdered their son, Zavier, because he was found with another young boy in a compromising position. After horrible abuse, they pushed both boys off a 4-story building and left them to endure a slow and painful death. Zara's parents were devastated, of course, and knew they had to get their daughter to a safer place, a place where she could have a normal, happy life. Zara was an exceptional young girl: beautiful, intelligent, and ambitious. She could be anything she wanted to be if she could just escape Gaza.

Farrah Nader heard about Zara's plight from a colleague at the zoo, a cousin of the al Tajir family. By the end of that conversation, Farrah felt a connection to this family and this young girl. Her husband, Nisim, agreed immediately after Farrah explained the situation, and together, they decided to sponsor Zara. Zara would live with them, become educated in Israel, and have every opportunity to be free and happy. Not so secretly, Farrah had hoped she would be a match for their son Omar, who, after his service in the Israeli Defense Forces, had just graduated from Veterinary College. Omar was following in his father's footsteps and specializing in large animal veterinary medicine. Despite Farrah's hopes, Omar and Zara became close, but not in a romantic way. Eventually, Omar met his bashert, his soulmate, Nadia, with whom he has been very much in love for over two years.

Zara rushes into the small kitchen. "Sorry, Mamma. How can I help?" Farrah points to the pile of bell peppers and onions on the cutting board, and Zara immediately begins chopping.

Farrah's daughter, Iman, is at the stove, busily preparing the spices and educating Zara on her Middle Eastern cuisine preparation.

"The ratio of paprika to cumin is the key to a perfect Shakshuka."

At nine years old, Iman is already a great cook. She loves spending time in the kitchen with Mamma and Zara, who is every bit of a big sister to her, blood relatives or not. Iman is so happy when she is making food for her loved ones; it is most definitely her love language. The girls learned all about love languages from reruns of *Dr. Phil.*

Zara has come to love this family as her own and takes immense pleasure in fulfilling her role as daughter and sister. She truly feels like Iman and Omar are her siblings. She mentors Iman when Iman isn't mentoring her, and Omar is very brotherly, always looking out for her. It is a warm and loving environment, and Zara feels like she is home.

"I'll take out the jachnun for Abi; you know how he loves his pastries." Zara calls Nisim "Abi," father, just like Iman and Omar. They are family.

Farrah enters the kitchen, freshly showered for her day at the zoo. Farrah, Nisim, and Omar all work at the Negev Zoo, located just outside Beersheba. Nisim is a primate specialist and large animal veterinarian, Farrah is a herpetologist, and Omar is interning under his father. Omar hopes to open his own veterinary practice someday. Zara always loves their discussions about the animals they care for at the zoo. Many an evening, Farrah came home with a sick snake or lizard. Once, an iguana escaped their apartment and ended up making a nest and incubating her eggs in the building's service elevator. Old Mrs. Spielberg almost had a heart attack when she tried to load in her groceries the next morning. She still glares at the whole Nader family when they see her in the lobby.

Zara loves animals as much as the rest of them, but she wants to raise them, not heal them. She jokes with Omar that someday she and her American husband would consider hiring him on as their Ranch Veterinarian.

Nisim enters the kitchen and kisses his wife affectionately on her cheek. "My beautiful Farrah, this weekend will be 20 years since you generously agreed to be my wife."

You would never have known they weren't newlyweds. Nisim and Farrah have one of those rare relationships where they grow more in love every day. The children watch the public display of affection with different reactions.

"Ew, my eyes, my eyes." Iman covers her face in an attempt to blind herself to the romantic gesture.

Zara thinks it is adorable and silently prays to Allah to give her this kind of love.

"Iman, you don't know how lucky you are that your parents love each other so much." The girl rolls her eyes.

Omar loves love and joins his parents' happiness. "So, you two lovebirds are heading out for a romantic weekend in a few days?"

This weekend, Nisim is taking Farrah to her favorite resort in Tiberias, located on the western shores of the Sea of Galilee, Israel's largest freshwater lake. It is their go-to vacation spot. The Naders have been going there with friends and family since Omar was a small boy. There is something for everyone to do there. Farrah loves soaking in the hot springs and getting spa services with the ladies, and Nisim spends most of the time on the water with the men and the kids. They go canoeing, rafting, stand-up paddling, boating, and fishing.

Once Omar got a little older, he hung out with his peers, jet skiing and wakeboarding during the day, and had bonfires next to the Eucalyptus trees at night. That's how Omar met Nadia two years ago. Omar was jet skiing with a friend when they came across a young woman floating alone hundreds of yards offshore. She wore a life preserver, but she was terrified and visibly distressed. Omar helped her onto his jet ski while she tearfully explained she had bounced off the back of a Banana

Boat, and the operator never looked back. Nadia told Omar he saved her life, and the rest is history.

Omar has a goofy look on his face, and his mother senses something.

"Omar, what is going on? You look like you're up to something." After some wavering, Omar decides to tell his family the secret too big to keep.

"Okay, I can't stand it anymore. I have to tell you all, or I think I'll burst."

The family stares in anticipation. What could this be? Zara thinks she knows. They endure an awkward pause as Omar struggles to find the words.

"Next month, I'm going to ask Nadia to marry me in a hot air balloon while floating over the Sea of Galilee!" Omar smiles ear to ear.

"Omar, that's wonderful! Congratulations! We love Nadia!"

"Son, I'm very happy for you!"

"Omar, can I be in the wedding?"

Zara just sits and beams. She knew it. She is thrilled for Omar. Nadia is a sweet, warm, and nurturing young woman who will make Omar a wonderful wife. They are perfect together.

Each family member takes their turn hugging Omar and wishing him well. It is a tender and beautiful moment. Zara once again thanks God for giving her this family and this new life full of hope and happiness.

Omar reminds them in a stern tone, "Nadia knows nothing, so please keep this a secret. This moment only happens once in a lifetime."

They all assure him their lips are sealed as Omar shakes his finger sternly at Iman, who rolls her eyes.

Nisim takes a bite of Shakshuka and exaggerates his delight for his daughter's benefit. "Iman, did you make this? This is really fantastic! Seriously! Amazing! I will be the first investor in Café Iman."

Iman giggles and grins from ear to ear. She's been talking nonstop lately about becoming a Chef in one of those fancy restaurants in Tel Aviv, and Nisim and Farrah have been ardently supporting her aspirations.

Nisim turns to Zara, "So Zara, what does your day look like?"

Zara has taken a job at Mishmar Ha'emek, an agricultural kibbutz in the Jezreel Valley. It is an amazing operation. One thousand people live there, and together, they manage 1,600 acres of field crops and orchards, 240 Dairy Cows, and a high-tech poultry breeding program that hatches 16 million chicks annually—quite the difference from where she grew up in Gaza. Zara much prefers the wide-open spaces of the kibbutz over the concrete, crowds, and poverty of Gaza.

"Usually, I work in the fields picking dates, but today, I get to work with the cows. I'm so excited!"

Farrah loves to see Zara smile. She has been through so much and wants the best for the girl. "That's wonderful, Zara. Isn't that where your American friend Rachel works?"

"Yes, Mamma, she works at the dairy. Even though she's a few years younger, we have so much fun together. She's an old soul. You know her grandfather lives in Texas, right? She promised I could visit there someday, isn't that amazing? TEXAS! I cannot wait!"

Iman gushes, "Maybe you'll meet the American man of your dreams there!" The whole family lovingly teases Zara about her obsession with the American West as she endures the good-natured ribbing.

Omar interrupts the spirited exchange. "Remember, Mamma, Nadia, and I are joining friends at the Nova Festival outside Re'im this weekend. We'll be leaving Friday night and camping out, returning on the evening of October 7th.

Farrah has a bad feeling. "Omar, I don't like this. It is only 3 miles from there to the Gaza border. Why ask for trouble?"

"Mamma, we'll be fine. Thousands of people will be there; nothing bad will happen, I promise."

"I don't like it." Farrah is uneasy about the trip, but Nisim puts his hand on hers, allaying her fears.

"Farrah, please don't worry, Omar knows what he's doing."

Omar looks up the Tribe of Nova Festival on his smartphone and passes it to his mother. "See, Mamma, it's a huge traveling dance party celebrating friendship, love, and peace."

Farrah reads the website. "What is this trance music, Omar?"

Zara chimes in. "It's a form of electronic dance music, Mamma. Everyone dances around like stoned hippies, spreading peace, love, and togetherness. Hey Omar, maybe you'll see Yoko Ono there!"

Omar ignores Zara's quip. "That reminds me, Mamma, Nadia asked me to thank you, yet again, for that red pashmina. She really loves it! She's wearing it to the Festival."

"Tell that beautiful girl, yet again, that it is my pleasure to spoil her."

As breakfast wraps up, Zara and Iman clean the kitchen as the others get ready to head out to the zoo.

"Girls, I'm going shopping for some vacation clothes after work today. If you want to come, we can get our nails done."

Iman and Zara enthusiastically accept the invitation, hugging and kissing goodbye as they look forward to a happy and productive day.

CHAPTER 4

Maui, Hawaii
August 1, 2024

"Ima! Ima!!!"

A horrible smell permeates the dining hall, like burning tires. And blood.

"Ziva!" Her mother's voice cuts through the chaos as she appears through the smoke and fire. Eleanor yells above the cacophony of screaming. Moaning. Gunfire. Explosions.

Ellie screams, "Ziva! Ziva, go with Kimo … !"

"No, Ima, no! Don't leave me! No Ima, NOOOO!!!"

Ziva sobs in terror as Ellie holds Ziva's arms firmly with both hands, staring into her eyes.

"Ziva Anastasia Cohen, look at me. You have to be brave right now. You have to be strong. You'll be okay. You have to go with Kimo NOW. Go to the bunker!"

Pua appears through the smoke, screaming for her children, "LILIKOI!!! KIMO!!! KIMO, TAKE THE CHILDREN TO THE BUNKER!" Kimo appears through the haze, and Pua turns to Eleanor in desperation.

"Ellie, I can't find Lilikoi!"

Eleanor and Pua spring into action and run toward the chaos and disappear through the dense black smoke. Before Ziva can quarrel, Kimo whisks her off and starts shouting orders to the other children. They run behind the building to the bomb shelter. Twenty yards feels like twenty miles. They run as more bombs detonate around them.

Explosions violently shake the buildings around her— warning sirens blare. Screams and shouts fill the air. Ziva can see nothing through the thick black smoke. She chokes and sobs and shrieks with pure terror. "Ima! IMAAAA!"

The screaming. The odors. Gunpowder. Burning buildings. Burning flesh.

Ziva tries to run, but her feet won't move. She is paralyzed as she sees Kimo disappear through the smoke. He doesn't know she isn't behind him. He doesn't know he's left her to die. She tries to scream, but no sound comes out. KIMO!!!

Nothing. She is paralyzed and cannot escape as the terrorists close in. Ziva knows she is going to die. She screams for her mother.

"Ima! IMAAAA!"

Ana awakens with a start, a scream caught in her throat, her long hair soaked with sweat. She looks at the clock, and it's 4:00 am. Much to Koa's chagrin, Ana jumps out of bed and starts her morning routine.

"Not today, Satan." Ana was certain she was in the middle of some kind of spiritual warfare, the fate of her soul in question. She was haunted by the demons of her past.

While she fully intends to go down kicking and screaming, today, Ana just doesn't have it in her to go back to sleep and face another round fighting the nightmare. She knows the dream will just continue where it left off. It always does. It's like a scary movie that's on pause. Once you press play again, the horrors keep coming, and Ana is not going to stick around for the second act. She already knows how it ends. Ana isn't going to give in to the haunting memories and decides to take advantage of the early morning hour to get some training in.

Ana puts on her Lululemon yoga pants, a sports bra, and an old Powerhouse Gym T-shirt left by an old fling named Pete. Poor, Pete. He'd had an ugly divorce and came to Maui from California in an attempt to heal his broken heart. The gentle, soft-spoken chiropractor had come into the Krav Maga dojo to sign up for a few months of lessons during his respite. The moment he saw Ana, he became immediately smitten. Ana is 5'9 and 150 lbs of lean muscle in an athlete's body. She has been a tomboy her entire life. Star of her high school rowing team and volleyball team, crossbow champion, and survivalist extraordinaire, Ana has it all. There's not a man with a heartbeat that doesn't notice her enter a room. The most attractive part is that she has no idea how striking she truly is. Ana is usually relatively self-absorbed and rarely notices the attention focused on her. Poor Pete didn't know what hit him. He never really had a fighting chance.

Ana's relationship with Pete was mutually beneficial: Ana helped Pete get over his ex-wife, and he helped Ana loosen up and become a little more social. He got her to let her hair down a bit. He was good for her. Pete was a nice guy, just a little too nice for Ana. They both knew it was a seasonal fling, and when Pete left the island, Kimo joked for months that they couldn't be sure he had actually left Maui. He was sure Ana had chewed him up and spit him out somewhere in the West Maui mountains. Poor Pete.

Darkness shrouds the property as Ana and Koa trot down to the barn, the beam from a flashlight guiding the way. Ana flicks on the light as she enters the space and walks toward her makeshift "locker," where she keeps her sparring gear. Ana and Kalia created a small private dojo at the back of the barn a few years ago when Kalia became serious about training. They lined one wall with mirrors and hung two heavy bags from one of the ceiling trusses. Thick pads covered the floor, allowing the girls to practice their groundwork. "Rolling" was an important part of Krav Maga. It is a fact that most altercations eventually end up on the ground, so it is important to hone your throws, holds, and, of course, strikes. Ana has been training Kalia for five years now, and she is so proud of the progress the feisty teenager has made. There is no doubt the girl can handle herself in a fight. Kalia has become a strong, confident, and capable young woman, what the locals would call a "tita."

Koa settles into his orthopedic bed in the corner of the barn while Ana puts on her boxing gloves. He knows he has time for at least an hour's nap as Ana loses herself in the primal physicality of her kickboxing workout. Ana works the heavy bag until the sweat is dripping in her eyes, off the tip of her nose, and down her chest. Sometimes, when Ana works out, she becomes lost in the memories and the rage of that day, entering a sort of fugue state. This morning, Ana emerges from her fugue, not knowing how long she'd been kicking and punching the monsters in her head. As the sun rises in pastel colors over the West Maui mountains, Ana completes her workout and heads back up to the house. Koa, right on her heels, is excited for breakfast.

Ana opens the door to the outdoor shower, her only shower, and is confronted by a huge, red, angry centipede. It's at least eight inches long and is rearing up as if to challenge her to a fight. Ana hates centipedes. She can deal with cane spiders, black widows, and even the occasional scorpion, and she's never seen a snake because there are none on Maui. It is the centipede that is her nemesis. Ana had reached the ripe old age of 28 without being stung by one, and she doesn't intend to break her streak now. A centipede sting is excruciating and burns and throbs for hours. Kimo had once been stung in the foot, and he said it felt like the little bastard was pulling off his toe! No, thank you. Ana removes one of her Oofos slippers and strikes the terrifying creature a total of 9 times until it finally stops writhing with loathing and vengeance in its heart.

"God, I hate centipedes!" Koa shnortles in agreement. Satan's worms. Spiritual warfare.

After her shower, Ana dons her usual attire – a bikini and board shorts – and heads up the lanai and into the house. She makes two cups of coffee, strong and black, no frou-frou flavors or creme, and puts them in travel mugs. Then she and Koa walk through the trees and across the stream to Uncle Kalama's "office," an old plantation-style house isolated among a forest of monkey pods and kukui nut trees. As they approach Uncle's hale, she can hear the constant chattering of his police scanner.

Uncle Kalama is a private contractor for various unknown clients (he could tell you, but he'd have to kill you) and is always involved in several projects with various law enforcement agencies. Uncle is part laid-back island boy, part international crime solver, part computer whiz. While the outside of his hale looks like it is a 100-year-old cabin, the inside is filled with the latest in computer technology and gadgets. A collection James Bond's "M" would be proud of.

Uncle sits on his lanai, three computer screens on the table in front of him. "Ana, dear, you're early today." Koa puts his head in Kal's lap for his morning pets.

"Sleep is for losers, Uncle. I have things to do, people to see, places to go." Ana is flippant, but Kal knows she is covering.

"The dream again?" He knows her so well. Uncle opens the door for Ana to share her feelings, but she slams it shut with a quick topic change.

"Can you believe it's almost a year since the fires? Are you and Auntie going to the Paddle Out next week?"

Kalama let it go. He knows it is no use pushing Ana; she will open up in her own time—or not. Besides, he has more pressing issues on his mind this morning and worries about how Ana will take the news.

Uncle and Ana sit on the lanai, sipping coffee in silence,

taking in the vast ocean views. They listen to the sounds of the mynah birds who fill the canopies with chatter in the trees above them. They watch the geckos crawl all over the lanai, searching for their tiny insect prey. A mongoose stealthily sneaks through the ground cover as the chickens and roosters peck the ground for entomological treasures. Kal seems distracted, and an uneasy feeling suddenly overcomes Ana. She notices the hair on her arms standing up and tries to shake off the feeling of impending doom. She asks Uncle if he thinks there's a storm coming. Uncle looks slowly up at the sky and doesn't answer. Ana can't quite put her finger on it, but something is off. Is Uncle acting a little odd, or is it just her? These flipping dreams are making her crazy; she feels off balance. She looks at her arms again: chicken skin. Ana is suddenly nervous and tries to cover with small talk.

"I found a centipede in the shower this morning. Is it me, or do they get bigger every year? I swore this one was going to grab the slippah out of my hand and start smacking me back with it!" Kal snickers and nods his head but doesn't respond. Something is definitely off with Uncle.

After a long but comfortable silence, Kal starts to reminisce about the past.

"It's been a good life here on Maui, Ana, yeah?" His

wistful tone worries Ana even more. This isn't normal for Uncle to wax sentimental. He usually isn't this … pensive.

"Yes, Uncle. I am eternally grateful for all you and Auntie have done for me." Ana feels a chill travel like a shock wave down her spine. Is Uncle sick? What is wrong?

"Ana, you don't have to thank us, you're ohana. Always and forever." His gaze is vague, unfocused somewhere far away. "Do you remember your 18th birthday?"

"Of course, Uncle. Grandpa Sid was here, and you and all the cousins gathered for an old-fashioned barn raising. It was the most amazing day of my life! I can't believe it only took a few months of weekends to build my hale. It is the best gift anyone could ever receive!"

When Ana turned 18, Uncle Kalama and Auntie Pua gave her a piece of the family property to care for adjacent to the main house. Just like on the kibbutz years before, her entire ohana came together to build Ana's hale.

Uncle teased that every unmarried man on the west side pitched in to help build it because they all wanted to gain favor with the beautiful and elusive Ana Summer. Auntie Pua had threatened to sell tickets to all the Aunties because they kept coming over to talk story just so they could watch the shirtless suitors pound nails in the hot sun. It was quite a scene. One time, they drank too many mai tais, and one of the Aunties started whistling and catcalling at the young men. Pua was equally entertained and horrified.

Ana remembers that time fondly. Kimo told her he'd only help her build her new hale if she'd let him name it, and she'd agreed. Days after the last nail was pounded and the last wall was painted, Ana had come home to a wooden sign hanging over the entrance to her lanai. It read, "Hale Lehua". Ana had been deeply touched. She knew what this meant. Kimo loved her, and he would wait forever for her. He was the warrior Ohia, and she was his Lehua, his one true love. They never spoke of the sign or of its significance. It simply hung there as a silent, steadfast reminder that when she was ready, he was hers.

"Uncle, is everything okay?" Ana can't shake the feeling of dread.

"Yes, Ana, all good. Don't you have better things to do than worry about some crazy kapuna?"

"You're not crazy, Uncle, but you are old." They both laugh as Ana rises and hugs Kalama, then she and Koa head back to Hale Lehua.

"Warmest aloha, Uncle".

Ana and Koa make the trek back to her property and continue their usual morning routine, taking comfort in the rhythmic nature of her daily schedule. It's predictable, steady … stable.

Ana heads down to the barn to feed the animals. She gets out the two 4-foot-long troughs and fills them, first with canned food and then with dry food. Ana cares for a colony of roughly 60 feral cats. She has been diligently trapping, fixing, and releasing them for years now, and she feels pretty good about the dent she's made: 45 of them are fixed to date. She has an area in the barn for them with various cat condos and feeding stations. Ana is an old softy when it comes to creatures big and small, except for centipedes. Screw them.

Next, she feeds the chickens and ducks and cleans out the water in their plastic pool. She spends a few minutes playing with the new ducklings and marvels at how gentle Koa is with them.

"Good boy, Koey. Aren't they adorable?" Koa responds by laying down and letting the ducklings crawl all over him—fierce but tender. Finally, Ana chops up the rotting fruit from the orchard and fills up two buckets. Ana puts the handle of one bucket in Koa's mouth, and she grabs the other one. Koa is a big help around the farm. The pair walk out about a half mile from the barn and dump out the fragrant fruit for the boar and the birds to eat.

On their way back to the barn, Ana wonders how anyone can be lonely. Alone is her favorite place to be.

She doesn't need anyone to make her happy or to feel safe and secure. She is perfectly fine by herself. Ana never stops trying to convince herself.

After the farm chores, she grabs her surfboard and hops in her old hoop-dee Ford truck, Hawaiian Reggae blasting. Koa jumps in the passenger seat, excited to go to the beach and visit the cousins. They always run into cousins. Koa is very popular at the local beaches and has endless opportunities for games, pets, and, best of all, treats.

Ana pulls off the side of a gravel road and parks outside a roadside food truck for breakfast and her 2nd cup of coffee. Ana and Koa walk up to "Auntie's Kau Kau."

"Howzit Auntie?" Ana approaches the window of the food truck as Koa runs up and puts his front paws on the vehicle so Auntie Kailani can see him. She tosses Koa a piece of bacon, and he catches it in midair. They both love this ritual.

"Ana! Koa! Howzit?" Auntie immediately begins cooking Ana's regular breakfast as they begin to talk story. "Where you been?"

"I've been around. Koa and I have been pretty much keeping to ourselves upcountry. How've you been?"

"How have I been? This VOG is killing my allergies." VOG is no joke. There is an active volcano only 200 miles away on the Big Island of Hawaii, and the volcanic dust and gases from Kilauea form a smog that follows the jet stream right over Maui. The locals call it VOG (volcanic smog), and it wreaks havoc with the air quality over the island, making a lot of folks sick.

"Auntie, I haven't seen you since Kaleo's ma'le; what a beautiful wedding that was. Your property never looked so amazing, and the grinds, all that gorgeous food, you really went all out!"

Auntie's son Kaleo had recently wed a girl from Kauai whom nobody knew until recently, so there was some suspicion among family members as to the reason for the wiki wiki nuptials. He'd only known her for six months.

"Yeah, 'ono loa. Delicious. The aunties got together to cater everything, and they each brought their best dish. Broke da mouth."

"How are the newlyweds? Are they getting settled into their new home?"

"You didn't hear about that on the coconut wireless? Tita is hapai. Pregnant. With child. Bun in the oven. Big surprise. I had that girl's number from day one." Kailani's demeanor belies her words. She doesn't sound too disappointed. In fact, she seems downright happy.

"Ooooh, sorry, Auntie. But look on the bright side; she really seems to love Kaleo, and now you'll have another grandbaby to love." Ana, along with the rest of the cousins, figured the couple were hapai at the wedding, so it wasn't really a shock to anyone.

"You're right. Everything is good. I'm just bustin' chops; she's a good girl and not the first one to ever put the cart before da horse." They laugh as Ana takes her coffee and breakfast burrito from Kailani's brown and weathered hand.

Kailani changes the subject as she tosses Koa another piece of bacon. "So, how's my boyfriend? Will he be on-island soon?" Auntie Kailani has a big crush on Grandpa Sid, who always flirts shamelessly when he sees her. Sid is charismatic, 6'4, and still in amazing shape for an old guy.

"You tell your granddaddy, next time he comes, I'm gonna climb him like a Cook Pine!"

Ana feigns horror. This is par for the course with Kailani. "Auntie! That's my 80-year-old grandfather you're talking about! Have some respect! Gross!"

They both laugh. "Happy Aloha Friday, Auntie!" Ana turns to leave but stops short as Leimomi blocks her way.

"E kala mai, Ana. Excuse me." Leimomi often translates for Ana when she uses Hawaiian words as if to rub in the fact that Ana isn't a native speaker.

"Leimomi! You startled me! Howzit?" Ana doesn't like the energy radiating from the recently jilted lover. She braces for a confrontation.

Leimomi can barely contain her contempt. "Howzit? Not too good, Ana, since Kimo dumped me, but you know all about that, don't you, malihini?" Uh oh. This wasn't good. Calling Ana "malihini," newcomer, is a low blow. Ana has lived on Maui for 18 years. Would she call Ana a colonizer next?

Ana struggles to remain calm. Clearly, she can knock the girl on her butt if she wants to. "I'm sorry, Leimomi, I know how much Kimo cares for you. I thought you two were good together; I even told Kimo … " Leimomi cuts her off. Deep breaths.

"Save it, Ana. Are you really this dense? Kimo is hopelessly in love with you, and you walk all over him, take him for granted, and give him false hope. He'll never be happy with someone else as long as you keep leading him on." Leimomi turns and storms off, abandoning her place as next in line at the food truck. Ana is left speechless.

Having witnessed the exchange, Auntie raises an eyebrow, smirks at Ana and says, "K den. See you at the Paddle Out, eh?"

Ana makes a face that says, "Yikes," throws Kailani a shaka, and walks toward her truck. "Oy vavoy, Koey …

that was awkward. Leading him on? I'm not leading him on. That's ridiculous. Kimo knows the score. He knows I'm broken. I told him to move on. I'm not leading him on." But the seed had been planted. Is Ana giving Kimo mixed signals? No. Maybe. Probably. Is it her fault he hasn't found his person? Is she keeping Kimo from being happy? Koa is distracted by an abandoned bagel and doesn't respond.

CHAPTER 5

Jezreel Valley, Israel
October 3, 2023

Zara happily tends to the dairy cows at Kibbutz Mishmar Ha'emek. Although she was hired to pick dates in the fields, Zara has been asking for more shifts at the dairy and she's thrilled about the assignment, even though it's mostly cleaning up cow dung. You have to start somewhere.

When Zara first heard about the dairy job at the kibbutz, she pictured herself raking out stalls and milking cows by hand. That's not how they do it here. Mishmar Ha'emek is a large, profitable farm and dairy operation with the latest technology. Instead of mucking stalls by hand, large skip loaders with special attachments rake the pens and the parlors, then scrape the alleys, pushing the cow dung to the end of the barn. Once the solid waste is in piles, another tractor pushes the liquids into trenches that run underneath the barns. It is a brilliant system.

Zara's job this morning is to gently coax the heifers, udders filled, toward the milking parlor. Zara gently persuades the cows, one by one, up the ramp to the holding area.

"C'mon, girl. The sooner you get through the milk line, the sooner you get breakfast and a nap."

Zara washes each of their teats so dirt or bacteria does not contaminate the milk. Once she cleans each teat, she dips it in disinfectant. Now they're ready for milking. She rushes through this part of her job so she can get to her favorite part, feeding the calves. She heard three new precious babies were born last night and is beyond excited to meet them.

Once all of the cows are cleaned and in the milk line, Zara heads to the milk room where her American friend Rachel is busy checking the pasteurizing holding tanks. She stops what she's doing and throws her arms around Zara.

"Shalom! I'm so excited we get to work together today; Uncle Lior said I can teach you how to operate the milk taxi and feed the newborns." Rachel knows how badly Zara wants to work with the calves, and they both beam from ear to ear.

"Yay! Thank you, thank you, Rachel. I'm ready to learn! I'm so excited!"

"Okay, first, this is the milk room. When the cows are milked, the milk is collected directly into the holding tanks here and then pasteurized. When that's done, we reheat the milk, fill the milk taxi, and feed the calves from there."

Rachel is enjoying showing Zara the ropes. She had only lived on the kibbutz for two months but feels very much a part of the extended family and loves contributing to the "family business."

Zara studies the milk room. She is surprised at how high-tech the operation is. Tanks, gauges, dials, and computer monitors are everywhere. It is both impressive and intimidating.

"And this is the milk taxi. You just attach this hose and turn this lever to fill the tank." The warm milk gushes freely into the milk taxi reservoir. The girls watch as the chamber fills to the top.

"Then attach the hose with the nozzle here. This is how we fill up the bottles and feeders." Zara is paying close attention. She doesn't want to miss one tiny detail. This is, after all, her future.

"Now fill up these last bottles and snap on one of these red nipples like this." Zara follows Rachel's lead, and soon the bottles are filled and ready.

"Wow, I'm amazed at how large this operation is. I wonder what Hoss and Little Joe would think of all this!"

Rachel laughs, "Haha, you and your American cowboy shows! It's not like that anymore, Zara; this is the wave of the future!"

Zara disagrees, "On my ranch, maybe we're going to do it the old-fashioned way. Hey, can I push the milk taxi?"

The girls enter the first room where the youngest calves are waiting impatiently. Every single baby is mooing, ready for breakfast. Rachel and Zara squeal in delight when they see the three newborns. "Omg, I can't! Look at these little angels! How do you know which ones are boys and which are girls?"

Rachel explains, "The red tags in the ears are steer calves, and the white tags are for heifers."

Zara has tears in her eyes. "I love them already. They're so excited to see us! I've never seen anything more precious in my entire life. I am obsessed!"

"Look, this little guy is a redhead!" After a few minutes of mooning over the newborns, the girls continue their work.

Rachel explains, "We'll have to come back here to bottle-feed these little guys. It takes a while for them to learn how to drink from the bucket."

As if to prove her point, a calf submerges his whole face up to his eyeballs into the bucket of milk. He drinks a bit, then comes up for air, shaking his head, milk flying everywhere.

The girls jump back and laugh at the unbearable cuteness. "See? He has to figure out how to keep his nostrils above the water line. He'll catch on."

Rachel and Zara push the milk taxi room by room, filling up the milk buckets for some of the calves and mounting the bottle feeder in the holder for the younger ones. As they work, the girls catch up on the latest goings-on.

"So, how is your Israeli family? Is Omar still seeing Nadia? Are you certain you don't like Omar that way?"

"Oy, Rachel. I've told you before Omar and I are just friends, more like siblings than sweethearts. And yes, Omar and Nadia are madly in love. Can you keep a secret?"

Rachel mimed zipping up her lips and throwing away the key.

"Omar is going to propose to Nadia next month!" The girls are genuinely happy for the couple and share a big hug. Rachel had never met Nadia, but she had heard everything about her and she sounds amazing. Nadia seems to be the perfect match for Omar.

After the bulk of the calves are fed, the girls go back to feed the newborns. These adorable darlings need to be bottle-fed and sometimes have to be taught how to find the nipple. Rachel and Zara hand-feed the babies, their tiny tails wagging as they suckle.

"Come on, now, take the nipple; there you go, good boy!"

"Take it, sweet girl. Good job! There you go!"

The two share a look of pure joy. Both girls are in their happy place. Life is good.

"I guess we should go back and help out in the milking parlor."

As they enter the milking parlor, Zara witnesses for the first time how the automated milk claws are attached to each cow's teat. She gasps as she sees the blood dripping from each cow as the milk claw is released.

Rachel agrees, "I know, it's horrible. Poor mommas."

Zara dreams of another life in America, where she is milking her own cows with her husband and children, looking out over the hills and open plains of Texas. Or maybe Montana. "This isn't going to happen on my farm. I'm going to invent a more humane milking process that does not hurt these poor girls' teats."

"I believe you will, Zara. Maybe next summer, we can spend some time on my grandpa's farm in Texas. I told you about him, right? My mom and dad used to take me there every summer."

"Is that your mom's father?"

"No. Grandpa Sid isn't actually my real grandpa. He's my dad's father-in-law from his first marriage to Eleanor, Sid's daughter. Dad's parents died in a car accident when he was in high school, so Sid always treated Dad like his real son. Even though Ellie died years ago, Dad is still close with Grandpa Sid, just like he's blood. He's a really sweet and generous old man, and he treats us all like family. I'm sure he'll love to have us help out there for a summer."

"That's amazing, Rachel. Blood does not make a family; love does. I think it's sweet that your Grandpa Sid is so close with your father and you."

Rachel agrees enthusiastically. "Yeah, and my mom, too. Grandpa Sid is family, for sure. Just like my cousins here on the kibbutz are like my brothers and sisters. And Uncle Lior, oy, he's even more strict than my bio-dad!"

Rachel becomes quiet and then reveals, "I have a half-sister I've never even met, and who may or may not even know I'm alive. Zara, you're more of a sister than she is, and I've known you only a few months. You're right;

blood has nothing to do with family."

Just then, the calf Zara is feeding lets go of the nipple and splashes milk all over her face. Rachel laughs as Zara sits stunned. What just happened?

"Yeah, I should have warned you about that." Zara wipes herself off with a rag as Rachel collects the bottles, and they head out.

"Next, we feed the cows."

The girls go to the feed room and fill several large buckets with pellets. "It's important to dump out the old feed and powder on the bottom of their feed basin before you put in the fresh food. Cows are picky eaters. You can just dump the old stuff right into their pen." Zara obeys, disposes of the powder at the bottom, then fills the basin with fresh pellets.

"Here, we check their straw and water troughs, and make sure everyone looks happy and healthy."

The girls happily go about their work as they chat.

"So, how did you come to live on this kibbutz, Rachel? You never told me?"

"My family has connections here. I'm staying here with my Uncle Lior, Aunt Aliya, and cousin, Joshua. Lior is actually my dad's brother-in-law from his first marriage. They also served in the military together, like 40 years ago, so they're brothers for life. I'm only working here for the summer. In a few weeks, I will be attending my senior year as an exchange student at Alexander Muss High School in Hod HaSharon, just outside Tel Aviv."

"I hear that's a great school, Rachel; you're very lucky."

"True story, girlfriend. I'm very grateful for the life I've been given. I know not everyone has the opportunities that I do. I plan on paying it forward, you know." Suddenly, Rachel is self-conscious about their two different realities and feels like a spoiled brat. Zara was raised in a war zone run by madmen and terrorists. Her family was poor and at the mercy of Hamas.

"I'm sorry, Zara, you must think I'm a typical self-centered, entitled American."

"No, no, no, no, no, Rachel. I don't. I'm happy that you've had such a wonderful life. God has shined his light upon you for a reason." The girls hug.

Rachel interrupts the sweet moment. "So, Omar's going to propose to Nadia? How exciting!" Rachel is a romantic and loves love, even though she hasn't had a serious boyfriend yet. "How's he going to do it?"

"He's taking her to Tiberias and is going to propose in a hot air balloon over the Sea of Galilee!"

"Epic! That's *SO* romantic!"

"Right?! Omar spoils her, but she deserves it. This weekend they're going with a group of friends to camp out at the Nova Festival outside of Re'im. I wish I could go; I love trance music."

"Why don't you go? I bet Omar and Nadia would take us."

"Us? Are you saying you want to go?"

"Yes! Yes! Let's go! It'll be so fun! I've heard it's an amazing experience."

"I don't know, Rachel, I don't think Mamma would let me. And what about your Uncle Lior? Will he let you go? You said he is so strict."

"Definitely not. What if I tell him I'm staying at your house on Friday night? And you can tell your parents you're staying with me."

"I don't know, Rachel. I don't want to be dishonest. Besides, Farrah and Nisim will be gone this weekend; they're going to Tiberias for their anniversary."

"Perfect. You won't have to lie to them. They'll never know."

Zara is uneasy about the plan. "I don't know. I'll ask Omar and see what he thinks. He's picking me up after work today so I can meet Mamma and Iman at the shops. I'll talk to him then."

CHAPTER 6

West Maui, Hawaii
August 5, 2024

The sunrise over Mauna Kahalawai finds Ana down near the gardens, replacing some wire on the chicken coop. She can hardly keep up with the damage caused by the deer and wild boar that come around at night. They treat her property like an all-you-can-eat buffet. Living off-grid is hard work. As Ana carefully opens a new roll of chicken wire, she hears shots fired off in the distance.

"Fucking poachers!" Ana realizes her rifle is stored at the main house, but she knows her crossbow is nearby because this is where she practices, shooting arrows into targets hung on hay bales.

More shots fired. Koa jumps up and runs to the edge of the gardens, looking back for direction from Ana, who quickly grabs her crossbow and a handful of arrows. Ana runs toward the gunfire, up the mountain in the direction of Pu'u Kukui, the summit of the West Maui mountains, Koa leading the way.

After nearly 10 minutes of covering rough terrain at a full sprint, Ana can hear two men talking. Koa walks cautiously toward the men and reveals himself at the edge of a clearing in the woods. One of the men raises his rifle and points it at the dog, who makes no move to advance or retreat. Ana walks up behind Koa, her crossbow raised.

"If you harm a hair on this animal's head, I will put this arrow between your eyes."

The young poachers laugh nervously. One asks, "Do you even know how to use that thing, hapa?" Hapa. It means half-breed. They assume she is half Hawaiian by the looks of her and the fact that she is on Akamai land.

Without hesitation, Ana releases the arrow, which tears through the air right between the two men's heads and lodges in the tree behind them. The one who called her hapa pees himself.

"It appears so." Ana laughs.

The men stand paralyzed as their eyes suddenly look to

Ana's right. There stands Pua with her favorite gun, an M-16 assault rifle, aimed at one of the men. Uncle had given her the rifle as a birthday gift ten years earlier, and she'd named it Keanu, after the Hollywood actor. The poachers' eyes simultaneously move left to find Kalama standing there with his SIG Sauer XM7. Nobody fucks with the Akamai clan.

Auntie speaks first. "Eh, you poaching on private property, you dumb mokes. You gonna get yourselves shot."

The men stare silently, then the one who hadn't peed himself begs, "Please don't kill us, Auntie."

Kalama laughs. "We ain't gonna kill you, lolo. Not this time." Then he looks at Ana. "She might."

They look at Ana, who is not amused and gives the boys her best Beth Dutton stare.

 "Only if I see you here again. Leave this property now." The men look at Uncle and Auntie for confirmation of their release. It is then Pua recognizes the would-be poachers.

"Eh, aren't you those Elliot boys? Your mama would whip you if she knew you were up here. Go on, get going!" The two terrified young men stumble over each other, trying to get away and run off like a herd of turtles up the mountain trail—clumsy fools.

Pua exclaims, "Meh. I wanted to shoot my gun today." Pua had been hunting since she was a girl and gets a kick out of showing up the men.

Ana loves her moxie. "Maybe next time, Auntie." Pua just shrugs.

Kalama laughs as they all turn to resume their previous activities. "You gotta love my wahine!"

Ana heads off in the direction of her hale while Pua and Kalama stroll together back to the main house. As they walk, Pua brings up what's been weighing on her heart.

"Kalama, I'm worried about Ana. I know she's been in therapy, but it doesn't seem to be helping. She's still as hard as a kukui nut and as closed off as she's ever been. I know Kimo is counting on her to come out of it, but how long is too long? You know I love Ana like she is our own, but there comes a time, Kal ... it's not fair to Kimo."

Kalama stops walking and turns to face Pua. He agrees with Kimo on this. Ana is a strong, intelligent, and deeply compassionate woman. She knows Kimo is waiting for her.

"Now, Pua, you better not let Kimo hear you talk like that. Our son has never wavered in his devotion to that girl. Fear not; Ana will come around. Your and Ellie's wish will come true. Be patient." Pua felt her heart in her throat. It had been almost 18 years since they lost Eleanor. They used to wonder if Ana, then Ziva, and Kimo would someday marry. They used to imagine their wedding and raising their grandchildren together. They were young then, naïve about the world before they knew that monsters did exist.

"I still miss her every day. You can't help but see her in Ana. Her beauty, her toughness. Even her mannerisms … and her laugh. She is so much like Ellie, it hurts. It's just not fair."

Kalama wraps Pua in a big bear hug underneath the canopy of the 30-foot-tall monkey pod trees. Rocking Pua slowly in his arms, her head buried in his muscular chest. "I know, my love, I know."

Meanwhile, Ana wraps up her barn chores, grabs her gear, and heads down the mountain with Koa happily riding shotgun in her old truck. She can't stop thinking about her encounter with Leimomi yesterday. Is she right? Is Ana sending Kimo mixed messages?

Ana tries to pull herself out of her funk and turns up the stereo. Miranda Lambert is lamenting her broken heart, and Ana can relate. Surprised by the tears that well up in her eyes, she gives in to the melancholy track and begins to sing along.

"Hey there, Mr. Tin Man, you ain't missing nothing 'cause love is so damn hard. Take it from me, darling, you don't want a heart." The tears come freely, and Koa puts a paw on Ana's leg, offering comfort with a tilt of his enormous head.

"Shit. This is bullshit, Koa. We don't need a man in our lives. We've got this." Koa acquiesces.

She joins Miranda Lambert, "You can take mine if you want it; it's in pieces now; if you don't mind the scars, you give me your armor, and you can have my heart." Ana wipes her eyes and abruptly turns off the stereo. She loses herself deep in thought, and they ride the rest of the way to the dojo in silence.

A good Krav Maga workout is exactly what she needs to get her attitude straight. As they pull up to the Krav Maga dojo, Ana sees Jud's truck in the parking lot.

"Shit! I'm really not up for this right now." Ana considers just leaving to avoid the imminent confrontation, but figures she'll get it over with. She does owe the poor guy an explanation. Ana gathers her gear from the back of the pickup and heads into the building. Koa follows, goes immediately over to his dog bed in the corner, spins around twice, and settles in. After greeting a few students in the lobby, Ana heads to the back of the dojo where the heavy bags are located.

There he was. Poor Jud. Another of what Kimo would call her war casualties. Jud is the local veterinarian and had been Ana's friend with benefits for the last year or so, but lately she'd been ghosting him. He wants more from her and finally gave her an ultimatum. She bolted. It's what she does. Ana is a runner.

Ana watches Jud work out for a minute. What the hell is wrong with her? He is gorgeous and kind and a vet for Pele's sake. Every single woman on the island would give their left coconut for this man. She knows it is time she let him go. She just hasn't told him yet. Ana hates conflict and wishes it would just go away.

Jud catches Ana's eye in the mirror and stops hitting the bag. He grabs his towel and is wiping his face when Ana approaches.

"Hey, you. How're you doing?"

Jud doesn't respond immediately. Was he pausing for effect, or was he grappling with what to say?

"Aloha, Ana. You look well." He isn't going to make this easy.

"Look, I'm really sorry I disappeared. It's just …"

"I understand, Ana. I'm going to save you the awkward apology and the cumbersome explanation. I know you. And if I'm honest, you were very clear about your boundaries. I thought I could do the no-commitment thing, but I was wrong. Bottom line: I fell in love, and you didn't."

Ouch. Ana wanted to cry. This sweet man. What the fuck is wrong with her?

"Jud, I …" She has no words. He packs up his gear, kisses her sweetly on the cheek, and walks out the door and out of her life while she silently watches him leave. And there goes another one.

Ana puts on her gloves, searches for some workout music, and blasts it through her headphones. The first song is "Another One Bites the Dust" by Queen.

"Unbelievable. Are you mocking me, Freddie Mercury?"

Ana begins her workout with jabs, roundhouse punches, front kicks, and spinning back kicks. Her frustrations erupt as she mercilessly batters the heavy bag. Eventually, Ana exhausts herself and ends the onslaught, dripping wet and short of breath.

"Howzit, Ana? Long time!" Ana turns to see Max Wright, the owner of Pono Security. She had worked for Max on some small jobs in the past, including tossing out drunks at the Makawao Rodeo Grounds and providing crowd control at the Maui Arts and Cultural Center. Once, he hired her as a personal bodyguard for a billionaire philanthropist. He was a big-time, high-tech guy from northern California who made millions in Bitcoin. It basically turned into a babysitting job, so she got to hang out with his kids at the pool while he golfed all day. A buck was a buck.

"Max, howzit? Yeah, I've been around." Ana towels off as Max puts his gear down on a bench.

"Hey, I'm glad I ran into you. I have a gig you might be interested in. It's at the old Hale Pau Hana resort where you used to work. Some billionaire haole bought the entire resort and turned it into his private compound. Ridiculous. He's throwing a huge party for all his billionaire friends and has hired Pono to handle his security. It should be a scene. You interested?"

"Hale Pau Hana? I used to work there guiding hikes for tourists through the lava tunnels." Ana loved that job, but the road to Hana was awful. She couldn't drive out there every weekend, so eventually she quit.

"I know, that's why I'm asking you. You're already familiar with the property."

"I don't know Max; Hana is a schlep."

Max doesn't push it. "Ok, then. Let me know if you change your mind. I always have room for another badass on my team." Max throws Ana a shaka and begins his workout.

Ana laughs and packs her gear. Koa rises from his corner bed, stretches, and prepares for their next stop. They exit the dojo, and Ana can't help but feel bad about Jud. And about Kimo. Shit! What the actual hell was she doing with her life? They jump in her truck, and Ana pulls out of the parking lot with Jelly Roll's "Lost Cause" blaring on her stereo. Ana looks at Koa and rolls her eyes.

That's me, Koey. I'm a lost cause.

CHAPTER 7

Re'im, Israel
October 7, 2023

Rachel and Zara marvel at the cast of characters roaming around the entrance to the Nova Festival. The group got a late start this evening because Nadia had to be home for Shabbat dinner, so it is just after midnight when they enter the gate of the festival grounds. Partygoers are everywhere: dancing, singing, talking, hugging, drinking, smoking. Everywhere you look, people are happy, laughing, hugging, and holding hands. Rachel and Zara stare, jaws gaping, at the scene around them.

"This must be what Burning Man is like." Despite being raised in San Diego, Rachel has never been to the Burning

Man event in the nearby Nevada desert, but this is how she imagines it would be. Zara, on the other hand, feels a little more out of her element. She has never attended any type of large concert, no less a music festival. She could never have attended one in Gaza, and her brief life in Israel has been all about her studies and work. Zara has never imagined an event like this.

"This is insane! Where did all of these people come from?" The crowd is robed in various manners of dress: some in costumes, some half-naked, others in nightclub attire. People are dancing around as if they are in a daze, becoming one with the music.

The girls stare out the car windows at the chaos before them. The Nova Festival is part of the psychedelic trance scene, and its main focus is promoting creativity, individuality, and freedom. The crowd is mostly people between 20 and 40, partying and dancing, embodying peace and love.

Nadia is almost as shocked as Zara. "Oh my goodness, look at all of these people! There must be thousands of them!"

"Yes, my beauty. I hear they are expecting 3,500 to 4,000 people." Omar had done his homework. "From what I read, the rave was billed as a 'celebration of friends, love and infinite freedom.' It looks like a combination of Haight-Ashbury in the 1960s and the Zombie

Apocalypse. This is crazy! By the looks of it, a lot of these people are on drugs."

Omar looks in the rear-view mirror at Zara and Rachel, mouths open in awe, still staring. "Look, you two, I don't want you talking to anyone you don't know, and don't take or drink anything anyone gives you."

Zara is offended. "Omar! How dumb do you think we are? Rachel and I don't drink or do drugs."

Nadia defends the girls. "Omar, the girls will be just fine. Don't be so bossy."

"Beshert, I am responsible for these two. It's bad enough that Mamma doesn't even know we brought them with us. I can't believe I let you girls talk me into this. Mamma is not going to be happy."

"Omar, don't worry, my love. You girls will make good decisions, yes?"

Rachel and Zara respond in unison, "Yes, of course!" "Obviously!"

Omar's friends had arrived at the venue earlier that day and had already set up camp. "Joshua said they'd meet us at the camping area." They drive up and down a few rows of raucous campsites before finally seeing Joshua and the rest of the group.

Omar parks the car, and they begin to unload. "Zara, I brought a tent for you and Rachel. Nadia and I have our own. Although I don't know how much sleep any of us will get, this place is a zoo ... I should know." Omar looks around for acknowledgment of his pun, but nothing.

"It's funny because I work at the zoo ..." Nadia pats his arm, "We know, Beshert, it just wasn't that funny." The girls all laugh at Omar, who sticks out his lower lip in his best fake pout, feigning disappointment.

"Omar, Nadia, over here!" Joshua and the others are drinking, laughing, and dancing around a small campfire. Everyone gathers around the car with a round of hugs and cheers.

After warm greetings and introductions, Omar warns all of the males in the group, only half in jest. "These two young ladies are my family. You will treat them like you would your own mothers." The men raise their hands and back away teasingly. Joshua bows and asks Zara, "Mother, may I get you a drink?" They all laugh, but Omar reiterates.

"Just behave yourselves. They are on my watch."

"Omar, stop! We're not children!"

"Yeah, knock it off!" Zara and Rachel are embarrassed by the attention.

Nadia laughs, "I'm so sorry, girls. Omar can be a little

overprotective. It's one of the reasons I love him."

The din settles as the crew returns to the campfire and begins arguing about Israeli politics.

"No, no, no, no, no! You are wrong! We are a democracy, yet we have a king!"

"Yes, but a bad ass king!"

Meanwhile, Omar sets up the girls' tent and then his own. After settling in, he and Nadia set out toward the grandstand a few hundred yards away, to get closer to the live music.

"Zara, we're going to the concert. You and Rachel, please stay together and stay close to the campsite."

The girls resist; they want to go to the concert, but Omar reminds them they promised they'd listen to him if he brought them along, so they reluctantly agree. Rachel and Zara stay up talking, giggling, and people-watching until after 2:00 a.m. and finally fall asleep despite the booming music and screaming partygoers.

The next morning, Zara and Rachel rise with the sun, excited about what the day will bring. They talk and laugh about all the crazies they saw last night. Neither of them has ever seen anything like it.

"How about that drunk naked guy who stumbled through our camp! Talk about TMI!"

"Gross! But then there was that nice man who was pushing his daughter in a wheelchair. That was so sweet. I guess it really takes all kinds, right?" The festival has already proven to be a multicultural education for Zara.

"Yes. I recognize them from the kibbutz, but I've never met them."

Zara exits the tent first and yells back at Rachel. "Omar and Nadia are still gone. They must be having so much fun! I'm jealous."

Rachel joins her and looks around the campsite. There were acres of tents and cars and trucks with tarps. Cups, cans, and bottles are strewn everywhere. "And we're stuck here. Let's get cleaned up and go over to the food court; I'm starving."

Zara and Rachel walk together to the bank of portable toilets at the edge of the camping area. As they wash up at the makeshift sinks, they run into the man and his daughter from the kibbutz. He struggles trying to put her hair in braids.

"Shalom. Would you like some help?" The man turns to Rachel, who is holding both of her braids in her hand. "I'm kind of an expert."

The man seems both relieved and embarrassed. "Would you mind? Her mother usually does her hair. This is a daddy/daughter date, so it's on me today, and I fear I'm failing miserably."

Rachel steps in and performs salon-worthy braids in minutes. "The trick is to wet it a little to smooth the flyaways, then keep each portion tight and even." She chats as she shows him her process.

"Aren't you the vet from Mishmar Ha'emek? I'm Rachel Cohen. I'm staying with my Uncle Lior for the summer." Zara offers her hand.

"Shalom, I'm Zara. I work there, too."

"Oh, yes, of course. I thought you ladies looked familiar. I'm David. Todah, todah. Honestly, I can't thank you enough. It means a lot to Rose to have her hair nice. She has cerebral palsy. It may seem like she's unaware, but she's actually conscious of everything going on around her, especially as it relates to beauty and fashion. Thank you so much for your kindness. Shalom aleikhem. Peace to you."

Zara is touched by Rachel's kindness and impressed by her confidence. She easily speaks with that man and offers what she can to help. Zara suddenly feels limited by her upbringing and vows to be more "American" in the way she approaches life. She feels she can be a more productive and useful person if she is less limited by her upbringing and less frightened to speak out. Zara resolves to be more open and outgoing like Rachel.

On their way back to the tent, the girls see rockets flying over their heads from Gaza into Israel. At first, it seems like a "normal" rocket attack. That is normal for Israel. Concert-goers cheer as Israel's defense system, the Iron Dome, intercepts and shoots down rocket after rocket over the skies of southern Israel. But something is different. There are more rockets than usual. Many, many more. Something feels wrong.

Rachel has only lived in Israel for a few months, and she isn't sure what to think. She looks around her, and most of the folks at the concert are looking up at the sky but don't seem overly concerned. Within minutes, Omar and Nadia arrive at the campsite - Nadia stunning in the red pashmina Farrah had given her. Omar tells the girls not to worry, but his demeanor reveals his concern. He keeps checking his phone and periodically walks away to make or receive a phone call. Something feels wrong. There are so many rockets. Thousands of rockets. Despite their apprehension, the group sets out to cook breakfast over the campfire. They all try to act normal, but the collective anxiety is palpable.

At 7:00 a.m., an attack warning siren sounds, urging all attendees to vacate the premises. Police and private security arrive to set up a checkpoint at the festival grounds' gate and begin directing everyone to leave the area and take cover at the closest bunker.

Omar acts instantly. He feels responsible for the three girls and is not taking any chances.

"Quickly, pack up your things and break down the tent. There are no bomb shelters out here. We need to get somewhere we can take cover. There is a kibbutz and a military base not far from here. We can go there and wait out the attack." The girls recognize Omar's grave tone and follow his orders like soldiers.

As Omar looks around him at the thousands of innocent people, he understands the danger they're in. Despite most of them having served their compulsory time in the Israeli military, most of the festival goers would be unarmed and defenseless. They are out in the middle of nowhere, less than four miles from Gaza, the home of the Hamas terror group, which has pledged "Death to Israel." The Nova Festival is in open terrain with no bunkers and precious few trees and bushes to provide cover. If the terrorists attack here, they will all be slaughtered. Suddenly, they hear gunfire off in the distance. Blasts are heard in central Gaza and Gaza City. The crowd cheers as the Israel Defense Forces begin to strike back at Hamas.

The campers and partygoers begin to get in their cars to exit the festival grounds, but quickly find themselves stuck in a motionless traffic jam as the gunfire and explosions continue all around them. For hours, thousands of people sit outside their cars in line, waiting for the blockade to be lifted. It seems everyone is on their phone. Some call first responders and loved ones; others take photos and videos of the chaos. Not one person anticipates what is about to come.

The unsuspecting partygoers do not know that at that very moment, the Israeli police are fighting for their lives defending the gates of the grounds, outnumbered by Hamas terrorists. Eventually, after four hours of fighting, the terrorists break through the blockade and enter the festival grounds. For 3,500 attendees, the world as they know it ends in this moment. Meanwhile, thousands wait in line, trying to exit the large compound.

"Where are the police? Where is the Army?" Nadia is becoming more anxious by the minute. She shares a look with Omar, and she can see he is worried too. Omar doesn't worry easily. Panic rises in her throat. The gunfire is getting closer. Nadia begins to cry. She looks off in the distance in the direction of the shooting and points. "OH MY GOD!!! OMAR!!!"

Omar looks up, off in the distance, and points his finger. "Look. See the birds circling the trees every time there is gunfire? That's how we know where the terrorists are." The three girls look in the direction of the gunfire and see it—hundreds of birds circling over the gunshots.

They all watch in horror as hundreds of people run towards them from the direction of the grandstand.

They are screaming, clearly terrified, but still hundreds of yards away; too far to discern what they are yelling. At that moment, Joshua, eyes as big as saucers, hands Omar his cell phone. On it is a video just posted to the Hamas channel on the Telegram app. It is a live video of Hamas terrorists slaughtering hundreds of civilians all over southern Israel, some right outside of the festival grounds. The video shows a line of cars on the side of the road riddled with bullets, burning, some completely destroyed and charred from rocket-propelled grenades. The terrorists are kidnapping families, the elderly, and children.

On the live feed, Omar sees hundreds of people lying dead in the street and hanging out of their cars, bloodied and limp. Hundreds of innocent Israelis slaughtered. Victims beg for their lives. Bodies strewn everywhere. The terrorists slaughter most and take some. They are gleeful, laughing, and taking selfies with the dead, calling them "Israeli dogs." As he watches in horror, Omar recognizes one of the girls taken by a terrorist on his motorcycle. She is screaming, "NO! DON'T TAKE ME! DON'T TAKE ME!" and reaching her arms out desperately for anyone to help her as her abductor rides away with her to an unbearable fate.

Omar is horrified and immediately realizes that they are all in mortal danger. He looks back at the frantic crowd running toward them. They finally come within earshot of the line of cars, and slowly, their screams can finally be heard.

"They're coming!!! Run, run, run! They're coming!"

"The terrorists are here! They're killing everyone!"

"Run! Everyone run! NOW! Run, run, run!"

"Hey, hey! They're here. Leave the cars! Run! C'mon, they're shooting! Don't stop running! RUN!!!"

Hundreds of people who had been waiting by their vehicles take off in all directions into the open fields surrounding the festival grounds. The shrieking and screaming are unbearable. The only sounds that penetrate the horror are the bursts of gunfire and explosions.

The terrorists infiltrate the festival grounds and blockade all of the roads entering or exiting the area. The Police are all dead. They had taken cover behind a tank that was blown up by a Hamas rocket-propelled grenade.

Where is the Army?

The terrain around the grounds is mainly open fields and farmland. There is nowhere to hide. Some run toward the sparse orchards and bushes along the border of the grounds, others run and hide in the portable toilets near the campground. They were first. Hamas executioners spray the whole bank of toilets with thousands of rounds of automatic weapons. There are no survivors.

Hundreds of Hamas gunmen arrive from all directions in vans, trucks, jeeps, and motorcycles – some in parachutes -- carrying assault rifles and hand grenades, firing in all directions. Bodies drop by the dozens.

Partygoers flee in panic as the terrorists massacre everyone within the range of their innumerable weapons. The gunmen whoop it up and scream victoriously, "Allahu Akbar!" -- God is great! -- as they gleefully mow down hundreds of innocent civilians in cold blood. Many of the assassins take gleeful selfies and videos with their lifeless victims as if they are on holiday in Corfu.

Omar screams, "RUN!!!" Rachel and Zara jump up, but Nadia is frozen. She is paralyzed with fear and cannot move. Omar grabs her arm, yanks her up, and forces her to start moving. He puts his hand on her shoulders firmly. "Nadia, look at me. We have to run and keep running. NOW!" Nadia snaps out of it, and they all begin running as fast as they can, joining the mass exodus of hundreds, screaming, bolting in all directions, fleeing for their lives.

Omar and the girls head for a small orchard on the edge of the festival grounds. Nadia trips and falls. Sobbing, she screams, "Omar. I'm slowing you down! Go on without me!"

Omar yells to Zara and Rachel, "Keep running, and don't stop!" Then to Nadia, "I'm not leaving you, Beshert, c'mon!" He yanks her up, and they begin to run hand in hand; screams of pain and panic surround them as the terrorists spray the running civilians with automatic gunfire. The bullets whiz by their heads as they run. All around them, people drop to the ground. One by one. It was like a shooting gallery. Omar and Nadia run for their lives. Omar scans ahead of them and cannot find the girls. He prays for God to watch over them.

Suddenly, Omar falls, taking Nadia to the ground with him. Nadia jumps up immediately, but Omar doesn't move. She yanks his hand. "Omar!"

The blood stain spreads quickly, soaking Omar's white shirt. "OMAR! NO! NOOO! OMAR!!!" Nadia looks up, and the terrorists are closing in. She tries to run but is almost immediately captured. Nadia shrieks Omar's name as they drag her, kicking and screaming, toward the nearby orchard.

Rachel and Zara watch the carnage from under a bush. In horror, they watch as Nadia is violently assaulted by three men wearing all black, black ski masks with green headbands displaying the Hamas symbol. Nadia screams as they tear at her clothes.

"NOOOO! NOOOOO! OMARRRRR!!!"

The girls are devastated and terrified, but their self-preservation instincts kick in. Rachel points to a farm in the distance. Maybe they can make it there? Zara shakes her head and points in the other direction, to the sky above the festival grounds. Rachel looks and understands. No birds. The gunfire is no longer coming from that direction. The terrorists had left the grandstand area. The birds are now circling above the long line of cars waiting to escape, so many targets at a shooting range. In the distance, they can hear screaming and Nadia begging for her life. Gunshots. Then nothing.

They take one last look back. Nadia's screams had abruptly ended, her red pashmina gently waving silently in the hot wind, and the moment of stillness belying the bloody massacre occurring before their eyes.

Under the cover of a low row of bushes, Rachel and Zara turn and run, hunched over, the mile or so back to the grandstand area. It is blazing hot, but they sprint there on pure adrenaline and faith. As the girls re-enter the fairgrounds, Zara stops short and gasps. There, lying in the dirt, is a wheelchair. A short distance away, they lay dead. The girl in the braids and her father, Rose and David from their kibbutz, his arms wrapped around his daughter in a final embrace. The girls keep running. As they approach the huge stage, gasping for air, they hear a loud whisper from underneath.

"Hey, if you don't want to die, get under here." As Zara and Rachel dive under the stage, the voice says, "They're here. The terrorists are here. They're killing everyone."

Rachel looks around and is surprised to see scores of people crouched down, hiding under the stage.

"Shhhh. Quiet! Quiet! Quiet!"

"Quiet. You're going to get us all killed!". They are all in shock. They lay silently, listening to the madness. Gunfire. Bombs. Begging, gunshots, silence. Suddenly, a blood-curdling scream.

"TERRORISTS!!! RUN!!! THEY'RE HERE! EVERYBODY RUN! NOW!" At once, the entire crowd underneath the stage scampers out and runs off in different directions as gunfire once again fills the air. Terrified, Rachel and Zara dart under the tents where the Food Court had been. Rachel points to a row of chest freezers and lifts up the top of one. It makes a screeching sound, and the girls freeze, fearing it will give them away. They look around, but they are alone.

"Get in!" They quickly jump in and close the shrill door above them. It is dark and cold. They can hear their hearts beating. They know they don't have enough oxygen to stay in there long. Zara prays. Rachel begins to panic and tries to control her breathing.

They hear gunfire, screaming, and begging. "No! No! No! Please!" Gunfire. Silence.

Zara whispers, "I see nothing. I hear everything." Then they hear it. Voice's approach, speaking in Arabic. Then, the screech of a freezer door.

Sobbing. "Why? Why? Why?" Gunfire. The question abruptly suspended in death.

Rachel and Zara prepare to die the same way as the girl in the freezer beside them. They hold their collective breath.

The screech of the freezer door. The girls gaze up pleadingly at the Hamas terrorists in silence. The men's smarmy, grotesque smiles are visible behind their ski masks, the only portion of their evil selves the cowards risk revealing. They laugh and high-five each other. Rachel and Zara realize this is the end. They hug each other and close their eyes.

"Today you die, Israeli dogs." A demon with missing front teeth aims his rifle at Rachel's head first. The girls huddle together sobbing and pray to their respective Gods.

A voice from behind them has a different idea. "Take these two alive."

CHAPTER 8

Maui, Hawaii
October 7, 2023

Kalama lay in bed listening to the wind blow wistfully through the areca palms outside their bedroom window. He turns to see Pua sleeping peacefully beside him, making the little squeaky noises Kalama has come to adore over their 40-plus years together. The pair had grown up together as "cousins" among a large Lahaina clan during the late 1960s and '70s. Although not blood-related, as children, they fought like brother and sister but became best friends in middle school and eventually fell in love. It dawns on Kalama that Kimo and Ana have grown up together, much in the same way, first on the kibbutz and now at the Akamai family compound on

Maui. Kalama has an unwavering belief that the two will finally figure out their feelings and smiles warmly at the future he sees for them.

Kal slowly gets out of bed so as not to wake his sleeping bride. He worries about Pua. She is haunted by the terror attack 28 years before that took their precious baby girl and her best friend. Pua struggles with horrible visions during the day and nightmares at night. Not unlike Ana, she is often awake for hours, fearing the horrors will continue where they left off if she falls back to sleep.

Kalama grabs his phone, leaves the room, and slowly, stealthily closes the bedroom door. As he walks toward the kitchen, Kal looks at his phone and sees an inordinate number of notifications and text message alerts. He opens his WhatsApp and sees the breaking news out of Israel. As the Akamai family had slept peacefully in their secluded island paradise, halfway around the world, Hamas had slaughtered thousands of innocent Israelis and abducted hundreds more. The terrorists massacred entire communities and kibbutzim. Men, women, children, the elderly, family pets … no one was excluded from their savage campaign of terror.

Dread sets in as Kalama recognizes the similarities between this terrorist massacre and the one at their kibbutz all those years ago. His heart breaks for the families and his first impulse is to immediately get on a plane for Israel and defend the nation; he is still an Army Reservist. But he knows he is needed more here; his family needs him now more than ever. Kal's mind races as he thinks about how this news will affect Pua, Ana, and Kimo. They were all traumatized by the attack on the kibbutz on Ana's 10th birthday, and this will definitely be a trigger. The unimaginable losses of Ellie and Lilikoi mirrored in this most recent slaughter of innocents.

Kalama rushes down the trail, through the wet cane grass, to his office and quickly boots up his multiple computers and police scanners. He reads every Israeli news source he can find on the topic: The Jerusalem Post, the Times of Israel, and Haaretz. The news is terrifying. Hamas terrorists have infiltrated the border in 19 places in a coordinated attack on Israeli civilians, murdering, raping, torturing and kidnapping civilians by the hundreds. Social media is even worse. There are live videos posted by both Hamas and innocent victims. The monsters have entered a music festival in Re'im and slaughtered thousands of civilians. There were lifeless, bloodied bodies everywhere. The images were too much to bear.

Just then, Kimo bursts through the door to Kalama's cottage, short of breath from his run through the forest. The two lock eyes, and Kimo's eyes well up with tears. Kalama embraces his son in a tight bear hug that would squeeze the life out of a lesser man. Both men fight their emotions, thinking only of Pua and Ana.

"Does Mama know yet?" Kimo can't help but remember that day. One moment, he was holding Lilikoi's tiny hand and singing Happy Birthday. The next moment …

"I don't think so. She was asleep when I left the hale. I need to get back up there. I want to be the one to tell her the news. You should … "

"I know. I'm going to Ana's now. Please tell Mama I love her." Kimo takes off, running up the mountain toward Hale Lehua, Ana's sanctuary. As he runs, memories of their shared nightmare come flooding in. The balloons, the singing, the explosions, the screaming, the smell of death.

As he approaches the edge of Ana's hale, Kimo hears screaming and glass breaking. Koa is standing on the lanai beseechingly, as if to say, "Hurry up, she needs you."

"Oh shit. She knows." Kimo takes the lanai steps two at a time and finds Ana in the living room, screaming at the television and throwing everything she can get her hands on. Koa follows but keeps a safe distance.

"You terrorist asswhores! I will fucking kill every last one of you fucking little cowards! I fucking hate you!" Ana drops to her knees, sobbing uncontrollably. The fury and the helplessness are too much for her to bear. Koa walks over and lies on top of Ana with a comforting embrace.

He rests his anvil-sized head in her lap.

"Ana?" Kimo speaks softly and gently. He understands Ana's trauma and wants to be a calming influence for her. "I see you heard."

Ana does not look up. She hangs her head, face in her hands, and sobs quietly now, repeating over and over, "Why? Why? Why?" Kimo gets down on the floor, wraps his arms around Ana, and rocks her slowly. "I'm here, beautiful girl, I'm here."

After some time, Ana's sobs subside, and she slowly becomes aware of her surroundings. She suddenly feels awkward about her outburst, and with Kimo's attention, she jumps up quickly, causing both Kimo and Koa to lose their balance and tumble into each other. Ana's walls reconstruct as quickly as they'd fallen.

"Don't worry about me, Kimo. I'm fine. Been there, done that, yeah?" She wipes her face, walks into the kitchen, and makes herself busy.

"You want some juice? Coffee?" Koa barks, and she throws him a liver treat. Treats trump trauma in his book.

"No thanks. Ana, you don't have to be tough with me. I know you. I know this is incredibly difficult for you, given what happened to your mother … and to Lilikoi. Anyone would be a mess."

"Kimo, shut up. I'm not a mess, and I don't want to talk about it. Besides, it's not me you have to worry about; it's Auntie. Does she know yet? We should be there right now, not here babysitting me."

Kimo watches Ana closely as she spoons some ground beef and veggies into Koa's food bowl, which he scarfs down in a matter of seconds. Ana avoids eye contact with Kimo and nervously fiddles with some kitchen utensils. Kimo decides to acquiesce to her denial. Pushing Ana never ends well.

"You're right; let's bring Mama a pot of coffee." Kimo eyes the Leoda's Bakery box on the counter. "… and some pastries, too."

Ana shoots him a weak smile and nods her head, her wavy brown hair falling in her eyes. As he often does, Kimo wonders how she can be so absolutely oblivious to her own stunning beauty.

"Here, use this basket and take some starfruit; Auntie loves those." Ana makes small talk as they pack to leave.

"Koa, wanna go to Auntie's?" The oversized canine jumps up and leads the way down the trail to the main house. Ana and Kimo follow in silence, each absorbed in their own thoughts.

As the house comes into view in the distance, Ana gives voice to her deepest regret.

"It's my fault."

Kimo stops on the trail and grabs Ana's hand. She stops and turns to face him as they stand face to face, just inches between them.

"What's your fault, Ana?" She can't bear to look him in the eyes. The one word, barely a whisper.

"Lilikoi." At the mention of her name, Kimo's eyes fill with tears. Ana can see his heart breaking all over again, and she instantly regrets bringing it up.

"No, Ana, no! It was not your fault! I was there too. We were both holding her hand, Ana, both of us. We were all knocked to the ground by the explosions. There was nothing that either of us could have done. Please, Lehua, please don't do this to yourself. Please, Ana." But it was done.

Ana feels the tears rise in her throat and quickly chokes them back. This is just all too much. It was just like that day … Ana turns away so Kimo doesn't see her weakness. If Grandpa Sid saw her now, he'd probably say she was as worthless as gum on a boot heel, and he'd be right. She is stronger than this. She must not give in to her fear. She must be strong. She must squash her feelings and embrace the numbness.

Kimo walks up behind her and wraps his arms around her, his hands holding hers. Ana can feel his breath on the back of her neck and his power embracing her. She can feel his love for her. Ana summons every ounce of emotional fortitude she has left. Not today, Satan.

Ana breaks free from the embrace, the comfort too much to tolerate. "Fuck it. Let's go see Auntie. She needs us." Ana will be damned if she lets this break her. She takes a deep breath and sets off down the trail. Kimo follows behind, shaking his head. Why is she so damned stubborn?

As Kimo and Ana climb the lanai steps, they can hear Pua's soft sobs. Kalama is holding her hand as they sit at the dining room table, watching the news. Pua looks up to see Kimo and Ana enter and stands with arms wide open. Tearfully, she speaks.

"My babies! Come here, come here. Can you believe this is happening again?" They all stand in the kitchen and hug, bonding over their shared trauma. They all cry. They cry for Lilikoi. They cry for Eleanor. They cry for themselves and the deep losses they'd all suffered. Eventually, Kimo and Kalama break off and go outside on the lanai. Pua and Ana sit silently at the table, holding hands, each lost in her own thoughts.

Once outside, Kimo explodes.

"Pop, what do we do now? We have to go back, yeah? We have to go kill these bastards, right?"

Kimo was shaking with fury, embracing the only emotion he could process at the moment. Rage. Having been born in Israel, Kimo holds dual citizenship and returned to Israel to fulfill his service in the Israel Defense Forces immediately after high school. He was a door-kicker and a sniper in the Tzanchanim paratroopers unit, 101st Battalion. Kimo is still in the Army Reserve and is ready to return to defend his country.

"I'll kill them all! I want them all to suffer!" Kimo's tears flow freely.

Kalama's heart breaks for his family; they've all suffered so much. When will this end? He struggles to find the right words to say. They don't need any more bad news, but it is unavoidable.

"Kimo, what I'm about to tell you stays between us, yeah?" Kimo notices the urgency in his father's voice. He stops his diatribe and dries his tears.

"Of course, Pop. It's in the vault."

"I heard from Lou Cohen this morning."

"Ana's biological father? Well, I guess that makes sense, you said he regularly checks up on Ana despite the fact she won't speak to him, so I'm sure he's concerned with how she's taking it, given what we all went through at the kibbutz all those years ago."

"Yeah …" Kal struggles to find the words. "Kimo … there's more. Lou's daughter, Rachel, Ana's half-sister, is in Israel. She went in June to live on the kibbutz with Lior and his family." The silence is palpable as Kimo waits for the next sentence, fearing the worst.

"Oh my God, Pop. Oh my God, no! Is she dead?" Kimo thought only of Ana. How would she handle another huge loss like this? She hadn't had time to resolve her feelings for her sister, now she might never be able to.

"No, no, no, no. Well … they don't know. They haven't been able to reach her. She was supposed to stay over at a friend's house last night, and today, both girls are missing. Lior has been trying to contact the family, but so far, no luck. It could be nothing. Everything there is in chaos right now. For now, let's think positive."

Kalama motions for Kimo to follow him. The men walk down the steps and through the tall pampas grass to the fire pit. They sit and talk in low voices.

"I assume Ana doesn't know?" Kimo's concern for her is unmistakable. Ana has never been willing to discuss her father or her sister with him or anyone other than her therapist, as far as he knows. She blames Lou for her mother's disappearance and for abandoning her in the years afterward. She's never even met her half-sister and never speaks of her.

"No, and neither does your mama. I want to have all of the facts before I worry them."

"Agreed. It might be nothing." Kimo says a short prayer, asking God to make it so.

Just then, Kalama's phone buzzes. He looks at Kimo intently. "It's Lou. I guess we're about to find out."

The two men walk toward the privacy of the woods as Kal answers the phone.

"Hey, Lou. I have Kimo with me, and you're on speaker." They continue to walk until they are well out of earshot of the house. Lou is clearly agitated and distressed.

"Kalama! Kimo! Oh my God, oh my God, oh my God …" Lou is frantic, and Kalama knows it is bad. Very, very bad. He's never heard Lou like this. Not in Beirut and not even after the kibbutz massacre when they lost Eleanor and Lilikoi. Very, very bad.

"Lou, slow down. Take some deep breaths. Tell us what's going on." They wait with bated breath for Lou to gather himself, and then they hear it.

"She was there, Kal. Rachel was there! At the music festival! Hamas massacred thousands of kids. She was there, Kal!"

Confused, Kal tries desperately to understand Lou's ranting. "Lior learned Rachel had snuck out and went to the concert with her friend Zara and her older brother. They were there, Kal, they were there at the Nova Festival! And now they're gone! Kal, she's gone!"

"Gone!? What do you mean by 'gone,' Lou? As in dead? Are you saying they're dead!?"

Kalama and Kimo could not believe what they were hearing. It felt like they had entered an alternate reality. This could not possibly be real. They exchange a glance of bewilderment, horror, and disbelief. This is not happening again.

"I don't know, I don't know, I don't know! No one knows! They're all missing! She's gone, Kal! She's vanished!"

CHAPTER 9

Maui, Hawaii
August 8, 2024

Ana awakens to the sunrise in a somber mood. Last night, the dream was unchanged. Mother and Pua laughing and singing 'Happy Birthday.' The children giggling and wrestling. The smell of challah baking. The explosions. The smoke. The odor. Kimo screaming, "Zivaaaaaa!!!"

Ana shakes her head as if to thrash the haunting memories out of her brain. Koa senses her mood and lays down on his bed in the kitchen, keeping a safe distance from the bad juju. Nobody likes a grump in the morning. Ana sees his furtive move and calls Koa out.

"What? You think I'm gonna kick you or something? Chicken." Koa's head pops up to his favorite word. Ana, at the kitchen counter chopping an avocado, laughs.

"Not that kind of chicken. Okay, here you go, boy." Ana throws a chunk over her shoulder, and Koa jumps up and catches it in one fell swoop.

Ana is wistful. "So today marks one year since the fires, Koey. Unbelievable. It feels like it was a couple of weeks ago." She can't help but become absorbed in memories of that dreadful day.

Hurricane Dora had been lurking outside the Hawaiian Islands, and the locals were preparing to hunker down. Hurricanes were not uncommon this time of year, but Maui had been lucky in the past. Usually, the big storms come from the south, and once they hit the Big Island, Hawaii Island, they usually break up and mellow before they hit Maui. Not this time. Locals battened down the hatches. Everything outside was either put away, tied down, or thrown in the pool if you had one. Flying furniture can cause a lot of damage.

The wind was so strong that the power went out early that day. The schools closed down, so all the keiki, the children, had to stay home. Many were left home alone by working parents who couldn't afford to take time off work. Ana remembers she had tickets to see the *Barbie* movie that day at the Wharf in Lahaina Town.

She was meant to go with a group of ladies from the women's auxiliary at the Yacht Club. They had bought their tickets ahead of time. It was out of character for her, and, as she often was, Ana had been sorry she had committed to attending the film and was happy when it was canceled. The ladies called and said the theater had closed because the high winds had caused a power outage at The Wharf. What none of them knew was at the exact time the movie was meant to begin, a massive fire was engulfing the entire complex and every adjacent building for miles. Had they been in that movie theater, they'd most certainly have perished in the blaze, blissfully unaware in a Barbie world.

Lahaina Town and the surrounding local communities were completely devastated on August 8, 2023. It wasn't only buildings that were destroyed. Yes, thousands of homes and businesses burned to the ground, but it turns out that wouldn't be the worst of it. Despite official death numbers at just over one hundred, the locals know that's not even close. Kimo, Ana, and Koa were at the retirement home in Lahaina that day, trying to evacuate Auntie Pakalana from the burning complex. Tragically, they were unable to save any kapuna from the retirement home, and they barely escaped with their own lives. More than 100 died in that building alone. Over the next several weeks, as the official numbers of dead and missing were posted, the locals knew it was a lie. The coconut wireless was buzzing with sightings of hundreds of body bags being loaded into a shipping container turned morgue down at the port. It is a small island, and secrets are hard to keep.

"Just over a hundred dead, my akole." The local government and leaders don't like to disrupt the aloha narrative for tourists. This is paradise. There is no crime, no death, no disaster. Just warm trade winds, mai tais, and happy locals living the aloha spirit. It's a bunch of bull: bullshit and corruption.

Another casualty of the fire devastation is the local culture itself. Entire neighborhoods with multigenerational homes burned to the ground, the occasional stone wall bearing witness to the ancestors who came before. Sadly, many of those people did not have insurance and will never have the resources to rebuild. Many of these local families, mostly Hawaiian, Tongan, Samoan, and Filipino, will be forced to sell to outsiders, changing the entire cultural composition of historic Lahaina.

Another victim of the horrendous fire is the local economy. Thousands of jobs were lost. Those jobs that remained took a huge hit from the abrupt termination of tourism, the chief income producer. Moreover, there is nowhere for the thousands of newly homeless people to live. There had already been a housing crisis on the island, and now it is impossible to find a place to rent.

Of course, the disaster capitalists, on cue, hiked up rents through the roof so normal working people couldn't afford to pay. FEMA was paying landlords exorbitant rents for fire survivors, so many locals who didn't lose their homes to the fire lost them to a greedy landlord looking for FEMA money. Thousands of people were forced to move off-island, and of those that remain, many continue to struggle.

After their morning routine, Ana and Koa head up the mountain to pick flowers for the paddle-out this afternoon. There is a huge patch of wild pua kenikeni about a mile from her hale, and she wants to bring a bunch of them. She thought of sweet Thumper, who always had a big smile and a kind word. Thumper loved the smell of pua kenikeni.

Finished with chores, Ana and Koa head down the mountain toward the beach. They pass Auntie's food truck and see a handwritten sign on the closed window. "Closed for Paddle Out." Everyone is going to the memorial.

When they arrive at Canoe Beach, the parking lot is overflowing, so Ana takes the off-road route and parks in the adjacent graveyard.

"Whaddaya think, Koey? Is this irony or coincidence?" Neither of them comes to a conclusion.

Ana grabs her paddleboard out of the back of the truck, locks the vehicle, and puts the key in a pouch in Koa's collar. They head toward the water, through a dense crowd of people, many of them she knows, most she does not. The press is there in full force, many from Oahu and some from the mainland. As Ana scans the crowd, she sees thousands of people partying on the beach. They are cooking out and toasting friends and family that had passed and celebrating that they hadn't. Ana sees some "cousins" who call her over for some aloha. They look like they'd camped out there all night and were feeling no pain. Ana takes a tequila shot from one of the girls and hits a joint from one of the boys, then continues to make her way through the crowd. Suddenly, Koa takes off. Ana looks up and sees Jud chatting with a local girl. Ugh. Ana yells after the eager pup.

"Koa, don't bother Jud." It was too late. The two had reunited in a flurry of barks, licks, and pets.

"Hey, Koa, how're you doing, buddy?" Jud gives Koa some love as the local girl glares at Ana and turns away, her nose so high in the air that she'd drown if it were raining.

"Catch you later, Jud." The girl struts off in her thong bikini, all ass cheeks and attitude.

Jud rolls his eyes, and Ana laughs. "Yeah, I didn't think she was your type." He looks at her questioningly as they endure an awkward pause. Jud breaks the awkward silence.

"Okay then. You have a good day, Ana. Koa, great seeing you, boy." Jud grabs his paddleboard and walks toward the ocean.

"Ugh. Thanks, Koey. You did that on purpose, didn't you?" Koa ignores her as he spies another cousin.

"Ana! Ana over here." Kalia is sitting with Auntie Pua and Uncle Kalama, camped out at the water's edge. They wave her over.

"Aloha, y'all! You're not going out on the water?" Ana sets down her board and paddle as Koa digs through Auntie's bag for treats. Pua swats the oversized intruder away.

"Get outta there, Koa!" He removes his head from her bag, a bag of cookies in his mouth.

"Give me that, you thief!" Koa gently puts the cookies in Pua's hand and retreats to the corner of the blanket, spins around twice, and settles in.

"Good boy."

"Hi, Auntie!" Kalia sees Auntie Kailani and runs off to talk story. Kailani has her ear to the coconut wireless and always spills the tea.

Ana has eyes on the festivities. "Looks like it's about to

start. See y'all after the service."

People start getting in the water by the hundreds. Ana tells Koa to stay with Auntie and Uncle on the beach, which he is happy to do because they both spoil him rotten. She trots off with her board and paddle and enters the cool ocean water. She's never seen so many people at Canoe Beach. It looks like everyone on the island is there—people on surfboards and paddle boards, on jet skis and in canoes. There are even folks on rafts and various other floating devices.

Ana paddles out with the crowd toward the ceremonial circle, then sits up on her board and waits for the stragglers to arrive. Ana gets the pua kenikeni flowers from her mesh backpack and sets them in a pile on the board in front of her.

As she floats, peacefully waiting, Ana considers the legion of people around her. Many are somber as expected, but others are surprisingly joyful. Many came to mourn their loved ones, while others are there to celebrate the lives of those lost with joy and happiness. The crowd is a mix of every kind of person: young and old; Hawaiians, Tongans, Samoans, Filipinos, Mexicans, haoles; rich and poor; locals and tourists. Everyone together for one day, to share in their mutual sorrow.

"Ana! Ana! Up here!" Ana looks around but doesn't see anyone. The cries continue.

"Up here!"

Ana looks up, and there, on a huge sailboat about 30 yards away, at the very top of the crow's nest, was Crazy Daisy calling Ana's name and waving her arms. Ana laughs and waves. Daisy knows how to have a good time and was no doubt working on her second or third mai tai by now. Ana shouts back.

"Hey, Daze! Don't fall off there, girl!" Her comment is met with a "Whoop, whoop!" and a shaka.

Ana looks around her at the crowd of grieving people and thinks of all the stories she's heard over the last year—stories about how people barely survived or didn't.

Ana's best friend Tina was eating lunch that day at Cheeseburger in Paradise on Front Street in Lahaina Town with her two sons, Milo and Noah. The fire spread like it was consuming matchsticks through the historic whaling town – all brittle timber – people had no warning. One minute, they were eating their favorite fries and sipping on chocolate shakes; the next minute, Tina and her boys were jumping out the window into the ocean. They spent nine grim hours in the water that night, standing in waist-deep water, shivering, choking on the smoke that engulfed Lahaina Town, pushing dead bodies away from them as they floated by one by one.

Then there was Jeff. He was a good friend of the family

who had called Ana that afternoon, when they had just thought it was a brush fire. He wanted to make sure she wasn't in town and didn't need help. He had been on his way to evacuate his mother from her home in Wahikuli, just northeast of Lahaina Town. She never heard from him again.

So many stories. Lahaina residents were angry at the local government for failing them, and everyone was asking the same questions. Why wasn't the power shut off during the hurricane? There were hundreds of live power lines blowing in the wind, igniting everything that wasn't already burning. Why wasn't the emergency siren sounded? The fire snuck up on the town like a mongoose to a nest full of eggs. Why was Front Street blockaded? Scores of people were trapped in their cars with nowhere to escape. Why was the water shut off? There were countless stories of first responders trying to tap into fire hydrants only to find them dry. Why was there no emergency plan? And now, one year later, why was it taking so long to implement a recovery plan? The people were still waiting for hope and desperate for a break. Where was the leadership?

Everyone on the west side of Maui was traumatized that day by what they saw, what they heard, and what they lost. In the aftermath of the fire, there was no power, no cell phone service, and no Internet. Rumors spread faster than the fire itself. All services were down for weeks.

Residents were desperate to find friends and family. No stores were open, which meant no food or water, no prescriptions, no booze, no gas, no ATMs. The roads in and out of town were cut off from civilization, causing massive traffic jams and mass hysteria. There were looting and burglaries by fearful people who had lost everything, desperate to care for their loved ones. It was a terrifying time.

Feeling the government had abandoned them, locals and folks on neighboring islands rallied and began sending boats with supplies the very next day. Word quickly spread, and locals headed to the beach to unload supplies and donations from strangers. The "aid boats" had to come right up to the beach because Lahaina Harbor was destroyed in the blaze along with the rest of the historic town. The community formed human assembly lines, passing box after box from one person to another, all the way from the boat to the staging area on the beach. It was a sight to behold, the community working together toward a common goal. In those days, the survivors became one big ohana. They were family.

Someone splashes Ana from behind, snapping her out of her reverie. She turns to see Kimo sporting a pikake lei, a huge grin, and his ever-present shaka. He looks at the pile of pua kenikeni on her board and teases, "Geez, do you think you brought enough?"

"Shut up Kimo. I see you brought none of your own, so you should be thanking me for saving your ass."

"Many mahalos, my queen." His fake bow earns him a smack on the arm.

"Shut up Kimo. They're about to start."

Kimo and Ana find a place in the large circle of paddlers and join hands with the others. They see Leimomi across the circle, and she glares in their direction. Kimo and Ana share a covert giggle but keep it respectful.

"Shhh. Shut up, Kimo."

The Paddle Out is traditionally a spiritual symbol of surf culture. It is a tribute to the life and legacy of loved ones who have passed away; a floating memorial meant to represent the way the ocean brings people together. It is an opportunity for mourning, camaraderie, and self-reflection. The ceremony highlights connections and separation, departure, and continuity—the circle of life.

Ana and Kimo listen as the Kahuna blows the conch shell four times, once in each direction: north, south, east, and west, symbolizing the coalescence of the gods. There are thousands of people there, so not everyone can join the circle. Hundreds float just outside the circle, and others form smaller circles of their own. Kimo takes off the lei that Auntie Pua made for the occasion and puts it on his board. He takes a knife from his waist and cuts the lei into five places so the honu, the sea turtles, won't get tangled up in the string.

The Kahuna begins to chant a traditional Hawaiian prayer. Although there are thousands of people there, it is dead silent as each individual bows their head and weeps. People speak of those they lost. Many pray. Others talk story about how they survived that day and how their loved ones did not. Then, at 2:55 pm, the entire beach, seemingly all of Lahaina, observes 102 seconds of silence to honor the number of confirmed lives lost with reverence and hope. They all know the number was much, much higher.

Thousands of mourners begin to scatter their flowers in the ocean. Some emancipate the ashes of their loved ones in a ritual that releases their spirit into the timelessness and eternity of the ocean. Suddenly, the serene moment is interrupted as a deafening incoming helicopter drops enormous bales of flowers over the circle. As the crowd gasps, each bundle hits the water and explodes in a technicolor pool that promptly becomes a vibrant sea of rainbow-colored blossoms. The moment is charged with emotion. The water is covered with flowers of every kind. Acres and acres of flowers. Ana cries. She turns to Kimo and sees tears run down his flawless cheeks. As she looks around the circle, she sees she isn't alone. The solemn moment escapes no one as their collective hearts break.

Abruptly, one of the mourners screams out in what sounds like pain. His wounded roar gives way to hoots and hollers and turns joyful. The crowd follows suit, and thousands of people energetically slap the water in a combined emotional release amid celebratory cheers. The ritual is felt deeply by everyone there, as well as those watching from the beach and the boats around them. It feels like the formation of a deep and spiritual bond among a large family who has come together in a common sorrow.

After the ceremony, Ana and Kimo paddle back to shore in silence. Ana is lost in thought and appears to be far away. Kimo attempts to distract her with yet another little-known fact. Maybe he could bring some levity to the situation.

"You know, Ana. The exact origins of the memorial paddle out are not known. It's not actually a pre-historical Polynesian ritual, as many believe. It appears that it started only about a hundred years ago in Waikiki and remains rooted in surf culture."

Ana feigns a smile. "Fascinating factoid, Kimo." Kimo laughs and points to his head as Ana rolls her eyes. "It's all right here."

They emerge from the water and head over to where Kal and Pua are sitting. Ana senses a weird energy as Kalama and Kimo share a few furtive glances. Pua and Ana watch the two and suspect that something's up as the men walk away to talk. Ana has a bad feeling.

Pua gives voice to her concern. "Something is going on with those two. They've been like this for days now, sneaking off, having secret conversations."

Ana agrees. "Right? I've noticed it too. Something is definitely sketchy. They've both been acting strangely."

Just then, Kalia walks up in a huff. "Can you believe these politicians? They ignore our people for a year, but of course, they show up for a photo op when the press is here. Look at them. It's SO gross!" Kalia stomps off in disgust.

Pua and Ana share a fond giggle at Kalia's expense. Pua was proud despite her teasing.

"That girl never met a cause she didn't take up."

"I hear you, Auntie, but Kalia is going to change the world someday; you just watch."

CHAPTER 10

West Maui, Hawaii
August 9, 2024

Sweat pours down Ana's face as she battles to excavate a large rock from a grown-over patch in her yard. Her plan is to level the area, install a brick paver deck, and build an outdoor kitchen complete with BBQ, smoker, and pizza oven. That's her plan, but as her mother used to remind her, 'Man plans, God laughs. ' Koa sees her struggling and lends a paw by digging beside her.

"Mahalo, buddy, but that's not helping."

"Yikes. A little ungrateful, don't you think?"

Ana turns to see Kimo standing behind her, offering some sort of frozen drink. "Here, it's a fruit smoothie with protein and acidophilus. Mama worries you don't get enough nutrition."

"That's sweet. Please send Auntie my mahalos." Ana takes the smoothie and takes a few large gulps. "Wow, that's good. Want some?"

Kimo waves the cup away. "Drink up; I have to report back to Mama." He looks at her pile of rocks and tools. "You finally starting that outdoor kitchen you've been going on about?" Ana guzzles the last of the smoothie and lets Koa lick the paper cup.

Ana has been talking about this project for over a year, but never seems to find the time to get it done. The truth is, she's had a hard time finishing anything for a long time now. She starts projects, but somehow never completes them. Her therapist says it's part of her PTSD … or was it her depression? Perhaps her anxiety or agoraphobia? It's hard to keep the many diagnoses straight, but bottom line: Ana is broken and can't seem to get shit done.

"Yes, Kimo, I'm finally starting my outdoor kitchen. With any luck, I'll finish it, too. My shrink says I have to hold myself accountable and finish what I start, so this will be a test." Ana hates tests. It's not that she doesn't perform well; she excels at almost everything she does. It's the anxiety leading up to the tribulation that she could do without.

"Well, I'm happy to help, Ana, you know that. What can I do?" Ugh. Why was Kimo always so sweet, so helpful, so caring? What an asshole. Ana is tempted to tell him she can do it alone, but reconsiders—no use cutting off her nose to spite her face.

"Okay, muscles, how about you help me dig up this rock?" Kimo peruses the situation and heads off toward the barn.

Ana watches him walk away and can't help but appreciate his, uh, physicality. "Is that a 'no'?"

"Hold on, I have an idea." Kimo disappears into the work shed and, after no small amount of clanking and banging, emerges with a large iron pole about 10 feet long.

"This should do it. What we need is leverage. You know all about that, don't you, Ana?"

Kimo looks at her with a raised eyebrow, and she pretends to ignore his reference. Kimo holds his gaze, and Ana suddenly feels shy, almost coy. She turns away so he won't see her smirk. He chuckles and continues his task.

Kimo lodges one end of the pole deep under the boulder and, using it like a crowbar, pushes hard on the end to dislodge the stalwart stone. Ana watches Kimo's tan muscles bulge and ripple with the effort. She may not currently be dating, but she isn't dead. He catches her looking at his body, and Ana self-consciously averts her gaze. Eventually, after several attempts, the rock breaks free, and Kimo rolls it to the side of the future BBQ area. He stands and bows for Ana's benefit.

"Did you enjoy the show?" Kimo knows she finds him attractive and takes great pleasure in teasing her.

"Shut up, Kimo." Ana tries to cover and mumbles something about using the boulder in a future water feature, but her chatter subsides. They both enjoy just being together, and neither feels the need to fill the silence.

They quietly work together for about an hour until the area is cleared out and ready to level. Ana brushes the dirt from her clothes and heads up toward the house. Koa abandons the shade of the barn to follow.

"Come on, let's get something to drink; my mouth is drier than a rice cake." Kimo chuckles and wipes some dirt off Ana's cheek. She avoids eye contact and turns away. Kimo knows she can't resist him forever. He can feel something shift in her behavior towards him.

Kimo and Ana sit on the lanai, sipping iced tea and watching Koa chase a mongoose through the garden.

"That dog has the life. When I come back, Ana, I want to be your dog."

Ana teases, "You're already my dog, Kimo." Kimo tilts his head and acquiesces as they smile and lock eyes. It is becoming increasingly difficult for Ana to deny the connection between them. If Grandpa Sid were here, he'd no doubt tell Ana to shit or get off the pot. She's been living in an emotional purgatory for 18 years, and her inability to get her act together is hurting her best friend deeply. Ana knows she is at a crossroads. It's time to make a decision.

As they sit in silence, Kimo becomes pensive and distracted. His eyes gaze off in the distance as his mind travels halfway around the world. Ana wonders where he went and pokes his shoulder.

"Are you preparing another 'little known fact' for my edification?" Kimo turns to Ana, and she can see the sadness in his eyes. Goosebumps travel up Ana's neck as trepidation fills her being. Bad news is coming.

"Ana …" Kimo pauses and searches for the words that will lessen the blow.

Ana is suddenly filled with fear. "Oh my God, Kimo! What's wrong? Spit it out! My head's going to explode!"

"Ana, you remember the Hamas terror attack at the Nova Festival last October?"

"Of course." Ana feels like she's going to crawl out of her skin. Her heart races as her nervous system takes control of her body. She wants to reach down Kimo's throat with her clammy hands and pull out the words he can't seem to find.

Ana jumps to her feet. "Kimo, just say it. You're killing me." She waits nervously with bated breath.

Kimo rises and stands in front of Ana, taking her hands.

"Your sister, Rachel, was there." Long pause. "She was taken." Silence.

"Ana? Did you hear me?"

Time stops. Ana opens her mouth but is unable to speak. She cannot breathe. Ana feels she is going to pass out. Rachel was taken? Her sister was abducted by Hamas?

"Ana!" Kimo's concern for her snaps her out of her psychological paralysis. "Ana!"

She turns to him, confused, and asks slowly, "She was taken?" Ana sits back down in her oversized rattan chair and motions for him to do the same.

"Tell me everything."

Kimo sits and explains with as much sensitivity and compassion as he can muster, but there is no softening a blow this horrific.

"Rachel went to the Nova Festival with a girlfriend, Zara, Zara's older brother, and a group of his friends. They were waiting in line to exit the festival grounds when Hamas infiltrated the border. They fired on the crowd as 1000s of innocent civilians ran for their lives. Zara's brother Omar was shot three times and left for dead. It was touch and go, but he managed to survive. Omar's girlfriend was assaulted and murdered. Everyone in the friend group was murdered. They now know Rachel and her girlfriend were taken by Hamas."

Ana stares in horror at Kimo as he gently tells her what happened. Taken? Taken where? Taken by whom?

"How do we know they were taken?" Ana spoke slowly, in shock. Unbearable thoughts racing through her brain.

"Well, initially, they believed Hamas had taken them because they weren't identified among the dead, but they couldn't be sure. Now they've found proof. The scumbags posted hours of videos on their Telegram channel of them murdering, raping, and kidnapping innocent people." Kimo opens the Telegram app on his phone and hands it to Ana.

"That's where they found this." Ana watches a video clip as crowds of Palestinians dance and celebrate in the streets of Gaza. A small truck enters the frame and drives slowly through the hordes of revelers. Kimo reaches over and pauses the video, then enlarges the picture. There in the back of the truck are two girls huddled together, bound and beaten.

"Oh my God, Kimo. That's my sister!? How can they be sure?" Ana feels sick as the dreadful reality sinks in. Her sister is being held hostage by Hamas terrorists. There is no greater fear for a Jewish woman.

"They're sure, Ana. There's more. Papa's contacts at Mossad have intel that Rachel and Zara were sold to human traffickers. If the intel is correct, they are currently somewhere in the middle of the Pacific Ocean on a cargo ship, imprisoned in a Matson shipping container."

Ana cannot believe what she is hearing. Is this a nightmare? How can this be real? Those poor girls! She can't imagine what they must be going through. Rage slowly replaces disbelief in Ana's mind and body. She begins to shake violently, tears coursing down her face. Will this never end? Flashes of her own experiences 18 years ago fill her reeling head. Then it dawns on her. The furtive glances, the secret meetings, the whispering. Koa senses her upset, goes to Ana's side, and sits on her foot, leaning all 140 lbs against her leg.

"Is this what you and Uncle have been trying to hide the last few days? Neither of you are very good liars."

"Yes. I'm sorry, Ana. We didn't want to worry you and Mama until we had a plan."

"A plan? What are you talking about? You're not going to Israel?" Kimo smiles sweetly at her panicked concern. He knows she loves him, even if she doesn't.

"No, we're not going to Israel. We're staying right here on Maui."

"Kimo, what are you saying? I don't understand."

"Do you remember Hale Pau Hana? You used to work there on the weekends before the pandemic."

"Of course, I ran the weekend fitness program and led the tourists on hikes through the lava tunnels. It was a great gig, but the schlep to Hana was too much. They closed it down a few years ago, and some billionaire bought it. What does that have to do with my sister?"

"Right. Well, that billionaire is no regular rich haole. He's a psychopath who deals in drugs, weapons, and humans. Anything that makes him money, humanity be damned."

"Sounds like a real peach. Who is this guy?"

"No one knows for sure. He goes by Lawrence. Anyway, we have it on good authority that he is having a secret, invitation-only party next weekend. There are some incredibly shady people on the guest list. Big-name bad guys. In addition to various weapons and ammo, we believe he'll be auctioning off Rachel and Zara."

"Oh my God, Kimo, WHAT? I can't even wrap my head around this. How are you and Uncle involved? I thought you were finished with this mercenary shit." Kimo pauses, unsure of how much to tell Ana, but quickly realizes he needs to be honest and lay it all out for her. It's the only way.

"Papa has been talking with Lior and Uncle Lou about this new intel." Ana has not seen her father, Lou, for almost 18 years and refuses to acknowledge him. Kimo continues.

"Uncle Lou is understandably distraught over Rachel's kidnapping, and he's beside himself. Unfortunately …" Kimo's voice trails off.

"Unfortunately …? Come on, Kimo, you can't stop now. What has my father done now?" Ana still blames Lou for her mother's disappearance and for abandoning her in the years that followed. She has forbidden Uncle, Auntie, and Kimo to speak of him in her presence, even though she knows they are all still close and keep in touch.

"Ana, that's not fair. I'm sorry to tell you this, but your father is ill." Kimo waits for a response. Nothing. "It's cancer."

Ana feels dizzy and nauseous. Cancer!? Kimo continues.

"And Rachel's abduction has taken a real toll on him. Lou had surgery last month and is in treatment as we speak … both chemo and radiation. We're all hopeful he'll be okay, but he's in no shape to help find your sister.

He's asked us to be his proxy. Uncle Lior is bringing some ex-Mossad buddies from the kibbutz, and Pop has reached out to some ex-CIA guys. We're going to Hana, and we're going to save Rachel and Zara."

Ana is in shock. Shaken to the core. WHAT? She stands up and rushes down the lanai steps toward the barn. Kimo follows. She yells back at him.

"Who are you, Captain America? This is completely insane, Kimo. Psychopathic billionaire arms dealers selling girls into sexual slavery? Are you fucking kidding me? But not just any girls, NO! It's my half-sister, WHOM I've never even met! Of course, it is! Unbelievable. Truly. NOT to be believed. Is this actually happening? WHAT the actual FUCK?!" Ana stomps through the cane grass, completely embracing her outburst.

Kimo follows at a safe distance, being sure to give Ana her space.

"Ana, please ..." Kimo struggles to calm her, but she's enraged. Ana has let her crazy bitch run free, and there's no getting her back in the corral now.

"Fine, Kimo. Go, then! Go off to save Rachel and get yourself killed! You can be the next thing my father takes from me!"

"Ana, please. I'm not going anywhere. You have to listen. This is important. We need your help." This is not going well, and Kimo starts to doubt whether their plan is feasible. Ana is clearly still traumatized, and this is triggering her. He fears it is all too much for her. This is a really horrible plan.

"You need MY help? You cannot possibly be serious. I want no part of your farkakt plan. How can I possibly help? If you want to get yourself killed, that's on you. Billionaire fucking ARMS DEALERS?! I mean …"

"You're right, Ana, I shouldn't have asked. I'll tell Papa we're going without you."

Ana tries hard to control her rage and remain rational, but fears she is losing the battle. Her heart breaks for the sister she never met. And her father, he must be devastated. Cancer? It is all too much to process. It is simply too much.

"Kimo, why would a group of professional mercenaries need my help? I'm sure y'all have it handled between you. What aren't you telling me?"

Kimo takes Ana's hand and leads her toward the barn. He picks her up and sets her on top of the split-rail fence as if she weighs nothing, then hops up beside her. Ana rolls her eyes.

"This outta be good." Kimo puts his hand on Ana's thigh and takes a deep breath. Ana fights her attraction to him and fights to hold on to her rage.

"Lawrence has the place locked up tight with lasers and cameras and hired goons. He hires only the best security teams. We've gone over and over our escape plan, and there's only one way that makes sense. We have to escape from the property through the lava tunnels and make it upcountry." Ana looks at Kimo incredulously.

"You are certifiable. First of all, there is a mile of waist-high cane grass between Pau Hana and the tunnels. Not to mention, there are hundreds of miles of lava tubes up there. You could get lost and die from starvation before someone finds you. You'd never find your way out without a guide." The realization comes quickly.

"Aaah. That's why you need me. You think I'm going to join your random band of soldiers for hire, rescue hostages from a psycho drug-dealing, human trafficking Bond villain, and heroically lead you all to freedom." Ana laughs a little too loudly, hops off the fence, and walks briskly toward the Ohia forest, Koa instantly on her heels. Kimo stays, watching her tantrum erupt. He decides not to follow her and not to push. Ana yells back to him as the distance between them rapidly grows.

"Nope. Nope. Fuck no! Not a chance." She turns around just long enough to throw him the bird, then continues stomping through the weeds. "Fuck you, Kimo! You're a soldier and an ex-mercenary! I'm just an angry island girl with trust issues! Who the hell do you think I am?

Wonder Woman? I may be a mess, Kimo, but I don't have a death wish … Nope!" Ana's rant continues, but her words slowly drift off as she disappears out of sight, Koa faithfully by her side. Kimo sighs and follows them through the thick outcropping of monkey pod trees.

He finds Ana sitting on a rock, having a meltdown, Koa devotedly at her feet.

"Omg, Kimo! I'm sorry, I can't do it, I just can't! I'll fuck it up, Kimo. Just like everything else, I'll fuck it up. I'll get you all killed. I want to help, but I just can't. I'm not good enough. Please, Kimo, you can't count on me. I can't do this!" All the years of pent-up emotions and insecurities come pouring out as Ana finally reveals her deepest shame.

"It's my fault Kimo. I was holding her hand and then … I can't do it, Kimo, I can't. I failed Lilikoi, and I'll fail Rachel, too!"

"Oh, Lehua." Kimo holds Ana tightly as she sobs and strokes her hair softly. He isn't going to let Ana lose another family member. He will find Rachel and bring her home. He will do it for Ana.

CHAPTER 11

Hawaiian Archipelago
August 10, 2024

Rachel awakens groggily to what have become familiar odors: vomit, urine, and feces. The drugs she was given swim in her head as she listens to the sounds she has become accustomed to, the sounds of suffering, the moaning, and the sobbing of children and adults alike. In the pitch black, they can't tell just how many people are locked inside this floating prison with them. There are several cracks and holes in the sides and corners of the large, rusting metal container, which let in tiny spears of sunlight. It is the only way they can tell if it is day or night.

Zara sits up and leans against the cold metal wall, holding

her head in her hands. Huddled up next to her is a young girl. Rachel and Zara had learned the girl's story three weeks ago when they were brought to the ship. The girl told them her name was Charlotte, and she is 9 years old. She barely speaks, but she was able to tell them a few things. Apparently, she was riding her bike, and an older white man with a beard took her. He gave her to a woman with an accent who brought her here. Charlotte is terrified and cries constantly for her parents. Rachel and Zara are suffering their own unimaginable trauma and can offer her very little comfort other than their presence and some kind words.

The lady with the accent, Yasmin, is the woman in charge of the girls on the ship. She speaks to them in English and Arabic and is permanently accompanied by a man with an automatic weapon she calls Otto. Yasmin wastes no time with pleasantries. She demands complete submission, barks orders, and treats the prisoners like they are chattel. Yasmin never makes eye contact with any of the hostages.

Rachel knows something about human trafficking; she had done a research paper on the topic for her Sociology class last year. From what she can surmise, some of those present had been kidnapped, like the three young boys who she thinks are probably Eastern European, but others had doubtless paid dearly for passage into the United States. There is a large group of Chinese nationals in the container that she believes were most likely hired under labor contracts—a sort of indentured servitude—that would never be fulfilled. Rachel remembers her teacher saying that human trafficking in shipping containers is largely a myth. It doesn't feel like a myth to Rachel. She can't wait to get home to teach her Sociology teacher a thing or two.

They hear the large metal door slowly creak open, and the girls huddle together in fear. Charlotte's tiny body begins to shake violently. They cover their eyes as the daylight rushes in with a blinding hostility. Zara speaks to the girls in a whisper so as not to be heard by their captors.

"Shhhh. They're coming. Just stay together, don't make eye contact, and don't speak a word."

The large iron door screeches as their captors enter the shipping container; the light streams in like so many shards of glass. Yasmin enters with Otto right behind her. She looks toward the back of the container and shades her eyes with her hand, waiting for them to adjust to the darkness. Looking around, their abductor spots her prey and points to the three girls huddled together in the corner. Yasmin's voice is something right out of a horror movie, loud and shrieking like a witch.

"You three!" The girls say nothing. Zara feels the goosebumps travel up her arms and neck to the top of her head. Yasmin raises her shrill voice.

"You three! Come with me. It's time to get you cleaned up and fed. No one will want you in this condition. This way." She turns abruptly and exits the container. Otto points his weapon at the girls, and they struggle to rise, weak and exhausted from their ordeal. They slowly and nervously follow Yasmin as Otto slams and secures the large, bellowing door behind them.

As they exit their steely prison into the blinding light of day, all they can see is more shipping containers. There must be hundreds, some stacked four high, one on top of the other. The girls are led through a maze of containers, down a narrow staircase, and through a long, dirty hallway to a small room with two bunks, a toilet, a sink, and a tiny shower. When they enter, Otto points to a small closet. He speaks in broken English.

"Clothes there. Shower and dress." The girls stare at Otto in silent submission. The intimidating guard leaves and locks the door behind him. Charlotte collapses in a puddle of tears, her body wracked with sobs. Zara and Rachel look at each other, each one trying to be strong for the other but finding it almost impossible. Zara puts her arms around Charlotte and tries to comfort her. Rachel speaks first.

"I'll shower first. We don't want to anger them." She tells herself to just stay alive and struggles to perform the most mundane tasks, just as she had over the last ten months. Do what they say and don't resist. She thinks constantly of her parents and her life before October 7th. What must they be thinking right now? They surely believe she's dead. Or are they still looking for her? Rachel can't stem the tears as she thinks of home. Her mother working in her award-winning organic garden; her father in his big leather library chair, immersed in some historical fiction – in hardback book form, no Kindle or audiobooks for Pop. Her heart breaks as she thinks of her Labrador retriever, Frank. Poor Frank would be devastated by the loss of his best friend. He probably thinks she abandoned him. Will she ever see her family again?

Rachel enters the small, dark, grimy shower and braces as the cold water cascades down her head and over her filthy body. Her hair is matted with dirt, and her feet and hands are caked in grime. She takes a hard, bristled brush from the broken shelf on the wall and scrubs herself until her skin feels raw, as if she could scrub away the trauma and experiences of the last 10 months. Rachel knows she has to be strong if she wants to survive this ordeal, and, as she has every day since she was taken, she prays to God to save them.

Rachel opens the bathroom door to find Zara lying on a bunk, spooning Charlotte, who had cried herself to sleep. Zara rises and covers the child with a towel.

"She's inconsolable. I don't know what to do for her. I don't know what to do for any of us." As the oldest of the three, Zara feels a responsibility to be strong and show leadership.

"For now, we just do what they say and don't speak unless they ask a direct question. We don't know what will make them angry. Just cooperate."

"I agree. Here, take this." Rachel hands Zara a towel. "The water is cold, but you'll feel much better afterward. I'll stay with Charlotte." The child sleeps restlessly on the bunk beside them.

Zara turns on the water and steps into the cold shower. Finally, alone, she breaks down, her body shaking as she cries for herself and for her family. She thinks of her parents in Gaza and wonders if they're still alive. Would they even want to go on living after the loss of both of their children? Visions of that horrible day ceaselessly haunt her: Nadia's screams, her red pashmina gently draped over her ravaged, dead body. She cries for Farrah, Nisim, and Iman. How would they bear the loss of Omar and Nadia? She wonders if it would've been better to die along with them rather than living this nightmare. What was in store for the three girls?

"Stop it!" Zara reprimands herself aloud. She knows she can't let these thoughts in; she can't go down the rabbit hole. Zara knows she needs to live one minute at a time.

Just think about survival. One second at a time.

Zara and Rachel somehow get Charlotte into the shower and clean her up. The girl has stopped crying but isn't speaking now. She has a faraway look in her eyes that is worrisome. The girls summon their strength as they share a knowing look. They may never be free again, but they cannot lose hope.

Just then, they hear a loud commotion coming from the top deck. They can hear boat engines revving and countless men shouting to each other. Zara jumps up to check on Charlotte, who is curled up in the corner of the shower, hugging her knees and staring into space.

"Charlotte. Charlotte! Come here, honey." Zara pulls the wet child from the shower and dries her off. "Come with me, Charlotte. Come on, sweet girl."

The girls dress in the gray gym clothes their captors had supplied for them, and they sit in silence, awaiting their fate. Moments later, Otto appears with his gun slung over his shoulder, not anticipating any trouble from the three girls. He leads them down a long, busy hallway to a large room with tables and chairs. Some men are at one table, eating off of cafeteria trays. No one speaks.

"Sit here." Otto points to the nearest table, and the girls sit as instructed. A woman they'd never seen before comes and places trays in front of the girls, who just stare at the food. Otto barks impatiently.

"Eat!" Immediately, Rachel and Zara begin devouring their food, grateful for the flavorless meal of meat and potatoes after weeks of living on bread, protein bars, and water. Charlotte sits unmoving, her arms limply at her side, and her eyes stare at her lap. Otto shrugs and leaves the room. Rachel puts her arms around the traumatized girl and tries to feed her.

"Charlotte, come on, honey, you need to eat. You need to stay strong so we can get back to our families. Please, Charlotte, eat!" Rachel lifts a spoon filled with the watery stew to Charlotte's mouth. The child slowly opens her mouth, allowing Rachel to feed her. She chews the tough meat slowly, deliberately, as if in a trance.

"Oh, thank you, Lord. Baruch Hashem." Rachel and Zara are relieved for this small gift. The girls finish their meal and wait for further instructions. Random men come and go for their turn at the gray meat and spoiled vegetables. Not one of them looks at the girls. It's as if they don't exist.

Finally, Otto comes and leads them back down the long hallway. Rachel looks to her side, and through the portholes, she can see the side of a large white ship docked next to theirs. Rachel and Zara share a glance as Charlotte's eyes remain lowered. Otto leads the girls up a rickety metal staircase, and they emerge on deck to see an enormous private yacht moored next to the cargo ship. The spectacle is as long as an American football field and features a satellite dish on top and a helicopter pad at the bow. They see Yasmin aboard the yacht, speaking with a tall, well-dressed man with white hair.

The girls watch as the man hands Yasmin a briefcase, and they shake hands. Just then, three boys, the ones from the shipping container, appear, climbing a staircase from below and arrive on deck. They stand silently, heads down and eyes averted. They look broken and terrified. Rachel wonders how long they have been below deck and what horrible things have been done to them.

Yasmin speaks to the traumatized young boys, and they walk ahead of her as they cross the gangplank and return to their floating penitentiary. The girls watch silently as the small boys are led to the ship's rear in the direction of the shipping container that had been their prison for weeks. Yasmin waves to Otto and the girls.

"Come now, it is time to meet my friend Lawrence."

CHAPTER 12

Maui, Hawaii
Present Day

Ana sits in her psychiatrist's waiting room, exhausted by a restless night of little to no sleep. The nightmares came anyway, despite being awake. She can't stop thinking about Rachel and what she must be going through. It's been nine months! Where had they taken her? What were they doing to her? Ana feels sick and tries to steady her breathing.

"Get a grip, dumbass." Ana recognizes her self-deprecating language and makes a note of it. It's one of the things she's supposed to be working on in her therapy. Just breathe.

Ana is frustrated as she considers her lack of progress over the last twelve years. Dr. Gilad had initially been

Ana's court-ordered shrink when, at 16 years old, she was charged with assault. Of course, it wasn't her fault. Ana had been surfing at Ho'okipa when some local girls started cutting in and stealing waves. The trash talk turned into a surfside brawl, with Ana easily emerging as the victor. Ana insists the other girl threw the first punch, but the local girls stuck together, so she took the fall. The silver lining was that Ana really connected with Dr. Gilad, who, in typical Israeli style, tells it like it is and doesn't pull any punches. Dr. G reminds Ana a lot of her mother, and the older woman has become a sort of surrogate mother and mentor over the years.

The seconds sluggishly tick by as Ana takes comfort in the sounds of a fountain in the corner. As she scans the room, Ana rolls her eyes at the mountain of self-help books on the sturdy oak table before her.

"I bet I've read every one of these. I may not be cured, but not for lack of trying. Let's see here." Ana picks up a familiar book.

"*Complex PTSD: From Surviving to Thriving*. Yup. Read it. Still surviving, not so much thriving." She sets the book back on the pile and grabs another.

"*Fearful & Dismissive Avoidant*. Guilty as charged, Doc, now what? Oh, this is a classic *Healing Trauma*. Still waiting on this one to take hold."

Ana digs through the pile until she finds an unfamiliar title. "Here's one I haven't read. *Yes to Life in Spite of Everything*. Ugh. No, thank you. Oh, we can't forget my favorite, *Risking Intimacy*. Uh, also no." Ana is startled by the creak of a door opening.

"Shaloha, Ana, come in." Shaloha. The word comes from a combination of 'Shalom' and 'Aloha' and is a common greeting among Jews in Hawaii.

"Shaloha, Dr. G." Ana skips the pleasantries this morning. Lately, she has come to feel she's just going through the motions with her therapy. Ana takes a seat on the stained, yellow-flowered couch and tries to fluff the old, lumpy pillow to lean against.

"How are you doing today, Ana? You seem agitated." Dr. Gilad sits in her brown leather library chair and sets her clipboard on her lap.

"Hold onto your tits, Dr. G." The therapist raises an eyebrow but does not comply.

Ana tries to find the words. "You're not going to believe this. I just found out. It's horrible. My half-sister Rachel was apparently abducted at the Nova Festival in Re'im last October, and they've just learned she was sold to a human trafficker." Even as the words formed in her own mouth, Ana could not believe what she was hearing. It sounds like a Hollywood movie script, not her real life.

Ana is numb.

"Dear God, Ana! No! I have no words. I'm so sorry! Ana, this is horrifying! This must be taking a toll on you. How are you handling this?"

"How am I handling this? Hmm. I'm not. You know me, avoid, ignore, and deflect. Yesterday I was estranged from my father and my half-sister, and today …"

"Today what, Ana? Do you feel differently now that you know Rachel is in danger? Tell me what you're feeling, Ana."

"I don't know what I'm feeling! Shame. Guilt. Rage." Ana drops her head, and tears slip from her eyes. "Fear."

"Good. Now we're getting somewhere. What are you afraid of?"

"You know what I'm afraid of, Doc? I'm afraid I'll fuck everything up like I always do."

"And if you don't, Ana? If you don't fuck everything up? What's to fear then?"

Ana knows the answer, but somehow, saying it out loud is nearly impossible, so she pivots.

"Honestly, my fear of abandonment isn't the issue right now. You haven't heard the best part. Kimo, Uncle, and some old military friends are organizing a mission as we speak. They're going to rescue Rachel. Dr. Gilad, they want me to go with them."

Dr. Gilad is aghast at the thought. "Go with them! Where? Ana, you need to leave this to the professionals. This is insane!"

In retelling the situation, somehow it doesn't sound as crazy to Ana as it did at first. Ana's jealousy and resentment for Rachel have given way to rage and horror at what her sister must be enduring at this very moment. She thinks of her father reliving this nightmare yet again. Ana's resolve begins to build slowly. Is it possible she could help them rescue Rachel? She would only have to lead them through the lava tunnels, something she's done countless times already. Ana is torn. Part of her wants to help, but what if she fucks everything up? What if she lets them down? What if she gets them all killed?

"Ana? You'll leave the rescuing to the professionals, yes?"

"Of course, Dr. Gilad." Ana has made no decisions regarding her involvement in Rachel's rescue, but just in case, she doesn't want to allow the psychiatrist to talk her out of it. Ana already seems to be doing a good job of that herself.

"Dr. G, I'm sorry, but I can't discuss this anymore. Can we talk about something else?" Ana is afraid that if she hears Dr. Gilad's logical objections, she'll lessen her resolve, however weak.

Dr. Gilad is concerned about Ana and struggles to keep it professional. With some effort, she moves on.

"How are things going with Kimo? Does it feel different now that he's ended things with Leimomi? I heard you were together at the paddle-out on Saturday. How do you feel about that?" The coconut wireless strikes again.

"We weren't together. We ran into each other in the water, and that was it. It wasn't a date. He's like a brother to me, you know that."

Dr. Gilad smirks at Ana's denial. "Ok, so you're sticking to the 'we're just friends' thing, eh? Fine. How do you feel about the memorial?" Dr. G was all too familiar with Ana's fruitless denial of her attraction to Kimo.

"How do I feel? I feel pissed. I feel furious. I feel sad and hopeless. Like nothing is ever going to change. I feel like I want to stay in bed all day. Sometimes I feel like just giving up."

"Have you been practicing your breathing and meditation? Are you still microdosing the mushrooms?"

"Yes, yes, and yes."

"When you say you feel like giving up, what do you mean exactly?"

"I don't mean I'm going to kill myself if that's what you're getting at. I'm talking about giving up on trying to make a difference. I feel like there's no justice in this world. Good, honest people lose their homes, their families, and their jobs due to corruption and government incompetence. People leave you. Innocent civilians are brutally tortured and massacred by terrorists by the thousands, all without consequence. Where is the justice? What is the use? I'm better off just living alone and keeping to myself."

"And you believe that will keep you safe? No one can hurt you if you don't let them in?"

"I see what you're doing. Yes, I have a fear of vulnerability." Ana's tone turns mocking.

"I have an internal conflict between my desire for intimacy and my fear of it. I know all this." She stands up and begins to pace in the small office.

"My question is: What can I do about it? It's been 12 years now, and I'm still as angry and fucked up as I was at sixteen. I've made zero progress!"

Dr. Gilad remains relaxed and watches Ana with wry amusement. "I beg to differ, Ana. Back then, you didn't know what your issues were, and you had no desire to address them. Now you're here telling ME what's wrong with you and asking how you can change. I would call that immense progress. Please sit down, Ana."

Ana obeys and begrudgingly returns to the ugly couch, still agitated.

"So, what's the answer? How can I change? Sometimes I just want to live a normal life, but then I wonder if I even deserve it." Ana thinks of Lilikoi, and the guilt comes rushing back. "How can I ever be happy? I'll never forgive myself for Lilikoi. Some mistakes are so horrible you can never come back from them."

There it is. Ana feels responsible for Lilikoi's death. She was holding the child's hand … and then she wasn't. Ana can feel the tears rise, and they puddle in her eyes. She blinks, and they stream down her flushed cheeks.

"Ana, we've discussed this, yes? You are not responsible for Lilikoi's death. You were a child. You must give yourself grace. You were a child in a war zone."

Ana slowly gains control. "I know intellectually that you're right. I just feel so … it's just so unfair. It's all so fucking wrong. And now, poor Rachel …"

Ana thinks about how jealous she was of Rachel and her seemingly perfect life and family. Lou had apparently met Rachel's mother at an Ashram in India. He had gone there after getting sober to heal, and he met his future wife. Given the events of the past 10 months, Ana is ashamed of her resentment and is devastated that she never got to know her sister. She wonders how much more of this she can take.

"Ana, can we talk about your father? He must be devastated about Rachel." Silence fills the room as Ana's face turns to stone, then softens.

"Why not? I'm already a fucking mess. Pile it on, Doc."

"Ana, let's have a come-to-Moses moment, shall we? It's time for forgiveness. I know you blame your father for abandoning you, and those feelings are completely valid. However, it is doing you more harm than good to hold on to this resentment. If you truly want to change and find love, you must come to terms with Lou." This is not the first time Dr. Gilad has advised Ana to forgive her father and move on. She was hopeful this time, it would sink in.

Ana blurts out, "He has cancer." It feels good to get it off her chest. Ana is confused by her emotions. She thought she hated her father, but now, to say she is conflicted would be a gross understatement.

"Oy vavoy, cancer? No! How bad is it?"

"I'm not sure. All I know is he has cancer, and he's going through chemo, and Rachel's abduction has been very hard on him. That's why he can't help rescue my sister." It does not escape the psychiatrist's notice that Ana just called Rachel her sister for the first time. No progress, indeed.

Dr. Gilad takes advantage of the breakthrough and puts it all out there.

"Ana, it seems your sentiments towards Rachel have softened. Have you also been reconsidering your feelings about your father?"

Ana sits in silence as she considers the question. She finds it hard to focus; so many thoughts leave her mind as quickly as they arrive.

"No. Yes. I don't know. I guess. Ugh." Ana is physically and emotionally exhausted. She wants to run away. She could take Koa and move to Costa Rica, living off the grid where no one would find them.

"Ana, your father is not to blame for Eleanor's disappearance. As you yourself have explained, Lou was out of the country when your mother was taken."

"I don't blame him for my mother's disappearance. I blame him for abandoning me afterward. He just left me, a war orphan at 10 years old." Ana knows she is lying to herself. She knows full well that Lou spent years looking for her mother and that he was devastated and broken by the loss of his wife and daughter. Uncle, Auntie, and Kimo have all pleaded his case to her many times over the years. They all rationalize his abandonment because Lou couldn't deal with the loss and eventually turned to alcohol to escape his pain. They have all forgiven him;

why can't she? But he left her. She was only ten. He left her.

Ana is suddenly repulsed by her own self-pity. When did she become this weak and whiny little girl? It's time for a truth bomb.

"God, I hate myself!" Ana jumps off the couch and again begins to pace the floor. "I know what you're going to say, Doc. Lou has suffered as much as any of us. The loss of my mother broke him, and he lost everything too. And now … and now Rachel. I know all of that. And I'm still pissed! I know it's horrible, but I'm still fucking pissed! Aaaargh! I'm a horrible person."

"Ana, do you truly want to heal? Truly?" She continues despite Ana's refusal to answer. "You will never heal until you forgive yourself. Hear me. You are not responsible for Lilikoi's tragic death. And while we're facing facts, Ana, Lou may never heal unless you forgive him. What will it take, Ana? Lou has repented and asked for your forgiveness many times and in many ways. He's only human. You know why he couldn't be there for you. Now that he may be dying, can you forgive him?"

Ana sits. Her anger turns to sorrow as she realizes she may never have a chance to see her father again. This may be her last opportunity to mend fences. Can Ana forgive her father? Can she forgive herself?

"Ana, you were deeply traumatized, and you've been stuck in fight or flight mode for 18 years now. Your nervous system is overloaded. If you want to make changes, you need to do something drastic. You need to take control. You need to learn how to stop hiding behind your trauma. You are no longer that helpless little girl on the kibbutz. You are a formidable, intelligent woman who is strong enough to move forward. I wouldn't say this to just any patient, but I know you, Ana, you're powerful. You need to make a postulate and stick to it. Stop making excuses not to love. There is no love without loss."

Boom. Ana does want love. She thinks of Auntie Pua and Uncle Kal. They met as children, grew up together, and eventually fell in love and had babies. Neither of them had ever dated anyone else, and they never regretted it. They have lived a long and happy life together. But look at the loss they've endured because they loved so profoundly. Losing Lilikoi almost killed them both. Is it worth it to love that deeply? People betray you. People leave you. People die. Is it worth the trade-off?

Her thoughts drift to Kimo. She knows he's in love with her, and God knows she has feelings for him; she just hasn't untangled them yet. Ana has been telling herself all these years that she was protecting Kimo from herself. She's always said she is too fucked up and broken for love, and that he needs a solid, stable woman. It turns out she wasn't protecting Kimo from herself. Ana was protecting herself from Kimo, or more accurately, what Kimo represents: Love. Happiness. Ana doesn't believe she deserves these things, and she certainly doesn't trust they'll not be taken from her again.

Ana's head begins to pound. It's all too much to process: Her father, Rachel, Kimo … this fucking mission! It's completely insane. How can this all be real? Agitated, Ana rises quickly from the sofa. Dr. Gilad remains seated and calm.

Ana is already at the door. "Ana, we still have 20 minutes, are you leaving?"

"I just can't. It's too much, Doc, my head feels like it's going to explode, and I'm crawling out of my skin. I need to walk, or surf, or run, or …".

"Let's schedule your next appointment, then."

Ana, hand on the doorknob, pauses and turns to face the doctor, still sitting calmly.

"I think I'm going to take a break, Dr. Gilad. I need some time to process. This isn't working." Ana walks out the door.

The psychiatrist smiles as she watches Ana disappear down the empty hallway.

"You'll figure it out, my dear. See you soon."

CHAPTER 13

Ana sits on a log and stares at the crackling fire as if waiting for the flames to reveal some sacred truth about her path in life. She has never been so unsure of her next move. She wants to help find Rachel but feels paralyzed by fear and self-doubt. Ana looks for answers in the warm night sky and embraces the celestial landscape, awash in radiant stars. The Maui sky is untainted by the bright lights of the big city, the unrestrained darkness revealing countless heavenly bodies. Ana can see the Milky Way arc impressively across the sky, its dense band of bright stars creating a stunning contrast against the vast black background. The gentle echoes of nature provide a peaceful soundtrack to the magic of the warm tropical island night. Ana listens intently. She hears the fire crackling and a pueo, the Hawaiian owl, off in the distance, calling its prey.

Suddenly, Koa's head jerks up, his large ears perked and alert. He gazes intently toward the main house as a figure steps out of the shadows, stumbles, and mutters softly to himself. Ana makes out the silhouette of Uncle Kalama, who is carrying something under his right arm. At the same moment, Koa recognizes Uncle and bolts in his direction. Ana waves and shouts into the night. "Howzit, Uncle? You're gonna get yourself shot sneaking around in the woods like that!"

"Auntie wanted me to check on you. She said she could hear you chopping wood, so …" As he approaches, Kal grabs the smaller of the two objects in his hand and gives it to Ana, who laughs.

"I see. Auntie's famous banana bread. She must really be feeling sorry for me." Ana takes the offering and immediately dives in.

It is common knowledge around the Akamai compound that chopping wood is Ana's go-to anger therapy. It's also a clear indication that she is not in a good place, so it's best to steer clear. Uncle was brave in approaching, but knows how to diffuse the situation with baked goods.

Ana goes in for a second helping before she swallows the first. "Sweet Moses, Auntie should sell this; she'd make a fortune." Kalama laughs, nodding approvingly.

"Yes, my bride has many talents."

Ana gets two Coors Banquets from a small cooler next to her chair. They each pop the top of their beer can and sip silently as they look toward the heavens, listening to the anole lizards call and the owls screech.

"Ana, we need to talk." Neither looks to face the other.

"I know, Uncle. I'm a hot mess. Did Auntie tell you I saw Dr. Gilad today?"

"Yes, she mentioned you were in a sour mood when you got home. Wanna talk about it?"

Ana lets out a wry chuckle. "What's to talk about, Uncle? It's nothing new. I'm broken. Despite all the hours of therapy and self-help books … still broken."

"Ana, you need to love yourself before you can let anyone else love you. *Kahuna nui hale kealohalani makua.* Love all you see, including yourself. The first step to loving yourself is forgiveness. Child, you need to give yourself grace."

Ana struggles with the words she knows are true. She wants to purge this guilt and shame, but she doesn't know how to. After 18 years, it's a large part of who she is. Who would she be without it?

"Uncle, I don't know if I can ever forgive myself." The tears stream down as Ana buries her face in her hands. "Lilikoi…" Her whimper is deep and primal. Ana shakes her head in her hands, feeling the shame of her perceived betrayal. "How can you ever forgive me?"

"Ana, look at me."

Her heart breaks as she looks up to see tears on Kal's cheeks. "What happened to Lilikoi was the tragic result of generations-long hatred and violence. We do not blame you; it was not your fault, just as it was not Kimo's fault. He was holding Lilikoi's other hand, remember? You don't blame him, do you?"

Ana softly answers. "No, of course not." Ana sees the logic and knows it doesn't make sense, but this has been her reality for far too long.

"I know you're right, Uncle. I'm working on it."

Kalama hands Ana a 12-inch-by-12-inch wooden box. "I've been waiting for the right time to give you this." Ana takes the box and stares down at the hand-carved Star of David on the lid.

"I believe the time is now." Ana opens the box, and sitting on top of a stack of letters is her father's old service pistol. She takes out the pistol, sets it on her lap, and then stares at the letters. The ones addressed to Uncle Kalama are opened and worn. Others were still unopened. There, in the box, is a stack of sealed letters addressed to Ana. She knew he had written to her, Auntie had told her, but Ana had refused to read them. Now, here they were. Dozens of letters from her father. His words, his love, still unacknowledged.

Ana sifts through the pile of letters and is surprised she recognizes her father's writing after all of these years. She notices a return address in Hebrew and realizes it is from Kibbutz Mishmar Ha'emek. Lou must have written this when he was staying with Uncle Lior. Then, a unique stamp catches her eye, and Ana sees an old letter with a postmark from India. She feels a pang of jealousy as she realizes he must have written that letter from the ashram where he met his new wife. With a disapproving snort, Ana tosses all the letters back in the box while Uncle watches in silence. Kalama knows when not to push.

Ana and Kal sip their beers and gaze into the fire. Each lost in thought. Unexpectedly, the night falls silent, as if all living things have frozen in time. In the distance, faint sounds of drums and chanting echo through the canyons. Kalama rises from the log and looks upcountry toward the *heiau*, the sacred temples he knows are hidden in the caves.

"Do you hear that, Ana?" Ana stands and follows Kal's gaze toward the star-filled sky. Kal's demeanor gives Ana chicken skin. He stares trance-like toward the mountain peak. "It's a New Moon. *Huaka'i po*, the Night Marchers are on the move."

Ana has heard many stories about the Night Marchers over the years. They are the ghosts of Hawaiian warriors who had protected the ali'i, the chiefs, in ancient times. The ali'i were more than just leaders; they were believed to be the physical manifestations of the gods, filled with vast spiritual power or *mana*.

In the past, warriors would blow conch shells and beat drums to announce the arrival of the Chief as he entered town. The commoners were expected to look down at the ground and avoid making eye contact with the ali'i. Disobeying this taboo could result in death.

The Night Marchers are believed to continue their protection of the ali'i and the gods even after death. Many locals today report seeing a line of torches moving down the mountain at night, often traversing sheer cliffs and areas where there are no roads for miles. Others describe hearing sounds of marching, chanting, and the beating of drums. The legend advises that if you hear the warning sounds of a nearby procession, you should run and hide or lie down on the ground to let them pass. Most importantly, it's crucial never to make eye contact.

Ana and Kalama listen as the chanting stops and the drums fade away.

"It is a special night, Ana. The ancestors are speaking to us." Kalama walks to the cooler and removes two more beers. He opens one and hands it to Ana, then opens his own.

"It will be a beautiful sunrise from Haleakala, Ana. Be at the main house at 4:00 am. *E' holoholo*; we'll go for a drive. There's something I want to show you."

Long before sunrise, Ana makes breakfast burritos for the ride and packs what's left of Auntie's banana bread. She and a drowsy Koa walk down to the main house to find Uncle proudly wiping down his new truck.

"Good morning, Uncle." Koa puts his snout in Kal's hand to beg for pets.

"*Aloha kakahiaka*, child. And what a beautiful morning it is, eh?"

Kal beams as he finishes wiping his truck. "She's a beauty, yeah?"

Ana smiles. "Does Auntie know you're in love with another?"

"What's not to love? This baby is an F-250 Super Duty with a 7.3-liter V-8 engine and 485 pounds of torque! Not to mention seven high-definition cameras."

What is it with these Akamai men? "I see where Kimo gets it from."

"What? You don't wanna hear about the cast-iron block and forged-steel crankshaft?"

"OK, Uncle, now you've gone too far."

The 90-minute drive to Haleakala is uneventful. Kal and Ana catch up on the local gossip while Koa leans his massive head out the window, his jowls flapping in the wind and drool flying everywhere. They climb higher and higher through six climate zones until they reach the volcano's peak, 6,500 feet above sea level.

Kal and Ana arrive in the cold, dark morning and quietly… humbly, hike two miles down a rocky path into the volcano's crater. The temperature is a crisp 41 degrees Fahrenheit, and Ana can see her breath. She can't remember the last time she felt this cold. As the sun slowly struggles to pierce the darkness, Kalama walks toward a large outcropping of boulders and then disappears from view. Ana soon notices a small light coming from Kal's phone, and as she approaches, she discovers him sitting on a rock inside a small cave. She walks in and sits beside Kalama.

After a moment, Kalama speaks with reverence. "This is Pua's and my sacred place. On June 16, 1981, I asked my beautiful wahine to be mine forever while sitting on this very rock." Kalama's voice sounds ethereal in the cave, shadows dancing in the light of the new moon. He smiles at the memory.

"I was leaving for boot camp the next morning. I'd enlisted in the Marine Corps to make a good life for Pua and our future family. I gave her a hundred-dollar ring I'd bought on Front Street, and she cried and cried. It was magic."

Ana watches as Kalama happily reminisces. "I met your father the next day on the plane to Parris Island, South Carolina. We went through Boot Camp together, and then we were both assigned to the Marine base in Beirut, Lebanon, in the summer of 1982."

"Is that when Lou saved your life?" Ana remembers the story from years ago.

"Yes, a little over a year later. Hezbollah bombed the Marine barracks and killed hundreds of US military personnel. You know the story: I would have died that day, at 21 years old, if it wasn't for Lou."

Kal lets out a throaty laugh. "It took saving my life for Pua to finally warm up to him."

"Wait, Auntie didn't like my father? Why not?"

"Pua only met Lou a few times before Beirut. She'd visit for a week here and there, and I would always bring Lou with me on our dates." Ana groans.

"Uncle, you didn't?"

"I know, I know. But Lou seemed lonely. Lost. Anyway,

he sort of became a third wheel, and Pua wasn't happy about it. Then, one day, when we were stationed at the Embassy in Tel Aviv, Lou met Eleanor. We four went on a double date, and the rest is history. We used to call ourselves the Fab Four, like the Beatles." Kalama releases a big sigh. "Good times."

Ana smiles, thinking of her parents' courtship. She remembers how in love they were, even after over ten years of marriage.

"We had a good run. Your mother brought out the best in Lou … he was never the same after that day."

Kal takes Ana's hand in the dark and sniffs, wiping his eyes.

"Ana, Lou is a good man. He didn't abandon you; he abandoned himself. He didn't think he could go on without Ellie. He almost didn't."

"What happened, Uncle? Why did he just disappear like that?"

"He didn't disappear, Ana; we were always in communication. Lou searched for your mother for the better part of three years. He burned through every contact and called in every favor he was owed. Lou ran down every single lead we had until they ran dry. And then he crumbled. He became hopeless. He began drinking and went downhill fast."

Kalama shakes his head. "Lou hit rock bottom. He was a drunk with a death wish. He had lost Ellie, and he felt he failed us because he didn't find Lilikoi's killer. He got into trouble in Egypt and spent time in prison there. Lior called in some favors, bribed the warden, and brought Lou back to the kibbutz. He had basically burned his bridges with everyone but Lior, who, as you know, is more of a brother than a brother-in-law."

"I remember Uncle Lior. You three were like the three Musketeers."

Kal laughs. "Yeah, those were good days. Anyway, Lior somehow convinced Lou to go to rehab, and straight from there, he went to the ashram in India, where he met Rachel's mother, Lorie. Lorie was a yoga instructor at the ashram. She was vegan and a Jew Bu, a Jewish Buddhist, and had also gone there to heal. She had lost a child to cancer at 2 years old, so the two had a lot in common. They talked about everything, and as Lou told it, Lorie gave him a reason to live. Lou said she saved his life. Lorie worked three jobs to put Lou through graduate school, and now he's a Professor of Political Science at UCSD in La Jolla."

Ana sat silent as she processed this new information. Her father didn't choose to abandon her. He not only failed her. He failed himself.

"I never knew her name. His wife, Lorie. I don't know

anything about her."

"She's a warm and intelligent woman, Ana. You would like her. And your sister, Rachel, she's so much like you: strong and stubborn."

"Stubborn? Okay, that's fair. Oh my God, Uncle … Rachel!" Ana feels the familiar anxiety taking over. She takes deep, slow breaths until it subsides.

"Uncle, I'm not strong; I'm a mess. I'm afraid." The tears come again as Kal puts his burly arm around her.

"Ana, you and your mother are the strongest women I've ever known. You are powerful wahine; strong Jewish women."

"I don't feel strong, Uncle. I'm not my mother. I'm broken."

"Nonsense. Remember your lessons from the kibbutz, Ana. King Solomon said *A righteous man falls down seven times and gets back up*. The Torah defines someone who is righteous not as someone who has succeeded but who has persevered."

"Proverbs 24:16. I remember, Uncle. I just can't seem to move forward." Ana is mentally exhausted. It has been too much for too long. Something needs to change.

"Child, you cannot avoid making decisions out of fear of making the wrong one. It is the failure to make decisions that is the worst mistake you can make. *Yeshuat Hashem k'herefayin.* The salvation of God is like the blink of an eye. You must have faith, Ana. Redemption can come at any moment."

Ana remembers back to her home schooling in Israel. She smiles at the memories of her mother and Pua teaching her and her cousins about the Torah and the plight of the Jewish people. Ana had asked how they could bear all of the horrible things that had happened to them. Her mother had responded with words that are still seared in Ana's memory.

We are resilient, Ziva. We are powerful, and we have faith. We do not collapse under pressure. We rise to the challenge. And for our hard work and devotion, Hashem blesses us, and we emerge stronger, better, and wiser. To be a Jew is to not accept defeat. That, my love, is the meaning of faith.

"Ana, you can do this. Your father needs you. Your sister needs you. Kimo needs you. You may be bent, but you are not broken."

CHAPTER 14

Kimo exits the woods between the main house and Ana's to a cacophony of curse words. He can't help but laugh at her barrage of foul language. She is one of a kind. As he enters the clearing that borders her yard, he sees Ana stomp up the hill from the direction of the catchment tank, covered in mud and swearing like a truck driver. Koa, similarly caked in filth, happily trails behind her.

"Fucking good-for-nothing critters!"

Kimo teases. "Hey Pigpen! You must have a lot of cash in Kalia's swear jar by now, yeah?"

Ana sees Kimo and scowls. How does he always seem to show up when she's at her worst?

"Honestly, I can't even keep track anymore. I just put in $100 a week and figure it's close. At this rate, Kalia can go to Harvard if she wants." Ana attempts to wipe off the mud but quickly abandons the fruitless task.

Kimo chuckles and shakes his head. "No Ivy Leagues for Kalia; she's keeping it local. U of H all the way. Go, Warriors!"

Ana is in no mood for small talk. "So, what's up, Kimo? The meeting isn't for a couple of hours, yeah?" Today is the day the team is gathering to discuss the mission to rescue Rachel.

"I came to see if you want to hit the beach beforehand. The waves are macking at Honolua Bay."

Kimo is confident she'll say yes. He knows Ana can't say no to great waves at her favorite surf spot.

Ana's attitude instantly changes. "Bitchen! Okay, let me rinse off real quick." She steps into her primitive outdoor shower, whose bamboo walls cover chest to thigh only, and strips off her muddy shorts and tank top. Kimo can't help but stare, his imagination filling in the blanks. Ana has no idea how beautiful she is, which makes her all the more attractive to Kimo.

"Kimo, you're staring." Ana feigns ire but enjoys teasing Kimo, and if she's honest, she doesn't mind the attention.

"Koa, get in here. You need this just as much as I do." The muddy dog reluctantly steps into the shower, and Ana sprays him off with the handheld sprayer. Koa whines in complaint.

"You'd think I was drowning you. There, Monkey. Stay out of the house until you dry off." Koa exits the shower and shakes violently, thoroughly soaking Kimo in the process.

"Ugh. Koa! How on earth did you two get so dirty anyway?" The murky water continues to flow past Kimo's feet down toward the rock drain.

Ana turns off the water, and Kimo hands her the towel hanging outside the three-sided shower enclosure, being careful to avert his eyes.

Ana doesn't notice his discomfort and continues her tirade. "The flippin' catchment tanks are clogged again. Between the stupid geckos, the ants, and the wasps, I'm surprised anything works around here. I got them all cleaned out, but the whole area was a mud bath by the time I was done. Obviously."

Kimo isn't surprised by Ana's ability to fix just about anything. Their early life on the kibbutz was all about self-sufficiency, and life on a multigenerational upcountry compound isn't much different. They all learned at a young age to work hard, solve their own problems, and live off the land.

"Glad you got it fixed. I would have helped if you'd asked, Ana. You just have to ask."

Ana gives Kimo a smirk. Sometimes, she thinks he knows her better than she knows herself.

"I know, I know. I need to learn to ask for help. You can tell Dr. G I've been listening."

The pair drive north on Honoapi'ilani Highway to Honolua Bay in Kimo's new truck, a replacement for the one he'd lost in the fire. Ana rolls her eyes at Kimo's choice of music, some local Hawaiian rapper singing about the white man stealing the 'aina. She quickly pairs her phone with the stereo and hijacks the music.

"You focus on driving, Kimo; the beats are on me." She scrolls through her playlists.

"Okay, but no, Miley Cyrus. If I hear you sing 'I Can Bring Myself Flowers' one more time, I might spontaneously combust."

Ana laughs and is forced to agree. "Fair. I was obsessed with Miley last summer. Remember? I declared it 'the summer of me'?

"How can I forget?" Kimo had found her 'summer of me' cute, if not downright charming. No one can say Ana doesn't fully commit to a plan. Her feminist revolution was in full swing last summer, and God help the guy who dared to open a door for her … yikes!

"So, does that mean no more Pink, Adele, or Taylor Swift either? It was all the same playlist, you know."

Kimo reluctantly confesses his not-so-dirty little secret. "You know I'll never say no to Taylor Swift."

"Hahaha. Yup! Kimo loves him some T-Swizzle!" They both laugh and ride the rest of the way, enjoying their deep and easy bond, singing along to Swift's 'You Belong with Me.' Kimo's heart beats faster as he feels Ana beginning to thaw.

They park along the beach highway and walk down to Honolua Bay, boards in tow. Ana walks ahead and takes a shortcut through a condo complex. Ana can hear the surf before she sees it, and as she turns the corner, the bay comes into view.

Ana yells back to Kimo over the crashing waves. "You weren't lying; this place is going off! These waves were ankle-slappers just last week, and now they're huge!"

"Yeah, last week's mush burgers are this week's bombs!" Kimo's words fall on deaf ears as Ana eagerly trots down to the water's edge and quickly attaches the Velcro leash to her ankle. She grabs her board and paddles out, the cool water parting as she propels toward "the line," where a few local surfers wait for the next set of waves to roll in.

Kimo sits on the shoreline, smiling broadly as he watches Ana paddle out in the large surf, effortlessly piloting her board nose-first, over and through waves others would fear. He watches the surfers sitting on their boards, welcoming Ana as she approaches the line. She fist-bumps one of Kimo's cousins and starts to talk story. While local surf spots are notoriously unwelcoming to kooks and Barneys (rookies and tourists), Ana is as local and as talented as any of these mokes, and they know it. Ana gets respect because she earned it, haole girl or not.

It is one of those rare surf days when the waves form perfect barrels that gracefully yet powerfully peel down the line. Ana is a striking balance of strength and beauty as she paddles fiercely, charging her first wave of the day. Ana can feel the rush of power beneath her feet as it effortlessly takes her. She drops into the pocket and feels the familiar adrenaline rush as her board races down the face of the six-foot wave. Ana's strong legs confidently command her board as she carves, then cuts back, peeling her way perfectly through the barrel, shooting out just before the swell meets the shore with an imposing crash.

Kimo laughs out loud. "Woo Hoo! You go, girl!"

Not to be outclassed, Kimo dons his leash, paddles out, and joins the line. As he approaches, Kimo beams proudly as the local boys praise Ana's skills.

"Hey, Bruh, your tita can shred, yeah?"

"Kimo, Bradda, you taking lessons from the little lady?"

Kimo laughs without a hint of irritation. It reminds him of the old days when Ana and Kimo were young, bobbing on their boards in the cool ocean water for hours, talking story with the locals, surfing, laughing, and enjoying their island paradise. Maui no ka oi. Maui is the best.

Ana paddles back to the line and glides up to Kimo. "I'm so stoked! That was rad! Did you see that perfect barrel, Kimo? I can't remember the last time we rode waves like this. I almost took a header over the falls, but man, what a rush!"

Kimo smiles. "You know, Ana, surfing produces a rush of neurochemicals that lead to a state of euphoria, not unlike a runner's high."

They both laugh at Kimo's latest little factoid. Ana splashes him, then cuts him off and takes his wave. Kimo is amused and lets it slide. He's thrilled to see Ana happy and playful again; his heart is full.

"Oh, Lehua."

Ana paddles hard and drops into a massive wave. Her adrenaline spikes as she is pulled down the face of the wave by a power to which she has no choice but to submit. Surrendering is the only option. Ana aligns her board in speed and tempo as she pursues the controlled slide. It's just her and the ocean. Everything slows down as she feels a familiar connection with the water, her soul intertwined with the sea, and her heart fully open. Ana looks up and sees the wave closing out. She tries to cut and exit off the lip, but she is too late. The white water closes in as the wave crashes down, and Ana gets caught in the impact zone.

Time creeps slowly by as Ana is tossed around like a towel in an angry clothes washer. She resists the intrusive fear as she calls upon her experience. Confident she can hold her breath for at least 2 minutes, she doesn't fight it and lets the ocean toss her in circles. Her mind drifts during the chaotic spin cycle, and she realizes she can see herself from above. Ana has a vision from her childhood. Her mother, Ellie, is reading from the Torah.

"Be strong and courageous. Do not be afraid or terrified because of them …"

Is she dreaming? Is she dead? The spinning abruptly stops, then only blackness.

Ana wakes up on her back in the warm sand and sits up, coughing up salt water. Kimo stands over her, frantic.

"Ana, Ana, are you okay? Damn, that was a nasty wipeout! Ana?"

Ana says nothing as she lays back on the warm sand, with her eyes closed, trying to catch her breath and gain her composure. The warm breeze plays over her wet skin, creating tiny goosebumps.

"Ana, say something. What can I do?"

Ana slowly speaks, but her eyes remain closed. "Oh my God, Kimo. Calm down, I'm alright."

"Baruch Hashem. Thank God. Thank God. Tell me what I can do."

Ana is touched by Kimo's concern and tries to diffuse the situation, eyes still closed.

"Kimo, aren't you the one who told me that wiping out is an underappreciated skill? Show me some appreciation, will you?"

"Ana, this isn't funny. You could have …"

Ana slowly sits up in the sand and teases. "Kimo, geez, chill out, will you? I just got the wind knocked out of me. Give me a minute. How about you tell me one of your little-known facts? That should cheer you up. Anything wipe-out related you'd care to disclose?" She knows Kimo can't resist the opportunity to share his obscure knowledge of, well, just about everything.

Kimo begins to calm down, and, for her sake, he plays along. If Ana is teasing him, she must be ok.

"Well, only because you mention it …" Kimo and Ana

share a look of relief, and both smile.

"Your wipeout does bring to mind the ancient Japanese art of Kintsugi, where broken pottery is mended with powdered gold. They believe something broken and repaired is something to celebrate, not disguise. I figure we should celebrate your wipeout."

"Nice, so you're saying I'm broken?"

"No, Ana. I'm saying you're resilient. You survived and are stronger for it."

"Wow, Kimo. That is deep. Honestly, I was expecting more of a pep talk and surfing metaphor, you know, "Hang in there and keep paddling because there's always another wave. Kintsugi. That's impressive, Kimo. Well done."

Ana stands up and brushes off Kimo's attempt to help steady her. "Oh my God, stop! I'm fine, Kimo. Good Lord!"

As in the past, their surf session leaves Ana and Kimo famished, so they stop at Joey's Kitchen for lunch before their secret meeting at Pu'ukoli'i Village. The hike into the old plantation village is more than two miles from the dirt access road, and they both need refueling. Kimo orders Loco Moco, a local favorite consisting of white rice, a hamburger patty, and brown gravy topped with a fried egg. Ana gets a mixed plate with teriyaki chicken and rice. They devour their food in silence, each lost in thought. No discussion of the elephant in the room intrudes on their quiet comfort.

After lunch, the pair drives up a dirt road toward the top of Ka'anapali Coffee Farm, the largest estate coffee plantation in the United States. Driving through the acres and acres of coffee trees, Ana is lost in thought and can't stop thinking about her vision. What did it mean? Was her mother trying to tell her something?

Just over a mile in, Kimo pulls off the road, and they prepare to hike down into the valley, each packing their own gear: water, protein bars, a first aid kit, guns, and ammo. Kimo laughs.

"This reminds me of Grandpa Sid and the six Ps …" Ana chuckles as they say it together.

"Proper Preparation Prevents Piss Poor Performance."

Ana and Kimo hike half a mile down steep switchbacks to the bottom of the ancient canyon. It was less than one hundred years ago that this area was a thriving village, before expansionism moved in and took control of the water.

As they follow the winding trail over massive river rocks into a clearing, they come upon an old wooden building that once served as a community gathering place. There, seated in dilapidated chairs, is a ragtag team of warriors, sharpening knives and cleaning guns.

A motley crew awaited Kimo and Ana at the old Pu'ukoli'i Village. Ana's eyes examine the men seated in front of them, each dressed in some form of camouflage and survivalist gear. She sees a familiar face in the group, her mother's brother, her Uncle Lior. Lior stands, his misty eyes seeking … Ana is unsure … forgiveness? Lior had sent cards and letters over the years, but he has not seen Ana since she was ten. He marvels at the beautiful woman she has become and her resemblance to Ellie. Lior chokes down the tears, and for a brief moment, he cannot breathe.

"Ziva." Lior opens his arms, and on impulse, Ana goes to her uncle like a child to her father. Lior holds her in a tight embrace as she melts to accept his comfort.

"Uncle Lior. It's so good to see you." Ana's uncharacteristic vulnerability does not escape Kimo's notice. She's been different lately. After a long moment, Ana steps back and wipes her eyes as Kimo comes forward to shake Lior's hand.

"Uncle, e' komo mai. Welcome. It's good to see you." Lior pulls Kimo in for a big bear hug and squeezes him tight.

"A handshake isn't going to cut it, son." Though they hadn't seen each other in many years, the connection –

and the shared trauma of the kibbutz massacre—endures.

Lior pats Kimo hard on the back and steps back. "Ziva, Kimo, I want you to meet the team."

They approach the others as they rise slowly from their chairs.

"Uncle Lior, it's Ana now. I don't go by Ziva anymore. It's Ana."

"Of course, my dear. Ana. Ana, come meet the team."

One of the men, handsome in a brooding way, with dark hair and a thick beard, comes forward and stands before Ana.

"I'm Omar." Kimo steps in and firmly shakes Omar's hand. He explains to Ana.

"Omar's hanai sister, Zara, was taken with Rachel. We've reason to believe they are still together."

Ana is jolted back to the reality she's been avoiding all day. The reason they are all there now is to rescue the girls from their captors. Overcome with emotion, Ana steps forward and takes Omar's hands.

"Oh my God, Omar, I'm so sorry." Omar remains stoic, but there is a barely noticeable softening in his eyes.

"Thank you, Ana. And I am sorry about your sister, Rachel. I take responsibility." Omar's loss has been devastating for him, one from which he may never recover. He perseveres, sustained by thoughts of vengeance alone.

"Omar, it was not your fault." Lior gently explains to the group.

"Omar and his future wife Nadia were at the Nova Festival on October 7th with Rachel, Zara, and some other friends. As you now know, Rachel and Zara were taken by Hamas and sold into human trafficking. What you may not know is that Omar was shot several times during the attack and left for dead by those savages. By the grace of Hashem, Omar miraculously survived the long hours before the IDF found him and could administer aid." Lior looks at Omar, who is the epitome of a soldier preparing for war. His eyes glisten with unshed tears; his fierce expression scarcely hides his shattered heart.

"Tragically, Nadia and the others were not as lucky." Silence saturates the primeval canyon as the gravity of their mission settles in the minds and very souls of all present. This is war. Good vs Evil. They will succeed, because the alternative is inconceivable.

Ana's heart aches for Omar, and she is horrified by what she hears. Of course, she knows about the horrors of October 7[th,] and she understands all too well about terrorism and its far-reaching consequences. Ana has worked hard for the better part of 20 years to stuff it all away and bury it down deep in the recesses of her psyche. She has been safe and living her life in paradise, privileged to live in peace. Ana is amazed by how easy it is to ignore the evil in the world when it's not directed at you. Until it is.

The other men in the group rise and introduce themselves one by one to Kimo and Ana. Kimo takes Omar aside, and two tall, muscular men approach Ana. One is bald, and one has long, shaggy gray hair. Both have long grey beards. The bald one introduces himself.

"Hi, I'm Joe, and this is Tom. We worked with Kalama and Lou when we were overseas. I served in eleven missions with your father. He's a good man."

Tom pipes in. "Yeah, Lou's the best. Brothers in arms from the old days. We both owe your father our lives." They all shake hands and exchange pleasantries.

"Hey, Ana. You remember Kai, yeah?" Max from Pono Security throws a shaka and a big smile. His sidekick, Kai, throws a shaka but remains silent, stoic.

"Max? What are you doing here?" Ana is surprised to see Max but quickly remembers he, too, has a sister who was taken several years ago. She was only 7 years old, and they never saw her again. It makes sense that he'd want to help.

Unlike Ana, Kimo is not surprised to see Max. "Hey, Bruh, thanks for coming." Kimo and Max hug and share a rather complex handshake from their high school days. Back then, they led their football team to the state championships, with Kimo playing quarterback and Max his tight end. They considered themselves *hanai* brothers, everything but blood. Ana remembers that Max's little sister disappeared when they were in middle school.

What exactly is going on here? It slowly becomes clear to Ana that Kimo has not been entirely forthcoming with regard to the mission and his role in it. Kimo is much more deeply involved in this operation than he'd let on. Ana was under the impression that Kimo had been recruited after the fact, as she had. Apparently not.

Just then, impossibly, the sound of a loud vehicle roars and echoes through the valley. It sounds as if it is coming directly toward them down the mountain. They all look at each other, confused. How can there be a vehicle in the middle of the thickly overgrown forest coming from the direction of nothing by canyon walls? As they try to wrap their minds around what they're hearing, a large black truck breaks through the dense foliage and slowly drives down the rocky riverbed, the independent suspension crawling spider-like across the large rocks and boulders.

"What the ... ?" Max looks like he's seen a menehune, the dwarf-like creature from Hawaiian mythology. Kimo laughs and shakes his head.

"Don't get too freaked out, Max. Pop knows these valleys like the back of his hand, and he's privy to the secrets of the ancestors. He's not magical, just mystical."

"But …" Max is astonished but lets it go. He knows better than to question a kupuna with ties to the ancient ali'i.

Kalama slowly drives up out of the riverbed and parks on the trail in front of the gathering. He exits the driver's door wearing a hat made from banana leaves and a grin from ear to ear. Kal is pleased with the spectacle he's created. He raises his arms toward the dense canopy of trees above them.

"Warmest aloha! As soon as you all pick up your jaws off the ground, we can hui up and get to work."

After pleasantries and introductions, Kimo finally lays out the mission plan.

"We all know why we're here. We're going to rescue Rachel and Zara." Ana glances around at the serious faces of the men, intently listening to Kimo, who, she realizes, is clearly in charge of the operation. She knows he served heroically in the Marine Corps. Kimo had been recruited by the Special Operations Command straight out of boot camp. Now, she understands why he rose so quickly through the ranks. He exudes strength and leadership.

"Pop is our analyst and Mission Control. He'll handle all of the back-of-the-house technology and communications with boots on the ground. He'll also interface with our outside resources. We have friends at various agencies that have our backs ... off the record, of course."

Kalama smiles broadly and pats his truck three times like he would a loyal old dog. "Yup, this baby is a war room on wheels." There is an appreciative, hyper-masculine murmuring among the men in the group. Ana waits for one of them to beat his chest. They all agree: Kalama's truck is *no ka 'oi*, the best.

Kimo continues, ignoring his father's humble brag. "There will be an intimate, black-tie event at our perp's mansion in Hana, with a laundry list of bad guys in attendance. Our sources tell us they will be selling arms, drugs, and humans."

A shiver snakes slowly, eerily up the length of Ana's spine. What the hell is she doing here? This is the real thing, the big league. Ana teaches Krav Maga to little girls and old folks. Arms dealers and human traffickers? Suddenly, she feels like she's in over her head, and the old doubt creeps in. As if he could feel her confidence stagger, Kimo steadies Ana with one reassuring look. Ana regains her composure. She has this.

"What type of surveillance do we have on the property?" Tom's expertise is in Synthetic Aperture Radar (SAR) imaging. "It looks like the weather will be dicey Friday night, good chance there'll be too much cloud cover for optical satellite imaging."

Kalama fields the question. "Copy that. We'll have access to SAR imaging through a Low Earth Orbit satellite that will allow us a visual of the property for just under two minutes. Ideally, we'll coordinate the extraction with the satellite and be able to track the team."

Joe nods his head. "Good enough. The SAR operates in the near-infrared spectrum, so cloud cover won't be an issue. We can get heat signatures, but the images won't be as distinct."

Kimo continues explaining the mission. "Agreed. Not ideal, but we work with what we have. So, our host and resident bad guy, Lawrence, has contracted Pono Security to work the event. Max, Kai, and their team will be on the inside and have full access to the estate. Ana will pose as one of Max's employees and will be stationed at the front entrance. Pop called in some favors at the Agency and managed to score an invite, so I'll be posing as an arms dealer with an old colleague from MARSOC, Natasha, as my wife."

Natasha? Ana had heard about his old colleague and feels an unfamiliar sting of jealousy. She'd always wondered about the time they'd spent together. Were they just friends as Kimo had claimed? Or was it more?

"Joe, Tom, Omar, and Lior will be posted on the outskirts of the property with night vision goggles. Once we get a verified location of the girls, Pop will cut the power to the mansion, and Max's team will create a diversion inside. Omar and Lior will extract the girls while Joe and Tom provide cover." The men pay close attention and nod their heads in agreement.

Max confirms his part in the plan for Kimo. "Yeah, Bruh. We got this. You and Ana can slip out during the commotion." Ana and Max share a glance. This is not some security gig bouncing drunks out of the Makawao Rodeo grounds. The stakes are much higher. Much, much higher.

Kimo is all business. Large and in charge. "Exactly. Once Omar and Lior have the girls, they'll hui up at the edge of the property, mauka of the estate. We will meet you there, and Ana will lead our escape through the lava tunnels."

Ana joins in. "It's not an easy trek. There's nearly a mile of thick, waist-high cane grass between the property and the tunnels. It will be slow going. And we'll need lights once we're inside, it's pitch black. One wrong turn, and we could be lost for days."

"But that won't happen because Ana knows those lava tubes like the back of her hand, so stick close once we hui." Kimo's trust in her buoys Ana's confidence. She feels strong.

"It's about a mile and a half through the tunnels from the makai entrance. We'll need to move fast. The ground will be uneven, damp, and slippery, so wear non-skid boots and waterproof jackets."

Kimo sums up the mission. "Mahalo, Ana. So that's the plan. Once we get through the lava tubes, Pop will be waiting with the truck, and we'll make our escape with the girls. Questions? Comments? Concerns? Observations?"

Leadership looks good on Kimo, and Ana watches him with pride.

Lior has a query. "What about power redundancy? Once the electricity is turned off, they'll still have their solar power and backup generators."

Kimo is one step ahead. "Good question. Tom and Joe will have the generators and Tesla Power Wall disabled by then." He looks to Tom, who gives him a thumbs up.

The team works out the travel plans as Lior takes Ana aside.

Lior chokes on his words. "Ziva, sorry, Ana … I apologize about my part in Rachel's kidnapping. I never should have let her out of my sight."

"Uncle, please, it wasn't your fault. Rachel was …" Ana catches herself using her sister's name in the past tense.

"Rachel IS sixteen years old; you couldn't keep her locked up like a prisoner." Despite her assurances, Ana knows too well Lior's guilt. She knows that he, like she, may never forgive himself.

210

CHAPTER 15

The luxury yacht *Lost Boy* bobs gently a few miles off the coast of Maui in the most remote archipelago on Earth. The ocean air is thick and balmy. Yasmin yells again, her harsh voice tainting the tranquil scene.

"Otto, bring the girls over now. Lawrence is eager to meet his nieces." Otto points his rifle toward the bridge connecting the two vessels, and the girls obey, holding hands. Rachel goes first, followed by Charlotte and then Zara. Charlotte squeezes the hands of the older girls with the strength of an adult, seeking comfort from two young women who are just as terrified as she is.

Yasmin leads the girls to the vessel's Main Salon, which resembles the lobby of a five-star luxury resort. Various seating areas contain couches of all shapes and sizes clustered in intimate settings. Everything appears to be wrapped in gold or covered in marble, with hand-carved wooden banisters, stairs, and oversized tropical engravings. There is an enormous bar in the middle of the room whose inventory rivals that of the hottest club in Los Angeles. The girls are encouraged to drink it all in.

"Look around you, girls. This could all be yours if you fit in." Lawrence's dark eyes seem to glisten as he leers at the trembling girls. "Who wants to play nice with Uncle Lawrence?" Rachel feels faint, and as her knees begin to buckle, she somehow steadies herself. This isn't happening. It must be a nightmare.

Lawrence approaches Charlotte and touches her arm. Zara instinctively steps between her and the creepy old man, who laughs at the gesture. Zara sees pure evil in Lawrence's black eyes as a cold silence shrouds the moment. She immediately lowers her head in submission and quickly averts her eyes as Yasmin's shrill voice snaps.

"Girl, you do not want to displease Uncle Lawrence."

The sound of a boat engine grows louder as a large fishing vessel approaches the yacht and ties off at the stern. A crew of two men unloads several large trunks and carefully places them on the deck. Lawrence's crew quickly takes the trunks down the stairs and into the cabin below.

A tall woman dressed in an expensive-looking suit and high heels appears on the deck of the fishing boat and is assisted on board by a crewman. Her perfectly coiffed, short gray hair remains indifferent to the warm trade winds. The woman surveys the over-the-top opulence of the yacht, seemingly amused, and mutters under her breath. "*Lost Boy*? Oy, who is this guy, Peter Pan?"

Yasmin turns to Lawrence. "This is our broker, Jackie. She is here to prepare the girls for their debut at the party tomorrow night." Rachel is horrified. Their broker is preparing them for their debut? She begins to understand. Oh my God! The room begins closing in on her, and she tries not to panic. Just keep breathing.

Lawrence claps his hands together like a small boy at a circus, downright gleeful as Jackie enters the main salon and offers her hand. "You must be Lawrence."

"I most certainly am … in all my glory." Lawrence bows dramatically, unable to contain his excitement as Yasmin makes the formal introductions. The three exchange pleasantries as if they are mingling at a yacht party.

"Jackie, can I get you something? A martini or …" Yasmin plays hostess as the girls stand quietly by.

"It's a bit early for a martini, Yasmin, thank you, dear. But I will have some champagne with a splash of guava juice. I prefer Cristal, but Veuve will do." Rachel recognizes the

Israeli accent and is horrified to learn one of her own has betrayed them.

Yasmin motions to a crewman standing by, and he rushes off to fetch the champagne. Jackie walks over to examine the girls. She touches their hair and caresses their faces appreciatively. "Nice. This one is a bit young for my regular clients, but I think I can find a sponsor for her."

The girls look down at their feet as they are inspected like so many cattle at an auction. With Yasmin and Lawrence behind her, Jackie examines Rachel last and puts her hand under the girl's chin, lifting it to face her.

"Look at me, girl." Rachel looks up and directly into the eyes of her next jailor. However, what she sees is compassion, not evil. Before Rachel could process the dissonance, Jackie squeezes her hand reassuringly and winks. She turns to Yasmin.

"These girls need a lot of work. I'll need to get started immediately to get top dollar. Bring my champagne, cigarettes, and a lighter below. Let's go, girls."

Jackie and the girls are led toward the yacht's bow to a beautiful suite of rooms, and the door is locked behind them. The trunks had been delivered to the suite, opened to reveal a treasure trove of clothing hanging on racks, expensive-looking jewelry, and endless high-heeled shoes. The champagne and cigarettes are promptly delivered, and the door to the suite of rooms is locked behind them as Jackie barks like a drill sergeant. She shouts and claps her hands loudly.

"Let's go, girls! We've no time to waste!" The older woman quickly takes pen to paper and scribbles a note on the back of a gum wrapper as she beckons Rachel and Zara with a crook of her finger. The bewildered girls come quickly and read the note.

I am a friend of your father's. I'm here to rescue you. Follow my lead. Remain calm and obedient.

Rachel and Zara cannot believe their eyes. Rachel's eyes fill with tears. They look shocked as Jackie continues her performance for the benefit of their host and the guard at the door. She lights a cigarette and burns the note with the lighter as they all watch it turn to ash.

Jackie loudly commands the girls. "You, get dressed. We've much work to do!" Zara rushes to comply and looks back at Rachel, each gaining strength from the other. For the first time since their abduction, they have hope.

Jackie whispers in Rachel's ear. "What do you know about this girl?"

"Her name is Charlotte. She doesn't really speak much." Rachel looks at the young girl and smiles.

Jackie realizes right away who Charlotte is. She is the young girl who was all over the news a few months ago. She was nine years old when she went for a bike ride in her own neighborhood and never returned.

Charlotte, unaware of this latest development, remains terrified and shakes uncontrollably. Rachel goes to her and wraps her arms around the terrified child in a huge bear hug. Rocking her like a mother would her infant.

Jackie sees the child's state, and her heart breaks for the girl. She opens her Spotify playlist on her iPhone and cranks the volume, speaking exaggeratedly over the din. "You girls are such downers. Our clients want happy, beautiful models. Let's change the mood." Jackie puts her hand to her mouth as if whispering in someone's ear.

The girls look bewildered, but Rachel understands. She whispers in Charlotte's ear under the cover of Katy Perry's *Roar*.

"It's going to be okay, honey. Jackie is here to save us; she's a friend of my father's, and he was a great soldier. She's one of the good guys. We're going to be rescued. We just need to stay strong and play along with her for a little longer. Do you think you can do that?"

Charlotte looks over at Jackie, who gives her a big smile and a thumbs-up while she sings along loudly with Katy Perry. With tears in her eyes, Charlotte looks to Rachel and speaks for the first time in days, just one whispered word.

"Yes."

Rachel summons all her courage to put a smile on her face and to sound reassuring and hopeful for the terrified and trembling child. She holds Charlotte at arm's length, looks her square in the eyes, and whispers.

"We're going home, Charlotte. I promise you, we're going home."

After much primping and grooming, all three girls are beautifully made up and wearing the expensive loungewear provided for them. Jackie knocks on the door of the stateroom with a reassuring wink for Charlotte, who seems distant and confused.

"Guard, I wish to leave." Otto immediately opens the door for Jackie, stands aside silently as she exits, and locks the door again. A moment later, the door opens, and a valet summons the girls to the Bridge Deck for brunch.

The large table looks like it is set for royalty. Zara had only seen such feasts on television and is in awe looking at the food. There are platters of lobster and crab, piles of meats and cheeses, and pastries surrounded by tropical fruits, many of which she'd never seen or imagined. Various bottles of champagne stand amidst pitchers of freshly squeezed juices. In the middle of the enormous table is a perfect replica of the yacht, *Lost Boy*, sculpted from ice. Lawrence, who has changed his outfit to a pink paisley silk shirt with an Hermes ascot, white linen pants, and Gucci slippers, is seated at the head of the table. Yasmin and Jackie sit on either side of him like guests at a dinner party.

The valet pulls out the girls' chairs for them and places a napkin on each of their laps. Charlotte sits silently between Rachel and Zara as Lawrence watches approvingly.

"Girls, it looks like Jackie did a nice job with your hair and makeup. Did you thank her?" Rachel and Zara respond obediently, but Charlotte remains mute.

"Thank you, Jackie."

"Yes, thank you, Jackie."

Lawrence chatters happily, ever the gracious host, as a waiter serves him a pile of pancakes, bacon, and eggs. "You know, if you girls play your cards right, this can be your lifestyle, as well. We are having a small reception this evening in your honor, just a few close friends, but tomorrow night is the big event! You'll be meeting some very important people, my girls. One of them just might be your future husband!"

Rachel and Zara listen quietly to Lawrence speak with

no eye contact and no response. This seems to irritate him, and he looks sternly at Jackie.

"It appears your clients need a bit more tutoring in the charming small talk category. Let's not forget you guaranteed me full cooperation, Jackie. Do we have to amend our transaction?"

Yasmin speaks first. "Lawrence, the girls will obey. I will make sure of it." She looks severely at the girls. "Tell Uncle Lawrence you will obey." Zara and Rachel make timid assurances, but Charlotte remains disengaged. Zara speaks up.

"Charlotte will obey, as well, Uncle Lawrence. You don't have to worry about us. We will all obey."

Jackie looks at the girls and back at their captors. "Damn right, you will. Lawrence, Yasmin, fear not. You will be very pleased with their performance tonight. I assure you, you will get your money's worth."

Lawrence appears satisfied as he smiles and raises his glass. "To a fun and successful evening." Jackie and Yasmin raise their champagne glasses as Rachel and Zara each muster a weak smile.

After the toast, Jackie stands. "This is lovely, Lawrence. Thank you so much for your hospitality, but we have much work to do if we are to be perfect for this evening. Let's go, girls."

CHAPTER 16

Koa whines at Ana's fitful sleep. She tosses and turns and mumbles unintelligibly as he cocks his giant head in bewilderment. It is the dream again.

Ana and Kimo each hold one of Lilikoi's hands as their extended family boisterously sings 'Happy Birthday.' She looks around and sees the children laughing and playing, the parents singing, and her mother looking radiant with a smear of pink frosting on her sleeve and a huge smile. A dreaming Ana knows what comes next but is powerless to change it. The deafening explosions. Confusion. Screaming. They are knocked to the ground by the force of the bombs. Fear. Terror.

"Ziva! Zivaaa!" Her mother screams for her through the smoke and explosions.

"Imaaaaaa …!" She chokes on the smoke as she calls for her mother …

Ana bolts upright in bed, calling out for her mother, to find Koa staring at her curiously.

"This FUCKING dream!" Koa shnortles in agreement.

Ana makes coffee and avocado toast and sits on her lanai to watch the sunrise. She listens to the roosters bear witness to a new dawn, and the plentiful birds sing happily in the forest around her. Koa lay by her feet, reluctant to start his day.

Ana thinks about her sister and the mission. She hasn't hiked the lava tunnels in a few years and wonders if she'll remember the way. She quickly rejects her uncertainty.

"You've got this, don't be a little bitch." She makes another mental note to work on her deprecating self-talk. No one knows those tunnels better than Ana; she is certain of it.

"Early bird gets the centipede, eh?" Ana turns to see Kimo emerging from the woods, holding a tin of something. He yells ahead. "Mama made your favorite green tea mochi and insisted I bring you some this morning. She says you're *wiwi,* too skinny." Kimo's warm smile is a welcome distraction from her thoughts. This time tomorrow, they'd be packing up to head to Hana and the mission.

"Nonsense. I'm not skinny; I'm fit." Kimo opens the tin and offers her a piece.

"I had some on the way over, it's really ono." Ana takes a piece, pops it in her mouth, and rolls her eyes in appreciation.

"So ono. Mmmmm! Send Auntie my mahalos." She waves her hand toward the kitchen. "There's coffee if you want some."

"Don't mind if I do." Kimo enters the kitchen and sees Ana's swear jar is overflowing. He laughs, "Kalia will be going to college in diamonds at this rate!"

"Right? I'm trying, but I just can't seem to clean up my potty mouth." She shrugs. "I guess I'm just a vulgar bitch." They both laugh, and Kimo acquiesces. He sits on the chair beside her, and they fall into a comfortable silence, listening to the sounds of their tropical utopia awakening around them.

Kimo can feel Ana's agitation. "Hey, let's go for a hike and work off some of this nervous energy."

Ana is amused. "You're nervous, Kimo? Mr. Marine Special Forces?"

Kimo's look is serious. "The stakes are high, Ana. It's my mission, and failure is not an option."

It is Ana's turn to be the reassuring one. "So, we won't fail. We've gone over the mission several times now. Everyone knows their role. We've got this."

"Yes, Ana, but these guys are no joke. They won't hesitate to kill us and the girls if we're caught."

"Then we won't get caught." Ana stands and reaches out her hand. "C'mon, Kimo, let's go for that hike." Ana grabs her crossbow and shrugs at Kimo's raised eyebrow. "You can never be too prepared."

Thirty minutes later, Kimo, Ana, and Koa are two miles deep into a rainbow eucalyptus forest. Ana looks straight up in the sky and can barely see the tops of the trees towering above them.

"This never gets old. Look at the colors in these trees, Kimo."

"Magic." A mischievous look comes to Kimo's face, and Ana prepares herself for incoming edification.

"You know, Ana, Eucalyptus deglupta was first described by Carl Ludwig Blume in 1850. The word deglupta is Latin and means to peel off or husk. Its pulpwood is used for making paper." He starts to laugh before he can finish his diatribe. Even Kimo knows he's being obnoxious.

Ana peels off a strip of the colorful bark and throws it at Kimo. "You're ridiculous!"

Kimo dodges the bark, laughing. "You're just jealous of my vast knowledge of the world."

Ana rolls her eyes. "Yeah, that's it, I'm jealous. Oy vavoy."

They hike up the mountain for about a mile and descend into a canyon, climbing almost 500 feet down a steep and dangerous switchback trail. One slip would send them tumbling hundreds of feet down a sheer rock wall. The temperature drops by ten degrees as they reach the bottom of the canyon, and the rainforest canopy obscures the sky. The thick shelter of tropical foliage soars hundreds of feet above the cool, densely planted ravine floor as they hike over the winding river that was once the life force of the valley. The red lava rock walls of the canyon, hundreds of feet tall, act as a fortress, protecting early inhabitants from weather and enemy intrusion.

Most of the inhabitants of the West Maui mountains were forced out in the 1940s when colonizers diverted the water source to develop the land for tourism. Today, what remains is a mostly dry riverbed and some short rock walls that once delineated the homesteads of scores of families.

Kimo leads the way through the dense, wet brush, using a stick to clear spider webs from the trail as Koa runs in and out of the tall brush. When they come to a small meadow, Kimo stops abruptly as a wild boar piglet crosses their path just ahead. Ana quickly loads her crossbow, knowing the mother boar is never far behind. They freeze and wait in silence. Where's Koa?

After what feels like an eternity, they hear a loud rustling in the brush in front of them and the sound of a large animal running toward them. Its hooves pound the ground so loudly that Ana pictures a rhinoceros charging them. Suddenly, a large black boar burst through the cane grass about 100 feet away, coming directly at them. Instinctively, they both turn to run but quickly catch themselves. Ana remembers from childhood that a wild boar can reach speeds of 40 miles per hour, so running would be futile.

Ana yells, "Climb!" as she turns to see Kimo already halfway up a tree, the boar at his heels. When she realizes she's thwarted, the sow turns to face Ana, who stands paralyzed for one very long second, staring the defensive mother directly in the eyes. The boar pauses as if sizing up her opponent, then charges Ana.

Kimo yells from high up in a kukui nut tree, "The rock! To your left! Climb the rock!"

Ana snaps out of her trance, looks left, and scrambles quickly up a huge boulder just beyond the pig's deadly reach. The boar pounds her hooves and lets out a few intimidating snorts and grunts. After a few terrifying moments, she turns and victoriously trots off, disappearing back into the tall cane grass and heading toward her waiting piglets, hidden in the brush beyond.

First, a very long pause, then slowly, the adrenaline spike turns to laughter, and laughter turns to tears as the relief washes over them. "The look on your face …" Kimo could barely get the words out. " … priceless!"

Ana looks around for Koa. There he is, standing on a large rock 50 yards away, watching them. Koa knows better than to get in a scrap with a boar.

Ana joins in the laughter. "Me?! What about you? You scrambled up that kukui nut tree like a starving monkey after the last banana in the jungle." They were both hysterical now, bent over laughing and playfully mocking each other.

Kimo holds his stomach as he points at Ana. "And you … standing there like a boss bitch with a loaded crossbow, too scared to take the shot!"

"Stop, stop, it hurts." Ana holds her stomach, trying to catch her breath. "I wasn't scared, you jerk … I didn't want to hurt her."

"Sure, you weren't scared." Still laughing, Kimo gathers himself enough to climb down from the tree.

"Oh my God. So good." They head back laughing and teasing each other with Koa in the lead. The closer they get to home, the more serious Kimo's mood becomes. He picks up the pace.

"We'd better get back. I want to go over everything one more time before we leave tomorrow morning." Reality rushes in as they make their way back through the canyon and up the steep switchback trail, an exhausted Koa straggling behind.

As the sun's rays retreat for the evening, Ana makes a small fire down at the pit by the barn in anticipation of a relaxing and restorative twilight.

"Ana! Anaaaa!" The serenity of the Maui sunset is interrupted by Auntie Pua clumsily approaching Ana's hale.

"Ana, where are you?" Pua drops something she's carrying, picks it up, and continues on.

Ana calls out from the fire pit. "Down here, Auntie." Ana stands up, and Koa meets Pua halfway for pets, which he gratefully receives.

"This is a surprise, Auntie. Uh oh, what's in the bag?" Ana notices Pua has a cloth bag with several items. This isn't the first time Pua has shown up unannounced with mysterious cargo, and each time, it's been memorable. Ana is curious.

"Auntie? What is this? Are you smuggling puppies in there?"

"Smuggling puppies? Ana, where do you get these ideas?" Sometimes, Auntie was a bit too literal.

"It was a joke, Auntie." Ana motions toward Pua's bag.

"What's going on here?"

"Let's sit, and I will tell you, child." Ana motions to the chair next to her in front of the fire. They both settle in, as Pua explains.

"First, I have a message from Kimo regarding the mission I'm supposed to know nothing about." Pua gives Ana a look that says, *What am I stupid?*

"I'm sorry, Auntie. I think Uncle just didn't want to worry you."

"Girl, I know everything that goes on in these mountains. Kalama has no secrets."

Ana smiles knowingly. Everyone knows Auntie Pua wears the grass skirt in that family.

 "What is the message, Auntie?" Ana feels anxious about what's to come.

Pua repeats what she was told. "The kidnapper's yacht has been infiltrated by one of our allies. This woman, Jackie, is what you kids would call a 'bad ass.' She was in Mossad with your mother and worked with Lou and Kalama years ago. Ellie and I knew her well."

Ana's eyes well up with tears. She doesn't know how to respond. She realizes she'd stopped breathing and takes a large gulp of air. A friend of her mother's is with Rachel?

Pua explains. "The three of us were quite close. Jackie and her husband had moved to the kibbutz about a year before we lost Lilikoi and Ellie."

"I don't remember her." Ana's memories of that last year in Israel are still cloudy and come only in brief images.

"That doesn't surprise me. Jackie and her husband, David, were usually on assignment with Kalama and Lou, and they didn't have any children you would have known. We lost David that day as well." Ana listens somberly but rejects the memories that threaten to invade.

"Apparently, Jackie has been working undercover for two years, trying to gather enough intel to stop this monster that has Rachel and her friend."

"Zara. Her name is Zara. Omar, her hanai brother, is here to find her. I met him yesterday."

"Yes, Zara. And apparently, another girl. A child abducted from New York." Pua turns to Ana and takes both of her hands.

"Ana, Jackie is with your sister on a yacht off the southern coast of Maui as we speak. Jackie is deep undercover and posing as a human trafficker who will broker the girls. Rachel is alive and coping. We're going to bring her and the other girls home."

Silence envelops the cacophony of thoughts in Ana's

mind. She gazes intently at the crackling fire as Pua unpacks her satchel and lays its contents on the large tree stump before them: Patron tequila, two shot glasses, a saltshaker, a Ziplock bag filled with lime wedges, and an old metal Snoopy lunch box.

"Ana, do you remember how much your mother loved Snoopy?" They smile as Pua hands Ana the lunchbox.

"Of course. Ima was obsessed with all things Peanuts, but especially Snoopy."

Pua laughs. "Remember on your 5th birthday, Ellie made Kalama wear that Snoopy costume?"

"I do remember! Uncle passed out because he couldn't breathe in that thing. That night, I asked Ima if we could get a dog and name him Snoopy." A tear comes to Pua's eye, thinking of a life that had never existed.

"I really miss my friend." She wipes her face and shakes her head.

"No. Tonight is not about this. Tonight is about happy memories, laughter, and celebration."

Pua pours two shots and hands Ana a lime wedge. She licks the inside of her hand between her thumb and forefinger and pours salt there.

"This is the way Ellie and I used to do it. Salt, shot, lime." Pua demonstrates as Ana watches, amused. "Now you."

Ana obliges. Salt, shot, lime. Her face crinkles up in disgust. "Yuck!"

Pua laughs. "Smooth, eh? Okay, now open the lunch pail, Ana." Ana does as instructed, and her jaw drops. She looks up at Pua and then back at the contents of the metal container. Inside was an old pack of zigzag cigarette papers, a small baggie of what Ana assumed was marijuana, a small glass pipe, and two Bic lighters.

"Auntie Pua! You and Ima?!" Ana could not hide her shock.

"Close your mouth, child. Is that so impossible to consider?" Ana remains speechless. "Good Lord, girl, give me this." Pua snatches the Snoopy lunch pail from Ana's lap, rifling through its contents.

"Ana, your mother and I were once young, too, you know. We had a lot of fun in the old days." Pua takes out a cigarette paper, folds it in half, and sprinkles some marijuana inside. As Ana watches in astonishment, Pua rolls the filled paper in her fingers until it evens out and expertly rolls it into a joint. She raises it to her smiling lips and lights it.

"Auntie! What is happening right now? Does Uncle know?"

"Ana, of course, he knows. It's not a crime, you know. I do have a medical card. Here, try it. Tonight, we leave our worries at the door." Pua grabs her phone, and after a few taps and swipes, Jo Dee Messina's "My Give a Damn's Busted" comes blaring out of the tiny speaker.

Ana laughs. She is no stranger to marijuana; it is just surreal smoking it with Auntie Pua. Not to mention hearing that her mother used it, too. Just wow. Ana takes a hit of the joint as Auntie looks on appreciatively.

"Sometimes, Ellie and I would sneak off to the stables to smoke after we put you kids to sleep. The last time was the night before the attack at the kibbutz. We'd stayed up late baking that ridiculous, enormous pink cake …" Pua's voice trails off, the memory almost too much to bear.

"I remember that cake. It had all of the Wizard of Oz characters on it. It was beautiful." Ana can feel the pot begin to relax her body.

"Yes. That night, we talked about the future. We talked about you, Kimo, and Lilikoi, and what we wished for the three of you. Ellie seemed a bit sad that night. Wistful. She said it was because you were turning 10—double digits. She said it broke her heart to see her baby growing up so fast." Pua takes another hit, then passes it to Ana, who takes a puff and imagines her mother smoking down at the stables with Auntie on what would be her last night with family and friends.

"The last thing Ellie said that night was to quote her favorite Rabbi, the Kotzker Rebbe." Ana's eyes fill with tears. She remembers it all too well and recites her mother's mantra with Pua.

"There is nothing so whole as a broken heart."

CHAPTER 17

Ana awakens well before dawn, ready to start the day. Koa, sensing her excitement, sits watching, ready for anything. She had already packed their go-bags the night before, but she goes through everything once more to be certain. Food, water, protein bars, hiking gear, two small pistols, a change of clothes, and, of course, her crossbow and arrows. Koa's bag contains food, water, his working vest, a collapsible bowl, a canine gas mask, goggles, and booties. Unimpressed, Koa noses his go-bag and whines.

"You glutton. Ok, I'll bring you some treats and some jerky." Ana puts the items in his bag, and Koa sniffs appreciatively.

Ana grabs some fresh eggs, bacon, and cheese and quickly whips up a few breakfast burritos for the road. She wraps them in foil and tosses them in her bag with napkins.

"C'mon, Koey. Kimo will be here soon to get us." Koa looks toward the driveway a moment before they hear tires on gravel. "Speak of the devil."

Ana and Koa meet Kimo on the lanai, bags in hand. Ana sees that Kimo has packed the surfboards. "What's with the sticks?"

"Good morning to you, too, Sunshine. I thought maybe we could stop at Pe'ahi on the way out." Kimo was never one to miss a chance to ride the famous Pe'ahi surf break on Maui's North Shore. The locals call it Jaws because the waves there can be so massive that they instill the same fear and respect as a great white shark.

"Awesome!" Ana is always up for surfing. She turns to Koa disapprovingly. "You cannot harass the sea turtles this time, Koa. You know you're not supposed to approach the honu."

Kimo comes to his defense. "Hey, that's not fair. He usually keeps his distance … it was just that one time. He couldn't help himself. Koa grumbles softly under his breath in his own defense, and they both laugh.

"Fair enough."

They drive in a peaceful silence, noshing on breakfast burritos, each lost in thought. Kimo keeps running over each step of the mission in his head, ensuring that he'd thought of every possible contingency. Ana goes through the maze of the lava tunnels in her mind over and over again as if to burn them in her memory. She closes her eyes and envisions every turn, every rock outcropping, every air shaft, every dead end, and most significantly, the way out.

As they pull off the road at Pe'ahi, Auntie sends Ana a text that makes her laugh. She reads it aloud to Kimo.

"Haha, listen, this is from Auntie. *Akahele, child …*"

Kimo interrupts. "That means be careful."

Ana rolls her eyes. "Thanks for the man-splanation, Island Boy." She continues reading.

"Akahele, child. My boyfriend say big storm coming." They both laugh. Pua has had an enormous crush on the local weather reporter, Guy Hagi, for 20 years, and everyone, even Kalama, calls him her boyfriend.

"Let's hope he's wrong again." Guy Hagi was not known for his accurate weather reporting, so much so that many of the locals call him *Lie* Hagi.

Kimo parks the truck and looks over to see the surf is only about four feet high. "Awe. I was stoked to ride some North Shore monsters. We can surf these tame waves on the West Side."

"Dude, this is awesome. Shut up. And it's not as crowded as it usually is. Let's do this."

The three walk down a dirt trail to the beach, where Koa sits patiently near the shoreline.

"Koa, stay here and don't bother the turtles." Koa is indifferent. He spins around twice and settles in for a nap. This is not Koa's first surf session.

Ana and Kimo paddle out and take their place in the lineup, waiting for their waves. Kimo looks at the shoreline to see Koa sitting obediently about 30 yards from at least a dozen enormous sea turtles.

Kimo is endlessly impressed by Koa's intelligence and obedience. Ana has done an amazing job with his training. From stray to soldier. "What a good boy he is."

Ana follows Kimo's gaze toward the group of turtles and gets a gleam in her eye. "You know, Kimo, the Hawaiian Green Sea Turtle can hold its breath for up to five hours and can reach up to four feet in diameter."

Kimo laughs and splashes Ana as she paddles off the lineup to take her turn. He yells after her.

"Are you mocking me?" Kimo smiles broadly as he watches her. So athletic, so beautiful. He could not possibly love her more than he does in this moment.

They surf for about an hour until the weather begins to

turn and they are forced to come in by the downpour. Once on shore, Ana removes her leash and looks up at the sky. "It appears Auntie's boyfriend was right."

"Looks like a Kona Low storm. This is going to complicate things for tonight." Kimo is suddenly distracted by this glitch in the plan. "I'll call Joe when we get to the truck and make sure his guys are online to connect to the SAR imaging satellite.

Ana tries to be reassuring and distract Kimo. "You know Maui weather. It could change in a minute. We have plenty of time before we join the others, let's hop in the truck and take a detour at Twin Falls." They share a look. Kimo and Ana have a history at Twin Falls. It was the one and only time Kimo had kissed her. It was a sweet moment turned dreadful as Ana, after kissing him back for a few seconds, freaked out and ran crying from the pools. Neither of them mentions the elephant in the room, and Kimo acquiesces.

"Twin Falls, it is."

The rains stop just in time for them to pull off at the trailhead that leads to their destination.

"Looks like there aren't many tourists today. Must be the weather." Kimo leads the way into the rainforest to hike the 1.8 miles to the waterfalls. Ana and Koa follow behind, as Ana is saturated in memories. She laughs.

"Do you remember when Joey Elliot prom-posed to me here?"

"Of course, I remember." Kimo laughs. "I spent two hours out here in the dark helping that tool spell out *Will you go to Prom with me?* With rocks. What a bonehead."

Ana laughs. "I didn't even want to go with him, but he'd gone through all that effort …"

They turn a corner on the trail and can hear the distant roar of the waterfalls. Kimo runs ahead and disappears into the rainforest. Ana hears a loud splash. She runs down the trail and cannonballs into the pool, drenching Kimo as he surfaces. They laugh and splash each other for a few minutes, just like old times. Koa sits lounging on the trail, cooling off on the wet rocks.

Later, as they lounge together on the rocks beneath the mist of the waterfall, Ana begins to reflect on their past and reevaluates her behavior. Why did she run away that day they kissed in high school? Because she was a weak and insecure idiot. Clearly. But that was then. What is stopping her now? What the hell is wrong with her?

Ana climbs out of the pool and walks underneath one of the waterfalls, standing on a shelf between the waterfall and the wall behind it. Kimo stands up and joins her, looking at their own little Eden through a roaring screen of water. Ana can feel Kimo's shoulder touching hers as they stand captivated by the beauty around them. Towering trees draped in vines rise alongside smaller trees crawling with life. The sky is hidden beneath the tall canopy of vibrant foliage drenched in rain. Remarkably, the cheerful calls of countless birds rise above the thunderous roar of the waterfall. The moment is magical.

The energy between them is palpable. Ana feels literally pulled toward Kimo and is powerless to resist. She turns to see him staring at her. He looks deeply into her eyes, and she instantly knows everything he's feeling. She wishes he would kiss her; she wills it to happen, but fears he would never cross that line again, especially here. Ana is taken over by a force outside of herself, and she is enveloped by a feeling of power and confidence. Certainty.

She turns to face Kimo, standing inches from him. Ana stares into his eyes with a look that can only mean one thing. He looks at her confused, and she smiles.

Kimo is hesitant. "Are you sure, Lehua? I don't want to …" Ana grabs Kimo's face in her hands and kisses him passionately. Her body falls into his, pressing hard against his strong chest. It feels as if they've melded together as one, body and soul. Ana feels unsteady, and Kimo holds her tightly as they kiss, holding her steady as she melts in his arms. It feels like home for both of them. Kimo stops abruptly and holds Ana at arm's length, his stare intent.

"Ana, are you sure? I'll wait as long as it takes." For once, it is Kimo who fears their connection and endeavors to protect his heart. He stares, searching her dark eyes, expecting to see fear or hesitation. What he sees is trust.

"Kimo, you've waited long enough. We've waited long enough." Kimo is stunned. After a brief hesitation, he grabs Ana with a desire born of twenty years of waiting. Time stops as they surrender to the moment that would forever change their lifelong bond.

CHAPTER 18

Kimo, Ana, and Koa hike back to the car in silence; each lost in their own thoughts. Ana fights off the onslaught of questions and doubts rushing in. *What the hell was that? What has she done? Did she just make the biggest mistake of her life? Is she ready to make this commitment? What if he gets bored with her after the years-long chase? What if...*

Ana catches herself before she gets to the bottom of the rabbit hole into which she was swiftly burrowing. She takes a mental moment. *Stop. Breathe. You're being ridiculous.* Ana is proud of her small victory. *Look at me,* she thinks to herself, *I'm adulting.* With some effort, Ana climbs out of her psychological bunny nest and turns to look at Kimo. She wonders what he's thinking. Is he having doubts, too? Is he regretting the kiss?

Ana attempts to fill the awkward silence with small talk. "I thought the traffic would be worse at this time of day. Looks like we got lucky."

Kimo just nods his head and smiles. Ana wonders what's on his mind and reminds herself of the reason they are going to Hana. She assures herself that Kimo is likely preoccupied with the mission, justifiably so. Don't be a dick.

The rain falls steadily as Kimo drives deliberately around the slippery, winding road with ease and confidence. Ana feels safe with him at the wheel despite the storm and the dangerous conditions. She looks out the window at their stunning surroundings and smiles. The Road to Hana winds through lush, green rainforests, featuring countless amazing waterfalls that crash down lava rock cliffs, creating dancing rainbows. It is truly amazing … prehistoric. There is lush greenery everywhere you look. The ground is covered in green mosses and vines; the trees are so tall that they provide a dense canopy of tropical foliage, daring the sun to peek through. The breathtaking waterfalls lightly spray humongous succulents that seemingly defy gravity and nature as they sprout horizontally from the massive rock walls.

Despite the rain, Ana opens the truck window and takes some deep breaths. Koa whines from behind them, his large body huddled in the back corner of the crew cab as the rain interrupts his nap.

"Can you smell that, Kimo? That smell is the real Maui. You can almost taste it."

"Ono." Delicious. Kimo is suddenly a man of few words.

As they cross the first bridge on the Road to Hana, Kimo can't let the moment go without entertaining Ana with his knowledge of the island.

"Only 58 more bridges to go!"

They both laugh as Kimo reaches across the bench seat and casually puts his hand on Ana's knee as if it's totally normal. Ana's heart races. She looks at Kimo's hand, then at him, but he stares straight ahead. Ana enjoys the intimacy, no matter how modest, and she allows herself to relax in the moment, trying not to overthink the gesture.

Their usual warm, playful teasing is now charged with a new primal energy that buzzes between them. Between thoughtful, silent moments, Kimo and Ana chat playfully about everything and nothing in particular, intentionally neglecting the gravity of their mission ahead. There would be plenty of time to confront all that would entail when they reach their rendezvous point.

Kimo laughs. "Remember what Grandpa Sid said the first time he took us up here?"

Ana lowers her voice and does her best impression of Grandpa Sid. "The Road to Hana ain't for sissies!"

Kimo chimes in. "These curves are tighter than bark on a log!" Kimo loves Sid almost as much as Ana and Koa. They first met when Kimo was 13, a few months after they'd left Israel. Sid visited regularly over the years, and it was clear it wasn't just to see Ana. Sid was kind and generous with the entire Akamai ohana and was universally loved. Pua, as his daughter Eleanor's best friend, has a special place in Sid's heart. Being together makes them both feel closer to Ellie.

Ana smiles warmly. "Remember the first time Grandpa took us camping in Hana? It was the first time we'd ever seen the lava tunnels."

"Of course. It was the summer after we moved here. You were obsessed with everything volcano and insisted we go back and explore the lava tubes every day. You were so annoying."

Ana laughs and nods. She was annoying. "You know, I'm still in touch with the owner of that place, Chuck."

"Seriously? Great guy. Now, there's a man who knows how to commit. Legend has it that Chuck cleared out the tunnel under his property all by himself. They say he removed one ton of dirt and rock daily for 20 years. Just one man, a ladder, and a Home Depot bucket! Incredible!"

Ana laughs. "Yeah, the crucial term here is *legend*." Kimo smiles and nods.

"Fair Enough."

Ana interrupts their repartee due to a sudden call from nature. "Crap. Pull over at the next turnout; there's one at the Ke'Anae Lookout." Kimo chuckles knowingly. Ever since he could remember, Ana has had the smallest bladder he's ever seen.

They chat nonstop for the rest of the drive. The distance that had separated them for so long had dissolved with a single – albeit amazing – kiss. There is no talk of the future or even an acknowledgement of what had happened at the Falls. But something is different. Something between them has definitely changed.

"Ana, do you remember going to Krav Maga camp at the Hatzbani River when we were young? You must've been 7 or 8, but you were a total badass!"

"Of course, it was near Kiryat Shmona. That was so much fun! Wasn't that the summer you earned your black belt?"

Kimo remains humbly quiet, and Ana fills the silence.

"Yup, from Krav Maga phenom to war hero to hula dancer. Which one of these things is not like the other?"

"Don't forget I'm also a fire dancer; that's manly and dangerous, isn't it?"

"If you weren't wearing a dress." Ana laughs at the injured look on Kimo's face. In reality, she loves to see him perform at the occasional luau and has secretly admired his body since the first time she'd seen him in his traditional Hawaiian attire.

"Oh, c'mon! It's not a dress; it's a pa'u hula skirt." They both laugh, thoroughly enjoying their easy banter. Ana is disappointed to realize they are close to the rendezvous point as reality comes crashing in.

"It's just around this bend, at the turn-off to Chuck's property." Kimo pulls off the main road and winds around to find the team gathered in an empty field of cane grass underneath a large kukui nut tree, some sitting on tailgates, others standing. The skies are gloomy and dark.

Kimo pulls up, flanking the small crowd as it begins to rain again. Kimo is suddenly all business. The fun is over. It's go time. They get out of the truck and join the team. Kimo shakes hands with the men, then sees his old friend Natasha and goes to her. They hug a bit too long for Ana's liking as she watches keenly, fighting the pangs of jealousy that threaten her cool demeanor. Natasha is naturally stunning in jeans, a tank top, and not a stitch of makeup. Kalama comes forward and embraces Kimo,

Ana, and Omar. Soldiers preparing for combat.

Kimo takes the lead. "Natasha, I assume you've met the guys?" Natasha nods, and he motions toward Ana. "This is Ana Summer. Rachel is her sister."

Natasha steps forward and holds out her hand, her warm smile evident. "Pleasure to meet you, Ana. Kimo has told me so much about you. I'm very sorry about your sister."

She *seems* sincere. Ana shakes Natasha's hand as she sizes her up and wonders, not for the first time, if there was anything romantic between her and Kimo when they worked together at MARSOC. She silently scolds herself. Get your head in the game, Ana.

"Aloha, Natasha. Mahalo for coming." Ana has no reason to be intimidated by this woman. Kimo loves her. Get a grip.

Kimo steps away to join Kalama at his truck and examine the latest surveillance. Joe and Tom follow.

"Aloha, boys, mahalo nui again for coming. Joe, how's it going with the satellite surveillance?"

"Confirmed. We'll have heat signatures, at the very least. BTN." Better than nothing. They all look up at the sky, cursing their bad luck. A crack of thunder detonates as if to punctuate the gravity of the moment and ushers in a deluge of rain. The wind howls ominously as they all look up at the sky, lamenting the weather. Kimo remains positive and confident.

"This weather could work in our favor. Their surveillance will also be compromised, so that's good for us. Plus, the conditions will make it more difficult for them to track us once they realize we've taken the girls. We've come prepared for the weather; they may not be. Has everyone studied the map of the house and property? Do you have any questions about the plan?"

No questions. They are all ready.

The wind picks up, and a menacing bolt of lightning emphasizes the magnitude of the moment.

Ana shouts to be heard over the wind. "Have we heard anything new about the girls or Jackie?"

Kalama answers. "No. Jackie's being very careful not to blow her cover, so she's been out of comms." The rain momentarily slows to a drizzle.

Kimo seethes. "We've had some new intel. Apparently, this scumbag tonight, this Lawrence, is not the big boss. He's just a sleazeball middleman. Jackie and her patrons are after the puppet master, who they suspect is some muckety-muck in the US government." Ana has always had a healthy distrust for those with too much wealth or too much power, so this doesn't surprise her.

Natasha explains. "That's why we're going in Black Ops. This operation has to stay off the books so they don't tip off the Big Fish."

Max hands Ana a suit bag with her uniform for the evening. "You'll be posted at the front door tonight. Lawrence insists that every guest be pat down so you will be searching the women. As you know, once we locate the girls, my guys will arrange for a distraction. When the lights go down, you can go directly to our rendezvous point at the edge of the property."

Natasha reaches into her bag and pulls out a small box containing a dozen tiny devices resembling earbuds. She passes one to each of them. "These are our two-way comms. A gift from our friends in Mossad."

Kimo runs through the mission one last time. "Pop will run the operation from the extraction point at the far mouth of the lava tube, running satellite comms from there. Joe and Tom will remain under camo in the high grass just off the property to the east and cover the extraction. Omar and Lior, you will cover the southern perimeter of the property, down by the dock, and find the girls. Once we have their location, Natasha and I will follow and provide backup. Ana and Max's crew will head to the hui point during the diversion. Ana will lead us through the maze of tunnels to the final extraction point. All clear?" In unison, Kal, Joe, Tom, and Natasha chant the Marine Corps call, "Oorah!" Lior and Omar stand stoic, primed for battle.

Kimo responds. "Oorah!"

The team climbs into their respective trucks.

"Koa, stay with Uncle." Ana hands Kalama Koa's bag and gear.

"Make sure he wears his booties because the lava tubes are slippery and there may be sharp rocks." Kalama nods and Ana turns to Kimo. He looks deeply into her eyes and says nothing. He doesn't need to. Ana somehow knows his heart completely, and her heart aches as she says goodbye, not knowing what will happen this evening. Sensing her distress, Kimo longs to soothe her.

"Ana. There's no turning back now."

"I know, we can't. We have to free Rachel."

"No, I mean us-you and me. There's no turning back. I love you, Ana. I've always loved you. And I know by how you kissed me at the Falls today that you love me, too." Kimo grabs Ana and pulls her to him. He kisses her with a passion she's never known. Ana's knees buckle, and Kimo holds her steady against his powerful chest. Their hearts pound in harmony. Ana feels a rush of emotions: excitement, joy, and an unfamiliar feeling. She feels like she's finally home. Ana feels safe in Kimo's strong arms.

Kimo feels her body collapse into his. "I'm yours, and you're mine, Lehua. We are bashert. Soul mates. I'm going to take care of you forever." The rain begins to come down in sheets, and Lior shouts. "Let's go, love birds!"

Ana stands on her tiptoes and kisses Kimo sweetly on the lips, the rain dripping off his forehead onto hers. "Pomaika'i, Kimo."

"We don't need luck, Ana. We have our amakua – the ancestors will guide us."

CHAPTER 19

Ana stands confidently in the foyer of Lawrence's ostentatious lair, just inside the massive glass swivel doors through which guests hastily enter, taking respite from the storm. One by one, the partygoers remove their wet coats and hand them, along with their umbrellas, to a revolving assembly of beautiful young girls, who whisk the items away for safekeeping.

Ana examines the invitees, and it dawns on her that this looks more like Fashion Week in New York than an auction of kidnapped women and children—some of the world's most dangerous criminals parade by wearing Hermes, Fendi, and Prada. Ana feels like Alice in Wonderland without the benefit of the acid trip.

An older gentleman approaches wearing a white Dior

tuxedo, a silk lavender paisley shirt, and a purple fedora. On his arm is a young blonde girl in a red, skintight bandage dress. She acts like a child at the circus, her loud Texas lilt hushing the thundering storm.

"Oh look, Love, this house is amazing! Oooh, Marty! Look at her diamond necklace! Y'all, that's exquisite. It must've cost a fortune!" Her guileless excitement cannot be contained.

The gathering crowd shifts to avoid the spectacle as Bandage Dress ogles the woman in front of her and taps on her shoulder. "Excuse me, ma'am. May I ask who you are wearing?"

The woman turns around and haughtily replies. "Chanel, dear. Couture." Conspicuous by its absence was a reciprocal inquiry, but the newbie informs her anyway.

"I'm wearing a bespoke dress by an up-and-coming designer; you may have heard of her ..." But the haughty woman turns away before the revelation, bored with Marty's latest trophy.

A third woman remarks to her companion in a Southern accent. "Bless her heart. Miss Thing didn't know what *bespoke* meant before meeting Marty at a Las Vegas pool party. Poor dear was wearing only a thong bikini, a holster filled with tequila shots, and a smile. Now she's carrying a Birkin and wearing Manolos."

A woman in a floor-length mink coat behind her retorts. "God bless America." The ladies chuckle wryly.

Not to be demeaned, another twenty-something arm-bunny comes to the defense of her sister-in-arms.

"I, for one, love that for her." The older women share a look and roll their eyes.

"Bless your heart, Dear."

Ana works the door like a pro, checking purses and respectfully ensuring no contraband enters the property. Her task was made relatively easy by the skin-tight dresses the women were wearing. Not much more than a thought could be smuggled in these outfits. The partygoers ignore Ana even as she intimately pats them down, and they cluelessly continue their conversations. She marvels at their pettiness and finds them phony, pretentious, and pompous.

Once past the security check, guests are treated to a kiss on both cheeks and a fragrant pikake lei placed over their heads by half-naked, would-be supermodels wearing gold-embroidered bras, what appears to be dental floss panties, and a crown of fragrant tropical flowers.

Lawrence stands just beyond the lei presenters wearing a dark blue Tom Ford tuxedo with a flamboyant gold-print Hermes bow tie and matching cummerbund. He stands next to a life-size ice sculpture of a mermaid -- topless and well-endowed, of course. Lawrence exuberantly greets his guests as if it were his only daughter's wedding and not a coalition of dangerous criminals and sociopaths.

"Aloha! Aloha! Hello! Welcome. Welcome to my home. Oh, the Bernsteins are here! So nice to see you. Shaloha! Come one, come all!" Lawrence is giddy and plays his role as host to the hilt as his guests slither past wearing Jimmy Choos and Christian Louboutin.

Ana spies Kimo as he walks up the long driveway toward the door. He is dressed to the nines and perfectly embodies the billionaire trust fund, nepo-baby persona. Ana realizes she's never seen Kimo in a tuxedo before and is taken aback by the striking image he poses. Before she can catch her breath, Ana sees Natasha reaching out to take Kimo's hand and snuggle into his arm. Ana instantly feels sick. She knows it's an act, part of the plan, but the momentary distraction throws her off her game. Otto yells at her from across the foyer.

"Girl, look sharp!"

Lawrence notices Kimo from across the room and watches him, a creepy smile consuming his long, pockmarked face. Max notices Lawrence's fascination with Kimo and believes they can use it to their advantage. He whispers to the team through their two-way comms.

"Kimo, it looks like our host with the most likes your

look. He's been staring at you like a lion at a lamb."

There is snickering over the communication channel as the team teases Kimo.

"Go for it, Kimo!"

"C'mon, Kimo, take one for the team!"

Max silences the teasing. "Look alive, Kimo. He's coming your way." The ribbing quickly ceases as Lawrence makes a beeline for Kimo, his hand extended, ignoring Natasha altogether. He only has eyes for his prey.

"Welcome to Hale Ho'olaule'a." Lawrence seems spellbound by Kimo's presence. "I'm Lawrence."

Kimo flashes a broad grin. "Aloha, I'm Kimo. Hale Ho'olaule'a. House of Celebration. What are we celebrating?"

Kimo shakes Lawrence's hand firmly and looks him directly in his dark, lifeless eyes. He is disgusted by this slimy predator but puts on his game face. Natasha reads the body language and quietly excuses herself. She can be more useful elsewhere.

Lawrence takes no notice of Natasha's stealthy departure.

"We celebrate life, beauty, and love, my young friend." Lawrence places his right hand behind Kimo's left shoulder and pushes him toward the bar. "Let's get you a drink." And just like that, Kimo is in.

Natasha is impressed and speaks quietly into her comms. "I'm leaving the happy couple and will survey the grounds. Has anyone spotted the girls yet?"

Kalama weighs in. "Not yet. Jackie has gone dark. There are several large yachts anchored just offshore. We're assuming they're being kept on one of them."

Lior interrupts. "Wait! We have eyes on Jackie and the girls. They're disembarking a skiff with the name *Lost Boy* on it. That's them. There's Rachel. Baruch Hashem. That's Rachel!"

Omar cries. "There is Zara. Oh my God. She's alive! She's alive. My sister is alive." He is overcome with relief and gratitude and begins to pray in Arabic.

CHAPTER 20

Wearing a gray sweat suit and black slip-on boat shoes, Rachel steps unsteadily off the skiff with Otto's clumsy assistance. The rain momentarily eases as the stoic giant awkwardly offers his hand to Charlotte, then to Zara, as they disembark from the bobbing boat in matching outfits. Standing on the dock at Hale Ho'olaule'a, they look up the hill at the brightly lit mansion filled with animated visitors. They hear loud music and the unintelligible murmurs of the partygoers. Otto motions with his rifle for them to walk ahead across the dock toward the mansion, and they comply. Another guard helps Jackie off the boat. She hands him three garment bags, steps onto the deck, and follows the others. Two burly men with automatic weapons strapped across their massive chests wait for them at the end of the dock, then silently lead them to a Pool House at the lower level of the extensive tiered property.

One of the men opens the door of the Pool House and steps aside as the girls enter. He points to a large sectional sofa, and they sit obediently. Another guard walks in, hangs the garment bags in the closet, and speaks gruffly to Jackie.

"Get the girls ready. Someone will come for them soon." He exits the bungalow abruptly and heads toward the main house, leaving two equally bulky men outside to guard the girls.

Jackie whispers to the girls. "It won't be long now. Stay strong, you're doing great." Charlotte looks at the garment bags, and Jackie explains.

"Don't worry, you don't have to wear those stupid dresses. You girls can wear what you have on." Jackie knows they have a difficult escape route to maneuver and wishes they had rain gear and boots. Beggars can't be choosers, so sweats and boat shoes will have to suffice.

Kalama checks in with the team. "Joe, Tom, report?"

"They've taken the girls to the Pool House. We're headed down there now." Joe and Tom swiftly descend towards the shoreline, taking care to stay out of sight in the tropical landscape.

"Copy. Get down there and stay close. Kimo has Lawrence occupied. Natasha, head down to the Pool House and prepare for extraction. Lior and Omar, keep eyes on the girls. We need to know if they move them."

"Copy that."

"Copy."

Back in the mansion, Kimo follows Lawrence down a hallway and through two large walnut doors to a dark, wood-paneled room.

"This is my bourbon room. What's your pleasure?" Before Kimo can respond, Lawrence takes a crystal carafe from a tall liquor cabinet and pours an amber liquid into two lowball glasses: neat, two fingers high. He hands one glass to Kimo and takes the other for himself.

"This is my guilty pleasure. It's called Angel's Envy. Top-shelf stuff. It's Rye Whiskey finished in a Caribbean rum barrel. Nothing quite like it. Smooth and exotic. Like you, my friend."

Lawrence takes a sip and smacks his thin lips in appreciation, the whiskey dripping from his unusually small mouth. Kimo fights to keep his face neutral and not cringe with disgust. He takes a small sip as his host looks on expectantly.

"Right? Delicious, yes? Delectable, no? Divine?"

Lawrence's voice raises an octave with each question.

Kimo smiles. "Delicious, yes."

"I knew you were a man of taste when I first saw you, Kimo." Lawrence's eyes wander from Kimo's, slowly down his fit body, and stop at his feet.

"What size shoe do you wear, my boy?" Seriously? Kimo's discomfort escalates.

"Uh, eleven and a half. Why do you ask?" Lawrence claps his hands together like a trained monkey with cymbals.

"Perfect! Come, come!" He runs out the door and up a long, winding staircase, summoning Kimo to follow. "Come on, boy! I have something for you!" Kimo follows behind, secretly informing the team.

"I'm headed up the back staircase. Pop, egress from the second floor?"

Kalama responds. "There is another staircase on the corridor's east end, just past the primary bedroom."

"Copy that. Updates Lior?"

"The girls are still at the Pool House with Jackie. Two guards are stationed outside. Omar, Natasha, and I are in position for extraction."

Upstairs in the mansion, Lawrence impatiently beckons

to his new friend. "Kimo, my boy, hurry, hurry!"

When Kimo reaches the top of the staircase, Lawrence proudly reveals his private space. In a move worthy of Vanna White, he dramatically throws open two large, hand-carved mahogany doors.

"Welcome to my Sports Bar! Do you smoke? There is a Cigar Bar on the right. Do you fancy playing cards? The Poker Room is on the left." Lawrence giddily courts the man he hopes will be his new pet.

"Come, come. I promised you a surprise. Come, boy." Kimo reluctantly follows Lawrence further down the hallway to a locked room. "This is the inner sanctum, Kimo. Hallowed ground."

Kimo has had enough. "Mahalo, Lawrence, I appreciate the tour, but I must be getting back to my date."

Lawrence laughs heartily. "Relax, relax. You can't possibly be afraid I'll attack you. I'm an old man, and you are … well, you are quite a specimen. Honestly, you've got it all wrong. Come, I'll show you. My desires are not as banal or predictable as you might imagine."

Lawrence unlocks the door, and as he enters the space, warm lights softly illuminate a large room reminiscent of an old library with row after row of long shelving. However, closer examination reveals not priceless first editions of collectible authors but hundreds of pairs of men's shoes, categorized by designer.

Kimo is speechless, which tickles his host to no end. "Isn't it fantastic? Do you fancy a foot rub, Kimo?"

Suddenly, they are saturated in darkness as the power to the mansion is cut. Lawrence emits a high-pitched shriek, invoking the image of a Girl Scout in a snake pit.

"Kimo! Kimo, I hate the dark! What's happening? Kimo!!!"

But Lawrence's latest love interest is halfway down the back staircase, headed toward the Pool House. Downstairs, the crowd of criminals murmurs loudly, confused in the blackness of the ballroom. As they become increasingly agitated, the murmuring turns to yelling.

"What happened?"

"Don't they have a generator?"

"Or Tesla power walls?"

People move quickly toward the exits, guided by the light of their cell phones. Amidst the frenzy, Lior and Omar rapidly approach the Pool House and are spotted. They take on a barrage of gunfire, take cover, and return fire. From roughly 100 yards behind them, Tom fires his sniper rifle and takes out one of the assailants. The other runs into the pool house, where the girls huddle together in fear.

"Fuck! Cover me!" Lior takes off running towards the Pool House, Joe and Tom providing cover until he arrives and bursts in, expecting to come face to face with a gunman. What he finds is a situation very much under control. Lior looks questioningly at Jackie.

"Don't be too impressed; I had the element of surprise in my favor. He thinks I'm one of them." Jackie stood over the motionless security guard, who had a large gunshot wound between the eyes.

The girls watch, horrified and speechless, in the corner. Rachel sees Lior and immediately runs into his arms. He holds her tightly, crying. She turns to Charlotte and opens her arms, and the child runs to her, sobbing. Rachel repeats to her, over and over, "We're going home, Charlotte. This is my Uncle Lior. We're going home."

Omar enters just behind Lior and immediately runs to Zara, who is shocked to see him.

"Omar? You're alive? But … we thought you were dead." They just hold each other and sob. "Omar, thank God." They cry for Nadia, they cry for their families, and they cry for themselves.

Despite his emotions, Lior takes control. "There is no time for this. We must leave now!" He pleads with Jackie. "Come with us!"

Jackie is touched but doesn't waver. "I'm staying. I'm so

close to bringing down this whole ghastly operation. I have to go back." She steps forward and stands resolutely in front of Lior in anticipation.

"Knock me out."

Lior is horrified. "No way. I cannot hit a woman. My wife would kick my ass." Lior is old school and won't have it. Frustrated, Jackie turns to Omar.

"You do it." Omar is uncomfortable and hesitates. Before he can respond, Jackie is pistol-whipped from behind and collapses to the floor as gunshots ring out on the edge of the property.

Natasha holsters her gun with a big smile. "Men! I guess chivalry remains alive and well, but it's not always relevant, is it? Good thing I'm here. Long live equality. It's just a flesh wound. She'll be fine. Now let's get the fuck outta here."

CHAPTER 21

Kimo arrives breathless to see Jackie unconscious on the ground, blood seeping from a wound in her head. He looks at his former colleague.

Natasha explains. "I did what they couldn't. It's only a flesh wound. Looks worse than it is. She'll be fine."

Kimo hastily reads the room and doesn't question Natasha. "Looks like you have things under control here." Gunfire erupts in the distance, but Kimo remains calm.

"Sounds like Max's boys are keeping them busy up at the house. You gonna go for a swim, or should we get these girls home?"

Natasha quickly checks outside for guards. "Looks like

the rain isn't letting up." She gathers the girls and hurries them out the door. Kimo barks orders as they rapidly head away from the property.

"We have a couple of miles to go before we're out of danger. Girls, we'll be using the Buddy System. Zara is with Omar, Rachel is with Lior, and Charlotte, you go with Natasha." The girl looks timidly at Natasha, who flexes her bicep and gives her a thumbs up and a big smile.

"Me and you, Charlotte. Girl Power." Natasha holds her hand out, and Charlotte tentatively takes it. "Good girl. Once we're off the property, we will be running through a big field of tall grass for a while, so I'm gonna carry you. Is that ok? Sometimes it'll be like I'm a firefighter, and you'll be laying around my shoulders. Other times, you'll be sitting on my shoulders like we're playing chicken in a swimming pool. Have you ever played Chicken, Charlotte? Is that okay?"

Charlotte looks at Rachel, who smiles warmly and encourages the girl.

"Go with Natasha, Charlotte. She's one of the good guys. I promise." Charlotte nods, and Natasha kneels beside Charlotte, who climbs on her shoulders.

"Good girl." Natasha holds Charlotte's legs tightly and pats them reassuringly.

Kimo touches base with the team. "Tom, Joe, we have the girls and are exiting the Pool House. What's your twenty?"

"We're 50 yards south of you. We'll skirt the property as you exit and make sure you're not followed. Over."

"Ana, report. Ana?"

Ana responds, panting heavily. "On the move, stand by."

"Copy that." Kimo leads them out of the pool house in the pouring rain, toward the edge of the property and freedom beyond.

"Max, we are headed up past the main house to the rendezvous point. What are we working with?"

Max responds. "Abort. We've got six unfriendlies about to cross paths with you at the main house. Turn north at the pickleball courts and circle back around. We'll keep them busy here for a while to give you some lead time. We'll try to hui up at the cave."

Tom responds. "Joe and I will flank you and stay between you and the thugs."

Kimo puts his hand in the air and motions toward the pickleball courts. They change course as they hear more gunfire erupt, and they run further and further from the commotion.

While Max and his team exchange gunfire with Lawrence's goons, Kimo, Omar, Lior, and Natasha lead the girls along the perimeter of the property and away from immediate danger, when they finally reach the edge of the property and enter the cane field, they are a mile and a half north of the rendezvous point.

Ana joins the conversation, breathing heavily. "I'm headed west to the hui point, over."

Max chimes in. "If the large man in the front yard with an arrow in his chest is any indication, I'd say you've been busy, Ana. The team and I have your back. We'll help keep the bad guys busy up here at the house."

"Roger that."

Kimo is alarmed. "Ana, you killed a guard? Are you okay?"

"I'm fine, Kimo. I had no choice. He was waiting for you at the bottom of the back staircase. I saw him watching you as I was leaving the property." Kimo could not find the words. She'd saved his life.

Natasha snaps him out of his incredulity. "Kimo, we need to keep moving."

Trekking through the tall, wet grass is slow going, especially for the girls, who have to high-step the entire way. They are in no shape for such an exerting trek and, exhausted, they can't keep up. The group takes many short breaks while Lior, Omar, and Natasha take turns carrying Charlotte on their shoulders. Lior is alarmed at their slow progress and fears the guards will discover them before they've made it to the tunnels.

"We're close to the cave entrance. Let's push hard for the last stretch."

Kalama jumps in on comms. "I have your heat signatures. Kimo, Ana is headed due west and is 75 yards southwest of you."

"Copy. Ana, pulse your flashlight." Ana complies, and Lior sees it first. "There!"

Kimo is relieved. "Got you. Stay where you are."

Minutes later, they are all standing in a tight circle surrounded by acres and acres of wet cane grass, the moon fighting to show itself through the mercifully relenting rain. Omar stands protectively next to Zara, and Natasha holds Charlotte's hand. Lior has his arm around Rachel, fiercely holding her. The girls remain silent, catching their breath. Between the pelting rain and the tall, wet grass they'd been trudging through, they are soaked to the bone and shivering.

Kimo hugs Ana hard enough to take her breath away. Ana gasps, and he loosens his grip. "I'm sorry. I'm just so relieved to see you." Ana is thrilled to see Kimo as well, and struggles to maintain focus.

A quiet voice reaches out. "I am, too." Rachel stands there looking unsteady and lost, a child in shock. Ana's heart breaks as she sees her sister clearly traumatized. Dripping wet and vulnerable, she resembles a girl half her age. Ana cannot fathom what the younger girl has gone through these past 10 months. Surprised by the rush of compassion for this young woman she's never met, Ana goes to her and holds her tightly for a long minute as Rachel sobs. All Ana can do is apologize over and over. Her emotions are almost too much to bear.

"I'm so sorry, Rachel. Honey, I'm so sorry." They both cry and hold each other tightly.

The comms crackle. "We are headed to your location now." Tom and Joe, a quarter mile behind them, hasten their pace to catch up. "Be advised. Enemy is in pursuit. I repeat: Enemy is in pursuit."

Max's voice comes over the comms. "Incoming! They're headed your way in off-road vehicles! Four goons on four-wheelers. We'll stay here and keep the others busy."

"Copy." Kimo leads the way. "Quickly! We need to keep moving." They rush toward the lava cave as the sound of off-road vehicles in the distance swiftly approaches. Kimo realizes they'll never outrun their pursuers and stops abruptly—time for a new plan.

"Ana, Natasha, take the girls to the tunnels. Don't wait for us. Don't stop. Take them all the way to the extraction point. Pop will be there waiting. We'll misdirect them long enough for you to get to the tunnel."

Ana acts with complete confidence. "Copy. Remember, when you get into the cave, make a right at the first fork, then keep left after that." With one last look at Kimo, which says everything, she grabs Rachel's hand, and they take off running as fast as the tall, wet grass permits.

"C'mon, girls!" Zara follows as Natasha bends down so Charlotte can climb on her shoulders. The girls rush off toward the lava cave as Kimo explains the new plan to the remaining team.

"We're going to have to split up and draw their fire so the girls can get to the tunnel. Lior, go with Omar and take the north flank." Just then, they hear Joe and Tom approaching.

"Joe, Tom, we're drawing their fire so the girls can make it to the tunnel. You two take the south flank; I'll creep back and try to position myself behind them."

"Roger that." The men quickly take their positions and wait for the bad guys to show.

As the roar of the ATVs approaches, Joe and Tom prepare themselves.

Joe laments. "This would be a lot easier with a QRF."

"Sure, but only sanctioned missions get a Quick Reaction Force, Joe. Welcome to Black Ops. We ARE the extraction team." Suddenly, a pack of wild boar trot by, seemingly unaffected by the men hiding in the tall grass. Joe points his rifle at the boar, just in case.

Tom laughs at his friend. "You afraid of a little pig, Joseph?"

"Fuck you. That thing's as big as a horse."

Gunshots break out as Kimo takes out two of the men driving by him in the tall grass. The other two don't hesitate and follow the path the girls took. Lior and Omar see this and begin shooting to draw them away from the girls. Their diversion works, and the guards turn and head straight toward them, the headlights of their off-road vehicles revealing their position. Kimo jumps on one of the dead man's ATVs and rushes to save them.

"Fuck!" Tom and Joe jump up and take off in a dead sprint toward the escalating barrage of bullets. As the guards open fire on Omar and Lior, Joe, finally in range, takes a knee and, in the light of their gunfire, takes them both out with his sniper rifle. Their relief is short-lived as they hear more ATVs approaching in the distance.

Kimo takes charge. "Let's go! You four double-up on the ATVs and head for the lava tunnel. I'll distract them and try to throw them off the trail. Ana, Natasha, be advised that we have their vehicles and are headed your way. Keep moving."

"Copy that." Ana and the girls finally arrive at the mouth of the lava cave, out of breath. She hands out flashlights to everyone as they enter the tunnel, and they walk briskly into the cold, damp darkness. The lazy sound of water dripping surrounds them as it trickles slowly off stalactites hanging like icicles 20 feet above their heads.

Ana leads them, winding through the tunnel, over an uneven lava rock surface, through puddles, and over various rock outcroppings. Every few hundred yards, they have to climb through small openings that reveal huge, cavernous caves beyond. Charlotte looks around wide-eyed as Rachel and Zara follow in silence. They are wet and cold but feel safer in the darkness of the lava tube. Ana tries to distract the girls with some small talk.

"You know, I used to lead tours through these tunnels a couple of years ago. It's actually pretty fascinating. I bet you didn't know there are species living here that aren't found anywhere else in the world."

Rachel follows Ana's lead and tries hard to sound normal and interested so Charlotte wouldn't be so afraid. "Wow, really, like what?"

Ana looks at Rachel, and they lock eyes in the light of their flashlights. She smiles and points her light downward, illuminating the cave floor. "Like, for example, blind scorpions, albino crickets, white earwigs, diplurans, millipedes ..." Ana's voice trails off as they reach a fork in the path.

"I'll stay here to make sure they go the right way; it can be pretty confusing and the darkness is disorienting. Take this tunnel on the right, then stay left until you reach the end. Uncle Kalama and Koa will be there waiting."

Natasha confirms the route. "Take this tunnel right, then stay left until we see Kal and Koa. Copy. Don't worry, Ana, I'll get them there safe." Ana nods, and Natasha leads the three girls toward the tunnel on the right.

Ana takes off running, splashing her way back through the tunnel to meet Kimo and the boys. Before long, she sees the glow of a flashlight coming toward her. At first, she thinks it's her team, but then she hears a man speaking through a walkie-talkie. She realizes it's Lawrence's henchmen and quickly turns off her flashlight. She runs back through the tunnel for about 50 yards, where she knows there's a place to hide. When she worked here, she used to sneak ahead and play pranks, jumping out to startle her younger clients during some of her more entertaining tours.

Ana climbs up a large rock outcropping to the top, where a small ledge is not visible from the cave's main trail, and waits. Ana can hear footsteps walking through puddles on the cave floor, and soon, two large men carrying automatic weapons approach. One is severely claustrophobic and focuses his anger on the girls.

"I hate this fucking cave. I can't wait to kill these bitches when we find them."

Ana stands on top of the rock, aims her crossbow, and whispers.

"That's gonna be a long wait. You first, you prick."

As the men walk past her, Ana takes the shot. The arrow stealthily soars through the air and hits the man in the back, piercing his heart from behind. He falls silently to the ground, his partner walking ahead, still talking, unaware of the danger behind him. Ana loads another arrow and shoots, but her foot slips on the wet rock, and the arrow whizzes by the gunman's head. He hears Ana gasp as she catches herself and turns, his flashlight illuminating his partner dead on the ground. As Ana ducks back into her hiding place, the man turns his light and weapon toward her. When he can't find the source of the noise, he takes off running toward the girls.

"Fuck!" Ana scrambles down the rock and runs after the gunman, yelling into her comms. "Natasha, be advised. One bad guy headed your way. I'm right behind him. Hide the girls and double back. We'll trap him."

Kalama can no longer stand idly by while his team and family are in danger. He hastily straps on his gear and turns on the flashlight connected to Koa's harness. They are both ready for battle.

"Team, report in."

Joe speaks first. "Tom and I just entered the mouth of the cave. We're headed your way. Omar and Lior are holding them off. The gunfire sounded pretty bad. We haven't seen Kimo since we split up."

Omar is out of breath. "Lior took a bullet to the leg. We're almost to the cave, but it's slow going."

Lior yells. "I'm fine—just a flesh wound. I'm fine. Where's Kimo?"

Ana breathlessly reports in. "I'm in pursuit. Girls are hidden. Natasha's lying in wait; he won't get away. WHERE'S KIMO!"

Kalama has a bad feeling. "Kimo?" They wait for a response. Nothing. "Kimo, report. Kimo?"

Koa follows Kalama into the mouth of the large tunnel, water dripping slowly but steadily on their heads. Kal checks Koa's gear and tightens his vest and booties.

"Go on, boy. Find Kimo!"

CHAPTER 22

Koa takes off at a dead run into the tunnel, the light on his military canine vest illuminating his path as his booties splash through the puddles that pockmark the tunnel floor. Kalama follows behind much slower, his old war wounds protesting the dank, damp conditions.

Up ahead, Natasha finds a large crevasse between two enormous rocks and tells the girls to hide in there. Natasha looks at Rachel and Zara, her flashlight revealing the fear on their faces in the blackness.

"Okay, you girls are going to go back as far as you can. Do either of you know how to use a gun?" Zara shakes her head, wide-eyed, but Rachel nods. "Yes, Grandpa Sid taught me how to shoot on his ranch."

"Great! Zara, you go in first, then Charlotte. Rachel, go in after them, stand out of sight, and take this gun just in case. It's loaded and ready to go. Don't aim it at anyone unless you intend to use it. Just point and slowly squeeze the trigger. I'll be back as soon as I can. Leave your lights off and STAY PUT!" Natasha takes off, running back toward Ana, the echoes of her footsteps fading as she vanishes into the darkness.

Natasha ducks at a narrowing in the tunnel to pass under the dripping stalactites and sees the glow of an approaching headlamp. She turns off her flashlight and crouches against the wall. The gunman's light gets brighter as he advances, and Natasha can hear his heavy breathing.

"Come to Mama, asshole."

As he comes into range, Natasha squeezes the trigger of her pistol. The man is almost upon her when she realizes the gun has jammed. He turns toward the noise and shines his light on her. As the man goes for his gun, Natasha lets out a primal growl and pounces on him like a wild animal, clawing at his eyes. The man screams and rolls away as Natasha pounces again, but he manages to draw his gun. Blood oozing from his face, he slowly stands, his gun pointed at Natasha's head. Her would-be assassin places his large black boot on her chest, crushing her as she fights to breathe.

"Hey, Fucktard!" Startled, the man swings to his right, releasing his crushing boot, to see Ana standing ten feet behind him, an arrow already in flight. Before he can shoot his weapon, the projectile reaches its target, lodging itself deep in his sternum. The second arrow silently pierces his neck. Natasha scrambles out of the way to avoid being crushed by the large man's falling corpse.

She stands and looks at the dead man, then at Ana. "Brutal! Shit girl, you are badass with that crossbow. Look at the surprise on his face."

Ana smirks. "Four for five tonight. A little rusty, but I've still got it. Let's get the girls."

As they jog quickly through the winding tunnel to where the girls are hiding, Natasha and Ana each silently worry about Kimo, not wanting to alarm the other.

 Ana checks in with the team. "Any word on Kimo?" She remains hopeful and does not slow her pace. She knows they need to get the girls to safety. Kimo can take care of himself. Ana repeats it in her mind. *Kimo can take care of himself.*

They see the glow of a light coming from ahead of them and see Koa tearing around a bend in the tunnel. He can sense Ana before he sees her and begins barking excitedly as he comes upon them.

"Good boy, Koa, good boy!" Ana is thrilled to see him, but knows she must send him on. She kneels in front of him, holding his face with both hands. He stands obediently awaiting his command.

"Koa, find Kimo. Find Kimo, boy." She points back toward the mansion, and Koa understands. He takes off in the direction of the men behind them. Ana watches him go, then looks at Natasha.

"If anyone can find Kimo, it's my Koa. Best soldier I know." Natasha nods appreciatively. She's worked with military dogs before and knows their value.

"Roger that." They take off, trotting in the opposite direction—toward the girls and, ultimately, freedom.

Ana and Natasha arrive at the hiding place just as the glow of Kalama's light reaches them. Kal hugs Ana as Natasha helps the girls out.

Kalama is out of breath. "Did you see Koa? I sent him ahead."

"Yes, I sent him to find Kimo. Anything?"

"I'm afraid not." Kal tries hard to remain calm and confident, but secretly, he's terrified for his only son. "He'll be fine."

Ana is not convinced and can sense Kal's worry. She, too, puts on a brave face.

"He's a survivor. Only the good die young, right, Uncle?" They share a weak smile as Natasha emerges from the crevasse with the girls. Rachel hugs Kalama.

"Shaloha, Uncle," Rachel remembers Kal from several years ago and uses the phrase he taught her. She had come to Maui with her parents on vacation, and while Ana had refused to see them, Kalama and Pua welcomed them warmly and treated them like family, like ohana. She even came to know Kimo and Kalia.

"Shaloha, Rachel. Baruch Hashem. You're alive!" Kalama held the girl and was moved to tears with relief. He couldn't imagine what his friend Lou was going through, wondering if he would ever see his youngest daughter again.

Natasha stands holding Zara's and Charlotte's hands. "Kal, this is Zara, Omar's sister. And this precious girl is Charlotte."

"Aloha, Zara. Hi, Charlotte." Zara smiles quietly and bows her head. Kalama kneels, placing one knee on the ground next to Charlotte, and speaks softly and gently. "I am so happy to meet you both. How about we get out of this dark cave and get you gals back home? We can save the small talk for later, yeah? Over a hot meal." Charlotte nods, her large brown eyes filled with tears.

The group begins walking briskly toward the tunnel's exit. Natasha brings up the rear and radios the team.

"We are headed to the extraction point. Omar, Tom, report?"

Omar speaks first. "Lior and Joe are headed to you now. Lior needs medical attention. Tom and I just left the cave, and we're following Koa back toward the house. I think he's found Kimo's scent. Over."

"Roger that." The girls and Kalama continue toward the truck, each praying to their god for Kimo's safety. Ana's concern is palpable, but she tries to convince herself and the group.

"He's going to be fine. Kimo's the toughest man I know. He'll be fine."

Outside the cave and back in the shadow of Lawrence's evil lair, Koa barks furiously as he finds Kimo lying unconscious and bleeding from his stomach. He licks Kimo's face and nudges him with his long nose, but Kimo doesn't respond. Koa continues to bark until Tom and Omar catch up to him.

"NO! No, no, no, no, no …" Omar runs up and slides on his knees in the wet grass to where Kimo lay, still. He kneels beside Kimo and checks his vitals as Tom checks in with the team.

The comms click on, and they hear Koa barking in the background.

"We found him! We found Kimo! Stand by." The girls and Kalama stand silently in the darkness; the only sounds are the agonizingly slow drips from the lava rock ceiling, as if the cave itself weeps for their suffering. They wait breathlessly for news of Kimo's condition. Ana feels like she is going to explode and finally erupts with worry.

"Is he alive?! Tom, is Kimo alive?" She looks at Kalama, and as they lock eyes, they gain strength from each other. Kalama begins to pray in Hawaiian, beseeching the ancestors to watch over Kimo.

Tom finally answers. "Affirmative. Kimo's alive. He's unconscious and bleeding from a gut wound. We have to get him to a hospital stat. It's not ideal, but we have to move him."

"Oh my God! Kimo!" Ana tries hard to control her panic. Kalama, despite his dread, reassuringly places his hand on her shoulder.

"Think good thoughts, child. The Amakua are watching over Kimo. The ancestors will not let him die."

CHAPTER 23

Joe helps Tom lift Kimo over his broad shoulders in a fireman's carry. They jog back toward the cave as quickly as Kimo's condition allows, with Koa leading the way. Joe takes the rear position in case Lawrence's men send reinforcements. Tom reports in, his breathing labored.

"We're en route now. Almost to the tunnel entrance." Kimo moans softly and whispers something.

Ana yells. "Kimo? Kimo? Kimo, help is on the way. Hold on!"

Kimo's response is barely audible. "Lehua …"

"Kimo! Kimo, I'm here … Kimo?"

Tom interjects. "He passed out, Ana, but he's hanging in there."

Ana peers, panic-stricken, into the blackness of the tunnel they'd just come through. She fights the urge to run back toward Kimo. She knows her responsibility is to the girls.

Kalama wrestles with the same dilemma. "Ana, let's get the girls to the truck. Koa will lead them to us."

It's all Ana can do to maintain her composure. "Yes, Uncle. You're right. Let's get the girls to safety and get Kimo help."

Just then, they see the glow of lights approaching. Natasha confirms the source. "Joe, is that you guys? Can you see our lights?"

As the men turn the bend in the dank tunnel, Lior's arm around Joe's shoulders for support, they see the glow of light from Kalama and the girls.

"Affirmative. We're here." Natasha runs to the men and checks Lior's wound. Every bit the warrior, he balks at the attention.

"I'm fine, I'm fine. It's just a flesh wound. Stop hovering." Natasha confirms Lior's self-diagnosis.

"I've seen worse, you stubborn jackass." She looks at the team with relief. "He'll be fine. Let's get to the truck.

Kalama rushes off toward the exit of the tunnel. "I'll call Doc Sherwin; his place is nearby.

"Right behind you, Uncle." Ana turns to the girls with as much enthusiasm as she could muster. "Okay, ladies, just a little further, we're out of this creepy tunnel. Let's do this!"

"I've got Lior, Joe, go help with Kimo." Natasha takes Joe's place as Lior's crutch as they follow Kalama out of the tunnel. Joe takes off back into the darkness.

By the time the girls and Lior exit the cave, Kalama is on his cell phone, sitting in his truck, engine running, in the unrelenting rain.

"Mahalo, Cousin. We'll be there as soon as we can." Kal sees the girls and waves them into the truck. "Come on, come on. Get in and dry off. I have the heater going."

Kalama takes Charlotte's hand first and helps her up into the large 4x4, followed by Rachel and Zara. They huddle together in the back seat, soaked and shivering. Ana sits up front in the passenger seat.

"I'll stay here with the girls, Uncle." Ana tries her best to comfort the girls while Kalama, Natasha, and Lior stand just inside the cave's entrance, out of the rain. Their concern is unmistakable as they nervously await the rest of the team's arrival.

After what seems like an eternity, they hear Koa barking. Kalama throws his fist in the air.

"Yes! Here they come! Baruch Hashem! They're coming!" Koa's barking gets louder, and soon, they see the glow of headlamps as the men emerge. Joe is first, followed by Tom, and Kimo draped across his broad shoulders. Omar arrives last with Koa, walking backwards, assuring they hadn't been followed. The sight of Kimo unconscious and bleeding is almost more than Kalama can bear.

"Let's go. Sherwin is waiting for us. Joe, Tom, and Omar get Kimo in the back of the truck and keep him as still and as dry as possible. There are blankets and tarps in the bin."

"Copy that."

"Copy." The men prepare Kimo's makeshift gurney as the girls look on. Koa jumps in back with the team.

"Natasha, ride up front with Ana." Natasha complies, and Kalama quickly drives off through the dense forest as the rain stubbornly persists. "Sherwin is about 20 minutes from here; hold on."

When they arrive at Sherwin's home just after midnight, they see him and his wife, Nicole, standing on the lanai, waiting expectantly. Koa recognizes the property and jumps out of the back of the truck, excited to see Uncle and Auntie. They were the ones who had rescued Koa as a puppy and placed him with Ana. Sherwin smiles.

"Aloha, Koa. Good to see you, boy. You're looking good." He beckons to Kalama. "Aloha, Cousin. Bring him, quickly. Here, on the table." Natasha helps the men carry Kimo carefully into the kitchen and lay him on the sheet-covered dining table. Sherwin immediately begins to examine Kimo's wound, Kalama at his side.

Nicole goes to the truck and opens the driver's side door. "Aloha, Ana."

"Aloha, Auntie." Nicole looks in the back seat and sees the girls. She smiles warmly.

"And who are these lovely young ladies?" Without waiting for a response, she waves them in. "Come now, let's get you dried off and warmed up. Whaddaya say? Auntie has some nice homemade banana bread if you're hungry." Koa barks. He's always hungry.

The girls initially don't move, paralyzed by the trauma of the night's events. Ana jumps out of the truck and opens the rear door.

"It's okay, girls. We're safe now. We're safe. These folks are family. We're safe here."

The girls slowly exit the truck and follow Nicole into the house. Nicole keeps herself busy getting towels and blankets and settles them in front of the fireplace, making small talk in an attempt to distract the girls.

"Now let's get you some nice banana bread and milk." She looks at Rachel and Zara. "Or would you ladies prefer some coffee?"

Zara speaks up, her voice timid. "Yes, ma'am. Yes, please."

"Yes, ma'am." Rachel gratefully accepts.

Rachel speaks in a motherly tone to Charlotte. "Honey, how does some banana bread and warm milk sound?"

Charlotte nods almost imperceptibly and looks at the floor, still shivering.

"You poor dear." Nicole puts a large dog bed directly in front of the fireplace. "Come, now. Lay down here with this fluffy blanket, and let's get you warmed up." Charlotte does as she's told, and immediately, Koa lies down next to her, his large body protectively wrapped around her. Nicole is touched.

"Good boy, Koa. Charlotte, it looks like you've got a friend." The girl remains silent but leans into the large dog. Koa licks her hand and puts his head in her lap.

As Nicole fusses over the girls, the team stands around nervously in the kitchen, waiting for news. Omar goes to the living room to check on Zara, who gives him a weak smile.

"Zara, thank God you're okay. We've all been so worried. I've already sent word to Mama and Papa. They are going to contact your parents. They can't wait to see you."

Zara melts into Omar and cries quietly, her thin frame shaking. She feels so small, so vulnerable. Nothing like the strong, happy girl he remembered. His heart breaks for her as he realizes she will never be the same innocent young woman she once was.

Nicole brings them their food trays. As they eat, Omar wanders into the adjoining room, too restless to sit still. He sees medical supplies and a metal examination table that is too small for a human. Scores of photos of dogs and cats are on the wall, alongside Sherwin's diplomas. Omar realizes a veterinarian is operating on Kimo. He returns to the kitchen.

"Sherwin, you're a vet?" Sherwin chuckles and nods his head.

"Yes, I'm a vet. Don't worry. This isn't my first human, and this isn't my first gunshot wound. Things are a bit different here on Maui, son. A little more like the Old West than the mainland."

Omar smiles. "Apparently. I'm a veterinarian, too. But I've never operated on a man. Or on a gunshot wound, for that matter. We don't get a lot of armed bad guys at the Negev Zoo."

"Well, it's never too late to start." Lior stands there pointing at his leg. "I could use a few stitches."

Omar shrugs. "What could go wrong?" Things really are different on Maui.

In the kitchen, Kalama has complete confidence in Sherwin and stands by his flawed logic. "A vet is a doctor. My cousin is the best vet in the state. He'll get Kimo stabilized. We can get him airlifted to Queen's Hospital on Oahu when the weather clears."

Kalama asks the question that's been weighing on him. "Sherwin, we need a cover story for Kimo's gunshot wound; they'll need to report it when we get to the hospital."

Sherwin nods. "Already thought of that. We'll tell them you two were out hunting, got drunk, and you shot him. You'll get off with involuntary manslaughter." The look on Kalama's face is priceless, and Sherwin laughs.

"Don't worry, Cuz. The Chief of Surgery at Queen's is a good friend. He owes me a favor. We'll tell them it was an accident and we'll leave it at that. He won't contradict us." Kalama smacks Sherwin on the back of the head, then they hug it out.

Nicole enters the kitchen on a mission to make her guests comfortable. She cracks a dozen eggs into a pan and fries up several slices of Spam. "No one goes hungry on my watch. No matter the time of day … or night." Nicole doesn't wait for an answer and continues to chatter, the others somehow comforted by her grandmotherly presence.

"Ana." Kimo's weak voice was almost inaudible. He fights to speak. "Ana."

The sound of her name startles her, and she rushes to Kimo's side.

"Kimo? I'm here. I'm right here, Kimo." She holds his bloody hand and looks beseechingly at Uncle Sherwin, tears streaming down her tanned cheeks. "Uncle?"

"I've got him stabilized for now, Ana. We need to get him to Queen's ASAP."

A strained whisper. "Ana." Kimo tries to open his eyes, but his lids are too heavy. "Ana."

"I'm here, Kimo." Ana is sobbing and feels sick. "Kimo, don't leave me now. Please, God, don't take him. Kimo, please don't leave me. You promised you'd never leave me. Kimo, please. Hashem, please, don't take him."

Kimo smiles weakly and whispers. "I love you, Ana."

Ana's heart aches. "I love you, too, Kimo." But the words come too late. Kimo loses consciousness again, and Ana fears he may never know her heart.

CHAPTER 24

Three Weeks Later

Ana wakes up to another gorgeous day in paradise, birds singing and geckos chirping in the dense forest around her. She smiles at Koa, snoring serenely beside her. Best dog ever. Ana has been sleeping in lately, mercifully undisturbed by dreams of the past. For a moment, she recalls that awful night at Uncle Sherwin's house in Hana. She has never been so terrified in her whole life, and that was saying something. Ana had feared she'd lost Kimo forever and was absolutely devastated.

Thank God he's okay. It turns out that Uncle Sherwin is not only an excellent veterinarian but also a top-notch human doctor. He stitched and packed the wound enough to stabilize Kimo and stem the blood loss. The morning was ushered in by a withering storm, so the helicopter was able to land nearby and fly him to Queen's Hospital in Honolulu. The surgeon said Kimo was lucky. The bullet missed most of the major organs and only hit a small part of his liver. There was a clean exit wound, and fortunately, no complications. Kimo's youth and fitness played a huge role in his quick recovery, and he was back on Maui four days later.

Ana had insisted that he stay with her when he was released, so she could take care of him, and Kimo was happy to accept. Truth be told, he had healed quickly from his surgery and really didn't need much nursing at this point, but neither one of them will acknowledge it. Kimo is thoroughly enjoying the attention and lets Ana dote on him incessantly. Ana has yet to leave Kimo's side in three weeks, and they still can't get enough of each other. They have a lot of time to make up for.

Neither of them is prepared to leave their bubble of safety and gratitude to return to the real world just yet. Kimo is grateful for Ana's long-awaited acceptance of her feelings for him and her willingness to let him in. He'd always known they had a special bond, and his infinite patience has finally paid off.

Ana is grateful for so many things. She is looking forward

to getting to know her sister, Rachel, who will no doubt need the support as she processes her trauma. Ana has even spoken to her father a few times since the mission. Things are still awkward, but they've taken the first steps. Mostly, Ana is grateful Kimo didn't give up on her before she could get her shit together and she is determined to make it up to him.

Ana walks into the kitchen, followed by a sleepy-eyed Koa. She pours a cup of freshly brewed coffee and walks outside on the lanai. Kimo is on the side of the house, pounding in wooden stakes and tying red string between them.

"What is this?" Ana stands, long brown hair tousled, wearing only little boy shorts and Kimo's extra-large University of Hawaii t-shirt. She sips her coffee and peruses the situation with a smile. She loves seeing him work around her house, and he loves taking care of her. Kimo looks up and feels the familiar flutter in his stomach. His heart is whole.

"What this is, is your new room addition, milady." Kimo bows melodramatically, and Ana giggles.

"My room addition?" Ana had been talking about adding on to Hale Lehua for years, but never got around to it. "Does that mean you're moving in?" She lifts an eyebrow persuasively.

Kimo laughs and dodges the question. He walks to her and kisses her softly on the lips.

"I figure you need at least two more bedrooms. I think you've outgrown this place."

Ana wonders again how she got so lucky. This gorgeous, smart, brave, gentle man loves her, with all her imperfections and peccadillos.

"I love you, Kimo." He puts his arms around her, looks into her eyes, and brushes an errant strand of wavy hair from her face.

"I have to say, I'm surprised to hear you say it so much. I didn't take you for an overly expressive woman."

"Oh, am I overly expressive?" She teases him and they laugh.

"I just mean, I think you've told me every day since that first time when I got home from the hospital. I love it, I'm just surprised."

"Wanna know a secret?" Ana asks shyly.

"Of course." Kimo wants to hear everything Ana has to say.

"That wasn't the first time I said I love you. That day you came home. It wasn't the first time." Kimo looks curious.

"The first time was at Uncle Sherwin's. I told you I

loved you, and you promptly passed out. I thought you were dead. I thought you'd died without ever knowing how I feel about you. I was devastated. I wanted to die right there with you. Uncle explained you'd passed out from shock and blood loss, and you would be okay. I vowed right then and there that I'd tell you I love you every day for the rest of my life." She begins to tear up, remembering the moment. "I thought you died, Kimo. I thought you'd never know …"

Kimo holds her close and gently sways. "But I do know, Lehua. I've always known."

Ana pushes his chest away from her and looks up into his soulful eyes. "You don't understand, Kimo. It all came rushing in at that moment. How much time we've wasted … I'VE wasted so much time living in fear." She melts into Kimo's arms, and he holds her tight until her tears subside and she collects herself. Kimo looks at her with a stern but loving gaze.

"Ana, listen to me. I need you to hear this. I promise you, I will never leave you. I will always be here for you. You have my word."

"But you don't know that, Kimo. You can't make that promise. Things happen. You know that as well as I do." Ana suddenly feels a surge of panic as she realizes how much she has to lose.

Kimo smiles and kisses her deeply and passionately. She can feel his love for her and finds strength in his embrace. Ana surrenders to the feeling and gives herself a mental kick in the ass.

"I'm sorry, Kimo. I know I have more issues than *National Geographic*, it must be so tedious." Kimo laughs and shakes his head.

"I love you *and* your issues, beautiful girl. Now, let's go, we're already late for Mama's luau and we still need to shower." Kimo looks at Ana suggestively and takes her small hand in his as he moves slowly, seductively toward the house. Ana laughs but does not resist.

"Kimo, you're insatiable."

CHAPTER 25

Kimo and Ana walk hand in hand through the tall grass toward the main house, as Koa diligently sniffs the ground the whole way there. Today is a gathering for friends and family in honor of those lost and taken on October 7th, 2023. It is a grim remembrance. The observance of the anniversary of these horrific attacks is particularly distressing for the family because of what Rachel and Zara had to endure over the last year. Not to mention, there are still over 100 innocent men, women, and children being held by Hamas terrorists, chained up in tunnels and cages, tortured in unspeakable conditions.

Ana says aloud what they're both thinking. "I feel guilty being this happy when so many people are suffering."

"I know, me too, a little. But that's dumb. We both know it." Kimo puts his arm around her shoulder and kisses the top of Ana's head. "There is no right or wrong way to grieve. No one would begrudge us our happiness, Ana. We've been through hell and back ourselves. Our joy does not diminish our suffering or what we've lost. In many ways, we've earned this happiness."

Ana nods her head and remembers her mother. "There's nothing so whole as a broken heart."

As the pair approach the property, the sounds of music and laughter drift toward them. "See? It's okay to be happy." Kimo waves at Pua as they approach the house. "Mama, I'm starving. Where's the kau kau?"

Pua clucks her tongue and gives Kimo a huge hug, then Ana. "And where the heck have you two been? We were getting ready to call the National Guard! Are you not feeding my boy? Kimo's looking a little wiwi."

Ana blushes. "Kimo has been recuperating, Auntie, you know that."

"Mmm hmmm. Just don't bust your stitches, eh?" Pua knows exactly what they've been up to.

"Mama!" Kimo acts horrified but laughs, and Ana is embarrassed.

Pua ignores Kimo's fake outrage. "Have you seen your sister? She brought her new boyfriend, Jakob. He's in law school. She's gaga over him. Go check him out and get me the deets. Tell me if we like him."

They both laugh as Pua walks away and toward the house. Ana calls after her. "*The deets*, Auntie? Who have you been listening to?"

"I'm serious, child. Go check him out. I have to watch the huli huli chicken." Auntie takes the well-being of her children seriously, especially since her only boy was recently shot in the gut. She's not taking any chances.

As they walk away, snickering, Kimo calls back to her. "Ok, Mama, we'll check him out." They walk toward the yard and see Kalama waving them over excitedly.

"Come, you two, I have Lior on the Zoom." Kimo laughs as they follow Kal down the dirt path to his office.

"Pop, it's just Zoom, not 'the Zoom'." Ana swats his shoulder and whispers in his ear.

"Stop!"

"Hurry, hurry, it's four in the morning there. I can't believe he's awake." Kimo and Ana join Kal in front of the computer screen.

"Shaloha, Lior." They all wave at Lior as he looks sleepily into the camera.

Ana is anxious to hear how they're all doing. "Shaloha, Uncle. How was yesterday?" Israel is 12 hours ahead of

Hawaii, so they had already had their commemoration of the Oct. 7th Massacre.

"It was difficult, child, it was hard, but we're okay." Lior looked tired and melancholy. "We lost several members of our kibbutz that day. Our families here are still in shock and struggling one year later."

A voice enters the room. "Hey, is that Maui? Shaloha, guys!" Omar appears on camera, standing behind Lior with a big smile. "Really great to see you all!"

"Omar? You went to the kibbutz for the Celebration of Life?"

"Well, yes and no, Kimo. Actually, I'm staying here for a few months until they find a new vet." Omar laughs. "I guess Lior liked the way I stitched him up." Omar looks good, like he has purpose again. They are all relieved he seems to be moving forward.

Lior explains. "Our veterinarian was lost on October 7th at the Nova Festival. He took his young daughter there to see her favorite band. She had cerebral palsy. Tragic, just horrible."

Ana tears up. "Oh my God, Lior. That's awful, I'm so sorry."

Lior agrees. "Yes. So many losses. We are strong, child. We will persevere."

After catching up with Lior and Omar, Kimo and Ana walk toward the crowd by the pool where the kids are throwing a ball for Koa.

"Kimo, you're looking well." Uncle Sherwin stands next to the Tiki Bar, mai tai in one hand and shave ice in the other.

"Uncle, yes, I'm feeling great thanks to you. Two-fisted, eh?" Kimo is still a little sore but isn't about to admit it. He's healed faster than anyone had predicted.

Ana gives Sherwin a big hug, almost spilling his mai tai. "Mahalo nui loa for saving Kimo's life, Uncle. I'm forever in your debt."

"All in a day's … or a night's work, Ana, good to see you both looking so … happy." Without warning, Koa snatches the shave ice from Sherwin's hand and runs off.

Sherwin laughs. "I didn't need that anyway." He sees his wife, Nicole. "Hey, honey! They're here! Bring her over." Auntie Nicole approaches carrying a medium-sized dog crate.

"Bring who over, Uncle?" Kimo reaches out to take the crate from Nicole as she approaches and sets it on the lawn.

"Did you get a new dog?" Ana bends down to look inside the crate to see a brown ball of wriggly fur. "What is it?"

Sherwin takes the pup out of the crate and puts a leash on her. "It is a she, and she looks to be part Labrador, part Husky, and part Tasmanian Devil."

"Awe. She's adorable." Kimo is a sucker for a puppy—or basically any baby animal.

"We've been calling her Nalu. She wandered onto our property a couple of weeks after our evening together, pretty scrawny and sickly. We got her healthy, and turns out she's a great dog, and shows a lot of promise as a warrior. We thought of you." Sherwin picks up the pup and places her in Ana's arms. "I thought maybe you and Koa would like to show her the ropes."

Ana's face lights up. "Really!? We can keep her?" She had always talked about getting a companion for Koa, but never found the right one. Ana kisses the pup and starts with the baby talk. "Aloha Nalu. I love your name. It means wave in Hawaiian. Do you like the ocean?" Nalu licks Ana's face, and the puppy breath seals the deal. There is no turning back now.

Ana looks happily at Kimo, who is beaming from ear to ear. He loves seeing Ana this happy.

"We'll take her." Koa trots up to sniff his new companion and gives her a nudge with his giant nose. "Hey, be gentle, Koa, she's just a baby." In a matter of minutes, Nalu is learning her place in the pack, trotting behind

Koa, who instantly takes his new role as big brother very seriously as he micro-manages her every move.

Max and Auntie Kailani approach from the side yard. "Howzit! Hey, beware, Auntie Kailani is a cornhole shark. She just took me for thirty bucks!"

Kalama laughs. "Kailani, up to your old tricks, eh?" Auntie waves her hand and heads to the Tiki Bar.

Pua yells from the house. "C'mon, folks, kau kau ready!"

After dinner, Max sits across from Kimo and Ana at a picnic bench as they watch the cousins dance hula to Kalama on the ukulele. "Hey, I've been wanting to talk to the two of you about something."

Kimo and Ana share a look, and Kimo gives voice to their curiosity. "What's up, Max?"

"This might not be the time, but when you're ready, I have a business proposition for you."

"You have my attention." Kimo is curious about what Max is up to. Before the mission, he was feeling restless and looking for a fresh opportunity.

"Well, after working with you two in August, I got to thinking. I've been getting more and more requests to do investigative work as part of the security gig, but I can't handle both. I just don't have the time or staff. Have you guys ever thought about opening up a private investigation business? I could keep you busy enough to pay the bills."

Ana is immediately protective. "I don't know, Max. Kimo is still recovering from a bullet wound, and I'd like to keep him around for a while. How dangerous is this investigation work?"

"Oh, it's not dangerous at all. It's mostly background checks and jealous lovers. The occasional runaway teen. Some small business embezzling. Easy money. Listen, it's just an idea. No pressure. Just think about it, yeah?"

Kimo nods. "Okay, Max, we'll think about it." He gets a look from Ana. If she has her way, Kimo is going to be lying low for quite some time.

"No promises, Max. We're planning on taking some time off this fall. Anyway, Kimo has a room addition to build, don't you, honey?"

Kimo smiles at Max and shrugs his shoulders. "She's the boss."

Kalia and her boyfriend approach the table. "Aloha. Kimo, Ana, Max, this is my boyfriend, Jakob. He's studying at the Richardson School of Law at U of H." Jakob timidly shakes hands and repeats everyone's names in hope he can remember them. They exchange pleasantries, and Kimo immediately begins the debrief. "So, Jakob, what area of law are you focusing on?"

"Civil Rights and Environmental Law." Jakob seems nervous and uncomfortable talking about himself. Ana likes the fact that he's humble. It's a rare quality in a future lawyer. Kimo continues the inquisition.

"Interesting. And how long have you been seeing my little sister? Where do you see this going?" Jakob stammers, and Kalia chastises her brother.

"Kimo! Stop!"

Ana takes pity on him. "C'mon, Kimo, quit grilling the poor guy. I'm sorry, Jakob, Kimo can be a little overprotective. So, what are you two doing for winter break? Anything fun?"

Kalia answers excitedly. "Jakob and I are interning with a local non-profit, Aloha Ranch, in Lahaina. You know them, they help the fire survivors get everything they need to set up their new tiny homes. You know, they have nothing! We'll be delivering stuff to 20 families a week!"

Kimo is charmed by Kalia's enthusiasm and figures this kid can't be all bad if he's volunteering on his winter break to help the fire survivors. "Sounds like a great cause. I'm proud of you, Kalia." He gives Jakob a shaka. "Well done." Jakob looks relieved. He doesn't usually drink, but right now, a beer sounds great.

Kalama turns off the music and calls the group over to

surround him. "First, I'd like to share our warmest aloha with all of our friends and ohana, and mahalo nui for coming together to share this very important day with us. We come together today in peace and love, whether you say Aloha or Shalom, in honor of those lost, those taken, and those still suffering from the horrible attacks one year ago on October 7th. There is no need to belabor the dreadful details of what has happened to our people, each one of us knows all too well. I ask only that we bow our heads and pray for peace."

Kalama bows his head and prays, and the crowd follows suit.

"Oseh shalom bimromav, hu ya'aseh shalom, alenu v'al kol Yisra'eil. He Who makes peace in His heights may He make peace upon us and upon all Israel."

The solemn crowd pray together. "Amen."

CHAPTER 26

Thanksgiving Day, 2024

Kimo wakes before dawn and reaches for Ana to find only a pillow and some tousled sheets. He raises himself on his elbows to look for Koa and Nalu, usually either in bed or on the floor. No pups, either. Kimo smells coffee brewing and hops out of bed. He enters the kitchen in only his black boxer briefs to find his favorite mug waiting for him beside the coffee pot, which he promptly fills.

"Ana? Koa? Nalu?" As Kimo walks out the back door, Koa barks once, and Ana yells down to him happily.

"Up here on our private rooftop lanai! Built by my very hot lover!" Kimo laughs and climbs the stairs to find Ana sitting in one of two Adirondack chairs facing the infinite ocean view, the pups immersed in their first nap of the day. He walks over, kisses the top of her head, and settles in beside her.

"Whatcha thinking about, beautiful girl?" Kimo loves these moments together, sharing their island paradise, just the two of them. And the pups, of course.

"Spiritual warfare." Kimo begins to laugh but then realizes she's serious.

"Wow. You're not kidding. Deep. Okay, tell me what's going on in that gorgeous head of yours."

"I don't know, Kimo. I've been thinking about all that our family has been through. The attack on our kibbutz when we were kids, the fire last year, followed by October 7th. The girls' kidnapping and ... ugh." Ana groans. "I tell you, it's hard not to question your faith. Think about it. If there's God, then there's Satan, right? Is he winning? I mean, the Holocaust, for Moses' sake?" Ana struggles to grasp the meaning hidden deep within the hypocrisy of it all. *What is the lesson here?*

"If God is all-powerful, why does he let the innocent suffer?" She looks at Kimo, tears in her eyes. "Rachel ... the girls. Oh my God, Kimo. It's so cruel. Why do righteous people suffer, and wicked people prosper?" Ana seeks answers to the unanswerable.

"My love, these are all good questions. I remember you

asking Rabbi Mendy similar things soon after we moved here to Maui. After Lilikoi was killed and your mother was taken. Do you remember what he told you?"

"Not exactly. I do remember that he did not answer the question to my satisfaction."

"That's because there is no good answer, Lehua. Rabbi said suffering brings us closer to God. He explained that suffering benefits us as individuals and as a community, and it is our challenge to find how. Our task is to find hope and meaning in adversity." They sit in silence for a minute, pondering the wisdom of the Torah. Ana remains frustrated and confused.

"None of that helps. It doesn't make sense to me. What do you believe, Kimo?"

"I believe life is about balance and doingness. Balance like the yin and the yang, yeah? Good can't exist without evil. Joy cannot exist without suffering. Suffering is part of life. I guess I have more of a Buddhist approach. I don't really worry about good and evil. I believe in doing good things and being a good person, and in turn, good things come my way. I mean, yeah, we've been through a lot, but look at us now. We have each other and all of this." They both look around in appreciation. Hundreds of mynah birds chatter incessantly like a bunch of arguing old bitties in the 30-foot tall kukui nut tree beside them.

"Balance and doingness. Karma, yeah? Kimo, you're right. It's futile to torture myself with questions that have no answers. Okay, new plan. Be here, be now. Consider me a Jew-Bu." Ana forces a fake smile until she eases into the real thing and savors their relaxed silence.

Kimo and Ana sip their coffee and watch the lights on the resort strip below surrender their twinkle to the pink, glowing dawn. Kimo reaches over and takes Ana's hand, a smirk on his face. She smiles. Here it comes …

"You know, Ana. The problem of justifying God, despite the existence of evil, is known as theodicy."

"You goofball."

"I'm your goofball."

Later, Kimo and Ana walk hand in hand through the kukui nut trees to the main house. Nalu tries to keep up as Koa leads the way, revealing to his enthusiastic student the best places to sniff and dig on the way to Auntie's hale. Kimo wonders how Ana will cope with seeing her father after so many years. Lou arrived from Texas late last night with Grandpa Sid and the entire oddly blended family.

"How are you with seeing your dad today, Ana?" She pauses before she answers, wanting to be honest with him and with herself.

"I think I'm good. We've spoken on the phone a few times … I'm good. I guess they're all getting along famously, staying at Grandpa's ranch. It actually sounds like a lot of fun."

Rachel and Zara have been in therapy at a facility outside of Dallas that specializes in trauma therapy. Since Sid's ranch is less than an hour away, he invited both of their families to come and stay with him so they could be close by and visit the girls frequently. The ranch is large enough to comfortably accommodate all of them.

"I'm really looking forward to seeing my little sister and getting to know Zara and her family; they sound amazing. Grandpa Sid has really loved having them all at the ranch. He can't stop carrying on about how well they are taking care of him and the animals, and he raves about Iman's cooking. He says she's going to be a famous chef one day." She smiles. "He's going to be sorry to see them go."

"That's sweet. I'm glad it's worked out so well for all of them; they can be there for Rachel and Zara as they transition back to the real world. What do you know about how their therapy is going?"

"Not much. The doctors never seem to say anything of substance. They don't make any promises, and we're not supposed to ask the girls about it. It's important they set the pace of their own recovery."

"Understandable. Trauma is a tricky thing; you know that as well as anyone."

"Truth. Anyway, after getting last-minute permission from the girls' doctors, Grandpa surprised everyone at the ranch with a trip to Maui for the Thanksgiving holiday. He rented an Airbnb on the beach, and they're all staying there for two weeks. Hopefully, they can relax and have some normal family time, whatever that means."

Ana and Kimo can hear the ruckus from the main house before they emerge from the kukui nut grove. Koa and Nalu run ahead to join the fun, and they hear a woman's voice hoot with victory.

Ana laughs. "Sounds like Auntie Kailani is already dominating the corn hole competition."

Pua calls from the kitchen. "Ana, Kimo, come, come! You have to meet Farrah and Iman!

Ana and Kimo enter the kitchen to a flurry of activity. Pua makes the introductions and puts everyone to work. "Kimo, just in time. Make yourself useful. Take the turkey out of the oven and set it on the kitchen island. Iman, how is the kalua pork stuffing coming?"

"It's almost done, Auntie Pua. It'll be ready in a few minutes." Iman fits right in and is taking her first Hawaiian Thanksgiving very seriously. She immediately assumed the role of sous chef to Pua ten minutes after their arrival. Farrah is busy mashing potatoes, but makes a point to stop and hug Ana.

"It is wonderful to finally meet you both. I have heard so many amazing things from Sid and Rachel. I feel like I know you. We are deeply grateful for all you and your family have done for us. You saved our Zara, and we are forever in your debt."

Kimo hugs Farrah, too. "Please, we are just happy we were able to bring the girls home." Farrah wipes a tear from her eye.

"I'm sorry, I thought I was done crying. It's just …" Pua hugs Farrah and clicks her tongue.

"No more tears. Today is a celebration! It is a day to be thankful. We have so many blessings. Let's focus on those."

"You're right, Pua. You're right." Farrah collects herself and smiles broadly. "Your family is wonderful, and we are blessed to be a part of it."

Ana looks around. "Where are Rachel and Zara? She texted that she's here already."

Pua waves her hand toward the lower part of the property. "They're down at the imu with Sid and Kalama. You know, Kal, he'll have them down there all day debating the value of banana vs ti leaves if you don't rescue them."

Kimo laughs. "Yeah, Pop gets a little carried away with his imu lessons." He tries to embody Kalama's professorial tone. "The imu is essentially an underground steam cooker used by our ancestors during festivities or religious ceremonies …" They all laugh, and Ana swats his back.

"Kimo, be nice."

"What?" He falls back into his impression. "It's important that the first layer of hali'i is laid directly over the hot rocks and kiawe to prevent the food from being scorched …"

"Kimo, stop! You know the mango doesn't fall far from the tree, right? Let's go rescue them."

Ana turns to Pua. "Lou, uh, my father and Lorie here yet?" Ana feels awkward calling her father by his given name, as she had for so many years during their estrangement. She feels differently about him now. Is this what forgiveness looks like?

"They arrived a little while ago. I think they're out by the pool with Kalia and Jakob. Lou asked about you the second he arrived." Pua puts her hand on Ana's arm. "It's a good day for healing, child."

Down at the imu, Kalama doesn't disappoint. As they approach, he explains the fourth and final layer of the *hali'i,* the layer of organic material that covers the pig.

"Once the banana leaves cover the entire animal, the final layer is loose dirt shoveled over everything to prevent any steam escaping. Ana, Kimo! E komo mai!" Kalama is clearly thrilled to be in his element.

"Aloha, Pop. Aloha, Sid, Rachel, Zara." They all exchange hugs and greetings.

Ana runs up and hugs her grandfather. "Shaloha, Grandpa. It's so good to see you." Sid holds Ana tightly as memories of his own daughter come flooding in. Ana looks more like her mother every year.

Rachel approaches. "Can I have one of those?" Ana hugs her sister warmly, any old jealousies and resentments far behind them.

"How about me?" Ana looks up to see her father standing there with Lorie. She is taken aback by how old he looks, and the reality of his sickness rushes in. Ana pauses briefly, then goes to him.

"Shaloha, Daddy." Daddy? Wow. The depth of Ana's emotions takes her by surprise as she collapses in her father's arms, crying softly. Her once impenetrable walls crumble like a sandcastle at high tide.

Lou gently rocks his daughter in his arms as they both cry.

"Ziva, my beautiful daughter. I am so happy to see you. I

am so grateful for you. I love you, Ziva. Baruch Hashem. Thank God for you, Ziva. Thank God."

There is not a dry eye as they all watch the long-awaited reunion.

Lou takes Ana's hands and asks, "Can we talk?" She nods, and they walk toward the edge of the forest as the others head to the pool. Lou tires quickly, so Ana finds a fallen tree.

"Let's sit, Daddy."

They sit for a few minutes, taking in the beauty of the West Maui mountains. After his extended battle with cancer, Lou has a unique appreciation for nature and for life in general.

"Ziva … I'm sorry, Ana. I am deeply sorry. I know it's insufficient, but I must start there. I was wrong to have left you. That's the bottom line. I was wrong."

Ana's head is spinning. There are so many things she wants to say … where does she start? She takes a moment to process, and the tears return as she forces herself to remember that day.

"It was my birthday, Daddy. I was only ten years old. You promised you would be home in time …"

Lou listens intently, tears streaming down his face. "I know, honey, I know. We couldn't get home in time …

I'm so sorry."

Ana's gaze was far off, recalling the moment their lives changed forever. "Everyone was singing Happy Birthday and laughing. Auntie was carrying this amazing pink cake … it had … it …" Ana begins to shake.

"Kimo and I were each holding one of Lilikoi's hands, and then …" She hangs her head and sobs. "Daddy, it was awful. Horrible! There were these big explosions … and smoke … then the screaming, Daddy, the screaming. Mama was calling for me … she was screaming my name …" Ana's body is wracked by sobs as she is transported back to her childhood. Lou wraps his frail arms around his daughter and gently rocks her.

Kimo and Lorie watch from across the yard. Kimo's heart breaks seeing Ana in such distress, and he starts to go to her, but Lorie stops him. She places a soft hand on his forearm. "They need this." Kimo nods. He understands this has been a long time coming and quells his impulse to rescue his love.

Ana wipes her eyes and catches her breath. "After Mama …" She struggles to find the words. "… and then you left the next day. You just left me, Daddy. I felt abandoned. I lost everything that day: you, Mama, my home …"

Lou bows his head with shame and nods. "I know, Ziva. I will never forgive myself. I failed you. All I can say in the way of an explanation is that I was so focused on finding Ellie that I never thought what it was doing to you. I thought Maui would be temporary. I thought I'd find her, and we'd come get you and start a new life together. Everything I did was with that one goal in mind. Each day, I would think this is the day I find Eleanor. I wasn't going to stop looking until I found your mother and brought her home."

Ana's shoulders shake as she quietly sobs. Lou is devastated to see the depth of Ana's pain. He would do anything to take it away.

"I'm sorry, Ziva. I became obsessed and single-minded. I was weak and selfish. A month turned into two, and then years passed. I lost myself in the grief and rage. I couldn't face you. I began to drink." Lou shakes his head. "I was ashamed. At some point, I told myself I didn't deserve your forgiveness … that you were better off without me. I just gave up."

Ana collects herself. "Is that when you went to Uncle Lior for help?"

"Yes. Lior helped me get sober and helped me find a place to heal."

"The ashram?"

"Yes, I went to India. It took a year there, Lorie's support, and two more years of therapy and self-reflection to make sense of it all. I thought of you every day, Ziva. Every single day."

Ana listens closely, silent tears falling intermittently. "By the time I realized the damage I'd done, you'd already cut me out of your life … understandably."

"Daddy, I'm so sorry. I didn't know …"

"Please don't be sorry, Ziva. I understood then, and I understand now. It was completely justifiable. You were angry, and you felt abandoned. You were protecting yourself. It was how you coped with what must've felt like unbearable loss and betrayal. I didn't force it because I didn't want to open that old wound. Maybe I should have." Lou takes a deep breath and exhales slowly. "Ziva, can you ever forgive me?"

"I'm sorry, too, Daddy. I was so stupid. So stubborn. I've wasted so much time, and now …" Ana looks at her father, weakened by his illness, and wonders how much time they have left.

Father and daughter stand and hold each other, and they cry. At that moment, under an enormous mango tree, it comes. Forgiveness. Her anger softens and is replaced by anguish, not only for herself but for all of them. For the time and the moments like this that were lost. Awareness. It wasn't her father's fault that her mother was taken. He was broken by his despair just as she was. Her father had hurt every bit as much as she had, if not more. She gets it now. Ana feels she has been emancipated from the bonds of anger and guilt, and the healing begins.

They look across the yard to see Kimo and Lorie walking toward them. Lorie stands at Lou's side, affectionately rubbing his back, and Kimo puts a consoling arm around Ana's shoulders. Lou proudly introduces his daughter. "Lorie, this is Ziva."

Ana steps forward with a warm smile and extends her hand. "Shaloha. It's Ana now. It's nice to meet you, Lorie. Mahalo for saving my father."

Lorie is touched and takes Ana's hands in hers. "Mahalo to you for saving my daughter. It appears we're even." Ana can't imagine what Lorie suffered when Rachel was missing, and feels an instant connection. The bonds of trauma join them forever.

Up at the house, Farrah and Iman help Pua with the last-minute touches for dinner. While Iman sets the table, Pua waves over Farrah and whispers conspiratorially.

"I don't want to bring up the subject in front of the others, but you asked earlier about Charlotte. Yesterday, I reached out to Charlotte's mother and sent her our prayers and support. This morning, I heard from her. She called to tell us how thankful she is for us. Wasn't that nice? That poor family. Horrible, just horrible."

"That's wonderful, Pua, thank you for telling me. How is Charlotte? Did she say?" Farrah's compassion runs deep.

Pua shrugs. "It was a short call, and I didn't want to pry. She just said Charlotte is doing as well as could be expected, and they haven't taken their eyes off her. I just can't imagine."

Unfortunately, Farrah can imagine. "Horrible. There is no worse torture for a parent." Farrah knows exactly what it feels like. The months Zara was missing were the hardest in her life—ten long, agonizing months. Iman interrupts the moment, all business. "Auntie, we need more napkins."

The dinner table is crowded with traditional Thanksgiving dishes like turkey, stuffing, and cranberry sauce. The cranberry sauce has always been a point of contention between Pua and Kalama. Every year, Pua makes a beautiful, fresh whole cranberry sauce sprinkled with citrus zest. And every year, Kal picks up a can at Safeway, opens it with an electric can opener, and points out the beauty of the perfectly formed can ridges on the solid purple blob of cranberry "sauce." Traditions are everything.

But this is no traditional Thanksgiving Dinner. There is kalua pork, macadamia nut-encrusted mahi mahi, and Auntie Kailani's beef teriyaki with wontons. There is also fresh ahi poke, Okinawan sweet potatoes, kalua pork stuffing, boiled peanuts, and chicken long rice. On the buffet sits a stack of Hawaiian Sweet bread rolls, a dozen varieties of fresh tropical fruit, and various pupus brought over by friends and neighbors.

The mood around the table is happy and hopeful, with no talk of the horrors they'd all recently endured. Rachel sits between her parents, Lou and Lorie, while her mother dotes on her, piling her plate with every dish on the table.

"Mom! I'm not a linebacker. I can't eat all that!" Rachel rolls her eyes dramatically.

Zara laughs at Sid's storytelling while Farrah and Pua fuss over everyone and everything.

Nisim and Kalama pile food on their plates. "Make sure you get some kalua pork; it's delicious."

"Don't eat so fast, you'll choke."

"Don't forget the rolls!"

"Don't give the dogs turkey; the tryptophan is bad for them."

They fill their plates as they talk and laugh, and it finally feels normal and right—safe, happy, and carefree.

Lou stands slowly, his body weak from his ongoing health battles. He raises his glass of sparkling cider and looks around the table. Lou tears up before he utters his first word, and the crowd goes silent.

"I am so grateful to be here today with family, ohana; in Yiddish, we say mishpocha. It's a miracle that I can spend this day, a day of giving thanks, with both of my beautiful daughters, each of whom I came so close to losing. I have never had more to be thankful for." Rachel and Ana share a sisterly gaze, tears in their eyes.

"The seeds of this beautiful extended family were planted in Israel years ago, where we welcomed our children and built a life together. That life was shattered by evil people who took from us our loved ones, Ellie and Lilikoi."

There isn't a dry eye around the table. Pua cries softly as Farrah and Nisim console her. The agony in Lou's voice is apparent as he turns to Kalama.

"Kal, my brother. I saved your life in Beirut, and now you have saved mine. You provided a stable and loving family for my Ziva … sorry, honey, Ana, and you rescued our Rachel from the unthinkable and brought her home to us. I can never repay you. We will always be in your debt." Kalama raises his glass with love as Lou turns to his wife.

"Lorie, you saved me from myself. You helped me to forgive myself, and you gave me hope. You renewed my faith in humanity and in God. I love you three women more than life itself, and I intend to spend the rest of my days showing you."

Rachel and Ana get out of their chairs and rush to Lou's side. The three of them stand there hugging as everyone around the table hugs and cries. They cry for the past and the present. They cry for the time they lost with their loved ones. They cry for themselves and for each other. They cry for those lost in the Lahaina fires and for those who still struggle to regain their lives. They cry for the victims of October 7th, the innocent lives taken, and the families that continue to suffer. Lou ends his toast with Ellie's favorite quote.

"There is nothing so whole as a broken heart."

Lorie and Kimo hug while the girls hug Lou. They face each other, holding hands, and Kimo says, "Welcome to the family, Lorie."

Zara takes Sid's hand. He is the closest thing she's ever had to a grandfather, and he has been wonderful to her and her family, even offering to host her biological parents when they manage to escape Gaza. Zara puts her head on Sid's shoulder; they share a special bond, and she feels safe with him.

Kalama stands and taps his glass with his fork. Everyone dries their eyes, awkwardly laughing. The tears have somehow cleansed their pain, and suddenly, the mood is a little lighter. Kalama raises his glass, and Auntie Kailani chastises everyone as she wipes her eyes.

"Come on now, we can't cry all day. The kalua pork is getting cold."

Kalama stands and strikes his glass with his fork as the crowd simmers down once again and gives their host their full attention. Kimo gives Ana a look, and she giggles. Here comes another one of Uncle's infamous toasts.

"On this day of Thanksgiving, we come together as ohana, as family. In Hawaiian culture, family is not born of blood but love and nurturing, mutual caring, and commitment to each other's well-being and happiness. This is our *hanai* family." Ana looks around the table at her hanai family. A blend of people from all walks of life: Jewish, Christian, Muslim, and Buddhist. Brought together by love, loss, and life experience. United by pain and trauma. Kimo squeezes her hand. Ana looks at Rachel and Zara with admiration and awe. They seem so strong now, but she knows the path to healing will be long and arduous.

Kalama continues. "Together, we celebrate our blessings, however humble they may seem, in the wake of our suffering. Confucius said the man who moves mountains begins by carrying away small stones. As I look around this table, my heart is full. Each of us has suffered greatly, yet each of us continues the work of fighting evil because not doing so is unacceptable. We have been spared. We have been chosen. Evil is our mountain to move. We do what we can day by day, little by little. One small rock at a time. We do not surrender or abandon our faith. Our ohana, the people at this table, we persevere."

Kimo admires his father as he watches him shine in his role of patriarch. He so naturally leads this large, extended, multi-generational, multiethnic family with strength and wisdom. Kimo puts his arm around Ana and kisses her softly on the lips, and she feels it, too. Gratitude. Belonging. Family. They are exactly where they are meant to be.

Kalama continues. "In Hawaiian, we say *ho'omau*. We persevere. All of us here have borne witness to the battle between good and evil, and we have persevered. Ho'omau. We have all suffered unspeakable loss, tragedy, and savage indignities at the hands of wicked people, demons working in the dark. Yet, we, in the light, persevere and continue to fight. Ho'omau."

Kalama raises his glass. "*Ho'omoe wai kahi ke kao'o*. Let us travel together like water flowing in one direction."

They all raise their glasses and exclaim in unison, "Ho'omau."